KISS & Collide

T0407727

AMANDA WEAVER

SLOWBURN
A zando IMPRINT
NEW YORK

zando

The characters and events in this book are fictitious. Any similarity to real persons, living or dead, is coincidental and not intended by the author.

Copyright © 2025 by Amanda Weaver

Zando supports the right to free expression and the value of copyright. The purpose of copyright is to encourage writers and artists to produce the creative works that enrich our culture. Thank you for buying an authorized edition of this book and for complying with copyright laws by not reproducing, scanning, uploading, or distributing this book or any part of it without permission. If you would like permission to use material from the book (other than for brief quotations embodied in reviews), please contact connect@zandoprojects.com.

Slowburn is an imprint of Zando.
zandoprojects.com

First Edition: August 2025

Text design by Neuwirth & Associates, Inc.
Cover design by Caroline Johnson

The publisher does not have control over and is not responsible for author or other third-party websites (or their content).

Library of Congress Control Number: 2025938171

978-1-63893-189-8 (Paperback)
978-1-63893-188-1 (eBook)

10 9 8 7 6 5 4 3 2 1
Manufactured in the United States of America
BRT

FOR LILITH
BE BRAVE

KISS & Collide

PROLOGUE Monte Carlo

Even the breeze off the ocean felt different in Monaco. Softer, sweeter-scented, expensive.

Violet had been at some of the glamorous parties surrounding the Monaco Grand Prix before, but she'd always been working.

Now she'd be free to enjoy it.

She'd officially handed off her duties at Lennox Motorsport to her replacement, and she wasn't due to start her new job until the midseason break. Tonight, she was free to have fun, and she fully intended to enjoy every second of it, in *every* way she could.

She stood at the base of the megayacht's gangplank, taking in the spectacle, as an exclusive selection of the world's rich and beautiful people streamed past her. The yacht was owned by some billionaire whose company was a sponsor of the Formula One team, and the party on board was supposed to be the highlight of the race weekend at Monaco—a weekend that was already jam-packed with glamorous parties and exclusive events.

As she stepped on board, the man greeting guests smiled broadly at her as he scanned her invite code. "Violet Harper. Glad you could make it."

"Hi, Simon. Thanks for putting me on the guest list."

He leaned in to kiss her cheek and she caught a delicious whiff of his cologne. "Have fun tonight. I know you know how." He winked at her and she felt the subtle ripple of mutual attraction.

"For once, I'm not working the post-race party and I am going to *enjoy* it." She paused, her eyes roving down Simon's body. He was fit, and in his tight navy suit, he looked positively edible.

Yes, he'd do nicely. "Maybe you can help me out with that."

Simon gave her a similar once-over, and bit his bottom lip. "Yeah, well, unfortunately, I *am* working this party."

"That's too bad."

He shook his head sadly. "Sure as fuck is. Anyway, the hot tub and pool are open. Just ask the attendant for a suit if you want to swim. The helipad's been converted to a dance floor. Calvin Harris is DJing a set later tonight. And of course, there's all the alcohol you care to drink."

"If I'm still looking for company by the end of the night, maybe I'll come find you." She tilted her chin.

Simon's eyes smoldered with interest. "I sincerely hope you do."

Violet hadn't taken two steps inside the lounge on the main deck when she stopped short, just a foot away from a very familiar, tall, hot irritation.

"What are *you* doing here?" she snapped.

Chase Navarro also stopped in his tracks, his eyes dipping quickly down her body and then just as quickly back up to her face. "Installing the Wi-Fi? Am I in the wrong place?"

With his golden tanned skin, jet-black hair, and eyes to match, he was revoltingly good-looking, but here he was, in the middle of this glamorous party, wearing *jeans.* Just ratty, faded Levi's and a short-sleeve black shirt, like some random American tourist who'd stumbled onto this yacht accidentally. Unfortunately, he was still hotter than nearly anyone else here.

Since the moment she'd met him, Chase Navarro had annoyed her. Beautiful, but careless, counting on his looks and his charm to carry him through this cutthroat world. But since he was just a low-ranking Formula Two driver, she only crossed paths with him at tracks every once in a while.

"All this and a sense of humor, too. You're a real renaissance man, Chase."

The grin he flashed at her made something tickle in her belly. It was truly unfair that the universe had chosen to gift a weapon as powerful as that smile to someone who used it so lazily.

"Violet, you're always so . . ." He hesitated, narrowing his eyes at her as he considered her. She'd very purposefully worn next to nothing tonight, wanting to look good and *feel* good, but Chase's once-over was making her feel some *other* kind of way.

"Be very careful about the next word that comes out of that pretty mouth of yours."

". . . *clever*," he said at last.

"Well, I'm sure you've got any number of indiscriminate young women to seduce tonight. Don't let me get in your way."

When she brushed past him, he hesitated a beat and then turned to follow her through the crowd.

"You here with friends?"

She scowled over her shoulder. "Yes, I'm meeting Mira." She might be moving to a new job at a new team, but thankfully her best friend back at Lennox, Mira, would still be at every race, so they could still hang out.

Just then her phone vibrated in her hand. When she glanced at the screen, she sighed.

Something came up at Lennox HQ. We're flying back tonight. Sorry!

"Was. I *was* meeting Mira."

Well, this sucked. No Mira meant she was flying solo tonight. She stashed her phone in her tiny silver bag and surveyed the room. Time to make a new plan.

"Why don't I buy you a drink?" Chase said.

She pivoted to look at him. Was he trying to flirt with *her*? The audacity.

At that moment, a waiter carrying a tray full of champagne flutes paused beside them. She gave him a radiant smile and plucked one off the tray. "The drinks are *free* here, Chase. Now, if you'll excuse me, I'm off to make some new friends."

CHASE WATCHED VIOLET'S back as she skirted through the crowd. He'd crossed paths with her often enough, on the track and at various racing events, and he'd always found her stunning, but tonight he couldn't take his eyes off her. Her lips were blood-red, and beneath her dark bangs, her eyes were winged with black. The brilliant blue of them was startling enough to distract him from her outfit—a triangle of shimmery metal mesh somehow held on to the front of her with little silver chains crisscrossing her back, a skintight silver miniskirt, and silver sandals with sky-high heels.

But it all came attached to Violet Harper, prickly and kind of mean. He'd definitely thought about her in that way, more than once, and she might be the most beautiful girl at this party, but he only needed to get his hand slapped once to learn his lesson.

He turned away, taking a sip of his drink. This whole party felt like he was swimming way above his pay grade. The enormous buffet of food downstairs, the crowded dance floor up on the helipad, the glamorous crowd hanging around on the back deck, with Monte Carlo glittering in the background . . . parties like this were for the Formula One elite, not a low-ranking F2 driver like him.

He'd wanted to be an F1 driver since he was a kid. He'd given up everything—absolutely everything—to pursue it. And at twenty-five, he was trying to come to terms with never getting it. Over and over he'd told himself that the odds were stacked against him. There were only twenty seats on the grid, and thousands of drivers desperate to fill them. The vast majority would never make it. He'd gotten as far as F2. It was more than most would ever see. He'd tried to make himself satisfied with that.

It was impossible.

The want felt like it was gnawing away at him from the inside out, and with it, the frustrating realization that if it never happened for him, he'd be nursing this unfulfilled desire for the rest of his life, no matter what else he managed to achieve.

He was surprised when he'd landed on the guest list for his team's F1 counterpart, but he figured he'd better take advantage of it. In this sport you either moved up or moved out, and since he was probably on his way out after this season, this might be his last chance.

Out on the back deck, he ended up being cornered by some wasted finance bro who talked his ear off about crypto for an hour. By the time he shook himself loose, the crowd had started to thin out. He made his way back inside, to the main lounge, thinking to grab one more beer before he hit the road. But the second he was inside, he spotted her—Violet—across the room. He was uncomfortably aware of how his eyes had followed her all night long—hanging out by the pool, dancing up on the helipad. She'd had company every time, one guy after another, so why was she still here alone?

He didn't really think it through—he never did—he just started heading her way, skirting the low ivory leather chairs scattered across the space and the clusters of people standing in conversation. On the way, he snagged two glasses of Moët from a passing waiter. As he approached, she swiveled to look at him in surprise. Long black hair tumbling over those bare shoulders and arms, long pale legs under that barely there miniskirt—skin, skin . . . so much touchable skin. God, she was gorgeous.

"Hey." He offered her a glass. "You look like you need this."

VIOLET EYED CHASE warily before taking the glass he offered. How had she ended up back where she'd started the night, still flying solo and talking to *him*? She'd entertained plenty of options tonight, but she'd passed each one by. This one had a weird laugh, that one had a suspicious tan line on his ring finger—she'd found reason after reason to move on. But now tonight's game of musical chairs was nearly over and there seemed to be just this one chair left available.

It was undeniably a hot chair. And it would probably be a lot of fun. Chase Navarro wasn't someone who did serious, and neither was Violet, so there was no risk of things getting messy. He was watching her over the rim of his champagne flute, humor lighting up those jet-black eyes.

Taking a deep breath, she raised her eyes to his. "So, are we doing this? Sex?"

She enjoyed the deep satisfaction of rendering him momentarily speechless as he choked on his champagne.

"What?"

"Come on now. We both know why you came over here. You want to fuck me."

He lifted a hand to rub the back of his neck as he looked down at the floor. Good lord, she'd *flustered* him. Now this *was* fun. "Ah . . ."

"If you're not interested . . ." she drawled with exaggerated disinterest as she dragged her fingertips along her collarbone. His eyes tracked the movement, flaring with heat.

"Um, yes, we're doing this." He cleared his throat and looked her straight in the eye. "We're absolutely doing this."

Her nipples hardened at the low timbre of his voice. Something flared within her. Okay, she was *excited.*

"WHERE'S YOUR HOTEL?" Violet asked.

Oh, she wanted to come back to *his* place. He hadn't considered that. This might be awkward. "Ah . . . I'm staying outside Nice."

She blinked. "Nice?"

"Yeah, Nice. It's not far in an Uber and—"

"I *know* where Nice is. Why are you staying there?"

Violet was used to the elite world of Formula One and the Lennox championship team. She didn't get how it was for some of the drivers on the lower rungs. Every dime his sponsors managed to cough up went straight to the team. It was the only way he could hope to hang on to his seat. That meant living on the cheap whenever he could.

"Me and some of the guys from the circuit got an Airbnb—"

Violet's eyes went wide and she threw up a hand in protest. "*Oh no.* My days of hostel sex are over."

"It's not a *hostel.* It's an apartment. I have my own room." It was a tiny box. With a twin bed. And thin walls. But it was all his.

"I'm not going to Nice." The stony look on her face made it clear the subject was closed.

"Okay, then." Maybe they *weren't* doing this. That was tragic, because right now he wanted her with a desperation that was almost scary. "I guess you're staying here in Monte Carlo?" he asked hopefully.

She looked at him, her gaze assessing. He looked right back, almost pleading with her with his eyes. She caught her lush, red bottom lip with her teeth briefly as she considered.

Then she blew out a breath. "I can't believe I'm doing this," she muttered to herself. Then, to him, "Get us an Uber. We'll go to mine."

He did his best to suppress his grin as he pulled out his phone, but it was hard as hell.

Monte Carlo was pocket-sized, and in no time, their car had climbed into the hills and turned onto a dark, curving street.

"This is me," Violet said when the car stopped.

Chase peered up at the tall, white, obviously expensive apartment building through the window. "You're staying here?"

Damn, she really did swim in different circles than him.

"For the weekend," she said. He was transfixed, watching as she opened the door and unfolded those long, long legs of hers. She straightened and turned back to him, a willowy goth goddess, all black hair and red lips, shimmery silver, and so much bare, pale skin. Hands planted on her hips, she scowled. "Well? Are you coming?"

This time he didn't even try to suppress his smile. "Absofucking-lutely."

1

Eldham, England

Violet stood in the main atrium of Pinnacle Motorsport, eyeing the water damage on the ceiling and the scuffed paint on the walls, and wondered if she'd made a mistake.

This was a significant step down from the Lennox Motorsport factory.

Had she really left the number-one team on the grid to come here, to the team that had ranked last for the past five years?

This move was strategic, she reminded herself. At Lennox, she was always going to be Simone's assistant, and however great Simone was, Violet's prospects were limited there. Now, somehow, she'd talked her way into head of PR at Pinnacle. That was a big deal, even if Pinnacle was the worst team on the grid.

Whatever. This was a huge step up the career ladder for her, one she could parlay into something even bigger in a year or two. This wasn't forever. And in the meantime, she'd figure it out like she always did.

The double doors on the other side of the atrium banged open and a young girl with long, dark blond hair and a frantic expression raced through. She looked on the verge of tears as she scanned the atrium.

"Are you Violet Harper?" she asked in a trembling voice.

"That's me."

"I was supposed to bring you to meet Richard, but now he's been fired and everybody's cross and I—"

Violet's chest gave a thump of dread. She'd interviewed with Richard. He was the reason she'd landed this job. "Hold on. Richard Clewes? The team principal? He's been *fired*?"

The girl—who, on closer inspection was older than Violet initially thought, just a bit younger than herself—nodded shakily, her pale blue eyes filling with tears. "Just this morning and . . ." She pressed her knuckles against her lips, letting out a muffled sob.

"Oh, don't . . ." Violet shifted back onto her heels in discomfort. "It's not worth crying about. Personnel changes happen all the time in Formula One."

"It's not just that!" the girl exploded in a wail. "We've been *sold*! To *Americans*!"

"What??"

At that moment, her phone, clutched in her hand, vibrated with a text from Mira.

I've just heard some unbelievable dirt. Tell me it's not true.

Violet blew out a breath and typed out a reply.

Did you hear Pinnacle's been sold to some Americans? Because I just got here and that's what I'm hearing, too.

Sold to Carter Hammond! Mira replied.

Violet looked up at the girl currently weeping in front of her. "Carter Hammond?"

The girl let out another wail and buried her face in her hands.

She typed out another text to Mira. *Obviously walking into a shitstorm here. Will call later.*

You better!

Violet closed her eyes and took a deep breath. Okay, so the situation at Pinnacle would be a little more . . . volatile . . . than she'd been expecting. It was fine. She started her career wrangling an irresponsible rock band. She would need to handle this, whether she was ready for it or not. This was the problem with talking your way into things. Sometimes you ended up dumped into the deep end.

Opening her eyes again, she focused on the crying girl. "What's your name?"

She broke off sobbing and blinked at her. "Imogen Hubert. Assistant to the team principal." Her face, flushed and wet with tears, screwed up again. "Who *was* Richard . . ."

Imogen seemed like a far cry from Mira, who was also the team principal's assistant, with her spreadsheets and lists and scary competency. But then again, when she'd first met Mira, she'd underestimated the spine of steel behind the princess face. Maybe there were hidden depths to Imogen, too.

Imogen let out another wail.

Maybe.

"Stop crying," Violet said as gently as she could manage. "Crying doesn't solve anything."

Imogen sniffed, then stared up at Violet with a trembling lower lip, tears welling up in her eyes.

"Let's deal with one crisis at a time, okay? So Carter Hammond has fired Richard Clewes. He must have someone he wants to put in his place?"

Imogen nodded shakily. "His son. Reece Hammond. He's already here." Her lip wobbled dangerously.

Violet pointed a finger at her. "British stiff upper lip and all that rubbish, right?"

Imogen gave a shaky smile. Progress.

"You'd better take me back so I can meet him for myself."

Imogen nodded and turned to lead the way, but just then, the double doors she'd come through minutes before, evidently leading into the bowels of the Pinnacle factory, banged open, vomiting a stream of people into the atrium.

The one in front she immediately pegged as Reece Hammond. His American accent booming off the high atrium ceiling was a dead giveaway. She had nothing against Americans. Mira was American and she was her best friend. But why did he insist on being so *loudly* American? Violet sensed in an instant that she wasn't going to like one bloody thing about Reece Hammond.

He was younger than she might have expected, had she been expecting *any* of this. Maybe in his mid-thirties. Beginning to get a bit doughy in the middle but trying hard not to let it show. Dark haired, tanned, like he spent a lot of time on the beach. Expensive dress shirt, no tie, dark jeans that were too tight on him, *very* expensive titanium Rolex.

He was talking—loudly—at the older man next to him. She recognized him from around the track. Oscar Davies, Pinnacle's chief technical officer. Old-timer in Formula One. Hadn't designed a winning car as long as Violet had been alive.

When Reece reached her, he stopped, running his eyes down her body and back up. If she hadn't already decided she hated him, that would have sealed the deal.

"Who's this?" He must have thought his oily, overly whitened smile was charming.

She plastered on her brightest fake smile. After all, she worked in PR. She could bullshit with the best of them. "Violet Harper. Pinnacle's new head of PR."

"Great timing! Big changes at Pinnacle! We're going to want lots of media coverage."

She maintained her smile. "I'd like to talk through your vision for the team, so we can plan—"

"Hold that thought, sweetheart. I'm going to say a few words to the staff. That'll get you up to speed."

Good god, she loathed him. But she just kept smiling, gritting her teeth so hard it felt like her molars might crack.

More people had streamed into the atrium, filling the edges of the room two and three deep. There was an upper balcony, and people clustered there, too. She moved off to one side with Imogen, who looked on the verge of tears again.

"Everybody here?" Reece shouted. Imogen flinched. There was no response from the sullen, stone-faced employees of Pinnacle, but Reece's manic confidence didn't waver. "Okay, folks, are you ready to shake things up? Because I am here to shake it *hard*!"

At that point, he did a little shimmy. Violet could only imagine that's what he did on the dance floor, because he bit his lip, lifted his arms, and wiggled his ass.

If she were capable of feeling secondhand embarrassment, she'd be dying of it right now.

"Here's what I want you to do," Reece boomed, putting his serious face back on. "I want every person in this room to look to their left." He waited while they awkwardly did it. "Now look to your right." Another painful pause. "At the end of this season, only two of you will still be here, because Pinnacle is going to become a lean, mean, race-winning machine."

The deafening silence greeting his announcement should have told him he'd just massively fucked up, but Reece seemed to not even notice that he'd uttered all of five sentences and managed to turn every single person in this facility against him. Violet might have been impressed at the sheer volume of his awfulness if she weren't as fucked as the rest of them.

"There's no reason that world championship can't be ours if we're all committed to the grind. If we're all willing to give two hundred percent. If we're all on our hustle. If we're all ready to live, eat, and breathe Pinnacle Motorsport. What this team needs is a win! If we win a world championship, we can turn this thing around! Now, who's with me?"

More silence from the crowd.

"Winning a world championship. Why didn't we think of that?"

Despite the seriousness of the situation, Violet smothered a laugh. At least there was someone funny here. She turned to look at the woman next to her who'd muttered those words under her breath. Mid-forties, short, and Southeast Asian, she had her black hair pulled back in a messy bun, and was wearing a gray Pinnacle button-down shirt.

"So simple, right? Violet Harper, head of PR," she whispered.

"Rabia Dar. Associate design engineer." She raised her eyebrows. "Last year they gave me a better title instead of a raise."

"You work with Oscar Davies, then?"

"Lucky me," Rabia muttered. She blew out a long breath, ruffling a strand of hair that had escaped her bun, and squinted through her dark-framed glasses at Reece.

Understandable. Oscar had a reputation for being an out-of-touch blowhard. Working under him had to suck.

Reece was still talking, but a low-grade murmur had started up amongst the staff, so they could speak without being heard.

"How's the new team principal?" Violet asked. She'd formed her own opinion, but she wanted to get a read on the rest of the Pinnacle staff.

"He knows fuck all about racing, which is . . ." She shook her head grimly. "Honestly, we're sunk."

Reece was still out there in the middle of the atrium, making an ass of himself.

"Now let's take Pinnacle to number one! Woo!" Reece thrust his fist in the air and shouted. The sound of shuffling feet and a few scattered, tepid claps followed.

He turned to talk to Oscar Davies, oblivious to the black mood that had fallen across the room. People began escaping, first a trickle, then a stampede.

"Well," Rabia said, turning to face her and extending her hand to shake, "welcome to Pinnacle, Violet. We're all fucked."

After Rabia left, Violet took a minute to arrange her expression into something approaching pleasant and headed over to deal with Reece.

"Ah, the PR girl. Perfect. Now I'm sure the media will be fighting to get sit-down time with me, so I'm thinking let's start with ESPN. A prime-time interview. That'll kick it off right."

Then he pulled out his phone, as if he'd already forgotten she existed.

Yeah, absolutely not. Never. There was no way she was letting the media get within three meters of Reece. "I thought we'd start with the drivers first. Media likes to talk to them. Then we'll segue into the new management. So I'll contact Dieter Gruber and Joren van der Huizen to set something up at the earliest opportunity and—"

"Joren's out," Reece said absently, scrolling on his phone.

What?

"What's that?" she said with forced calm.

Violet looked from Reece to Imogen, who was hovering behind Reece looking like she was about to cry again.

"Um. Joren has to have surgery on his back," Imogen murmured. "He can't race."

"Since when?" Joren van der Huizen had been driving just fine right up until the start of the midseason break a few weeks ago.

Reece shrugged. "Yeah, I called him this morning to give him the good news about the sale and he told me he'd just talked to his doctor and he needs the surgery right away. Hell of a thing."

Violet fought the urge to roll her eyes. Joren was a veteran. A dozen years in racing, a known name in the sport. This season at Pinnacle was supposed to be his swan song before retirement. No doubt as soon as he got the measure of Reece Hammond, he'd decided he'd rather not have this disaster besmirching the end of his career and suddenly developed a pressing injury that needed immediate attention.

"It's no biggie," Reece said. "The . . . whadaya call it?" He snapped his fingers and glanced at Imogen. "The understudy is on his way here now."

"Reserve driver," Imogen whispered to no one.

"Which reserve—" Violet started.

"Oh." Imogen breathed out as the glass front door whooshed open behind Violet.

"There he is!" Reece shouted, brushing past her.

She turned to look.

Oh fuck. Oh fuck no.

Chase Navarro, looking like the star of some action movie in jeans and a battered brown leather jacket, lowered his mirrored aviator sunglasses and unfurled that deadly grin of his. Behind her, she heard Imogen sigh dreamily.

Reece crossed the atrium and raised a hand to high-five him. "Hey, Chase! Let's hear it for Americans, right? USA! USA! USA!"

If Reece fist-pumped one more time, she was going to duct-tape his arms to his sides. But there were more pressing issues at present, like—

"Happy to be here," Chase said with a smile. "You have no idea." His eyes suddenly landed on her and his grin grew wider. "Hi, Violet."

What was he doing here? How? Why?

Violet forced herself to move, one foot in front of the other, across the atrium to join them. She hadn't seen him since that night—that *epic* night—in Monaco. She wasn't supposed to see him *again* unless it was in passing in the paddock. Her brain was frantically working to solve this rapidly unfolding disaster.

"Come on back and we'll show you around," Reece said, clapping him on the shoulder. "Well, my assistant will, since I'm new here, too."

Imogen made a squeak of terror.

Reece turned to Violet and snapped his fingers at her like she was a fucking dog. "Why don't you tag along too, ah . . ."

"Violet," she said between gritted teeth. "Violet Harper."

"Right. You can keep the fellas company, Vi. Isabelle, lead the way."

Imogen didn't correct him as she led them across the atrium. Violet fell in beside Chase.

"What are you doing here?" she hissed. "You drive Formula Two for Hansbach."

"Yeah. I'm also on contract as a reserve F1 driver for Hansbach, Deloux, and Pinnacle." He clapped his hands together with satisfaction, his dark eyes lit up with excitement. "And now, as of a couple of hours ago, looks like I'm driving Formula One for Pinnacle." He looked at her sideways. "Funny seeing you here."

"Strategic career move," she said grimly.

"Congrats. Head of PR. That's a pretty significant step up."

"Yeah, that's what I thought, too. Now I'm not so sure."

She grimaced and stopped walking, watching him catch up to Reece and Imogen and head through the double doors into the factory. Overhead, that old ceiling leak was taunting her. Her gut had been right this morning. She should have turned around and run.

The team was a disaster and the new team principal was a nightmare. And she now had to work with a one-night stand—which, she begrudgingly had to admit, was the best one of her life—directly violating her *no-strings* rule.

But she'd already trained her replacement back at Lennox. The second half of the season was about to get underway in a matter of days.

There was no going back.

When Chase woke up this morning, he'd had nothing more interesting on his plate than a simulator session at the Hansbach factory. Then his phone rang, and some terrified girl—whom he now knew was Imogen—had asked him, between sniffles, how soon he could be at the Pinnacle factory.

While he'd driven at breakneck speed, he'd sorted out the details with his agent, Phil. At first it hadn't made any sense. In fact, he'd been so stunned that he'd asked Phil outright if Pinnacle knew how little sponsorship money he would bring with him. How was it possible that a Formula One team, even Pinnacle—*especially* Pinnacle, which everybody knew was strapped for cash—was okay with that, even if their star was out?

Phil had tried to stall, but eventually he had to confess that Reece Hammond, Pinnacle's brand-new *American* team principal, had handpicked him from the list of reserve drivers.

So he was only here because he was American, not because of his driving, and despite his lack of funding. But fuck it, he was used to being an afterthought in racing, dismissed as insignificant before he'd ever gotten behind the wheel. It just gave him motivation. He'd prove he had every right to be here. He'd done it his entire career.

And now, impossibly, because of the whims of one rich guy, he'd made a seat in Formula One, at last. He did not give one single solitary fuck how it had happened. All that mattered was that he was here.

The excitement, the flat-out euphoria, made him feel like he might just bust out of his own skin.

Ahead of them Imogen keyed in a code to unlock the door and ducked to the side as Reece pushed his way past her and through. It was early yet, and Chase was willing to give the guy some time to prove himself, but so far, it didn't seem like Reece was winning over any Pinnacle hearts and minds.

"Um, this is Engineering," Imogen murmured, so softly it was hard to hear.

Oscar Davies had been across the room with a couple of people but came to greet them with another guy and Rabia Dar, whom he'd seen around the track now and then.

"Welcome to Engineering," Oscar said with a wide smile. He was a barrel-chested white guy in late middle age, ruddy faced, with a thick head of dark hair. He reached for Chase's hand and shook it hard.

Then Oscar gave Violet a once-over that made his skin crawl. "And who's this pretty face?"

Seriously? That's how he talked to staff?

"Violet Harper," she ground out between gritted teeth. "PR."

"Nice to have you aboard, Violet," Oscar said to her breasts. Jesus. It was disgusting.

He took a step forward to say something to redirect Oscar's attention when Reece cut them all off.

"So is this where they build the cars? You guys build them, right?"

"Designed and built from scratch every season." Oscar turned to Reece, leaving Violet to stare daggers at him. He started describing the Engineering facilities to Reece, whose eyes quickly glazed over. Oscar had never bothered introducing Rabia or the other guy, and he didn't direct his conversation to anyone but Reece.

"Hey there," Chase finally said, reaching out to shake Rabia's hand. "I've seen you around, it's nice to finally meet you. Chase Navarro."

"Rabia Dar, associate design engineer. This is Leon Franklin, head of Engineering."

Leon, a compact Black man with long, thin locs held off his face with a band, leaned past Rabia and shook his hand.

"Good to meet you, Chase."

Chase gestured to Violet, who was watching all this unfold. "And this is Violet Harper. It's her first day, too."

He'd already been buzzing with adrenaline when he walked in the door this morning, and as soon as he set eyes on Violet, he started buzzing with an entirely different kind of energy. She was in a tight, wine-red striped suit that made her legs look somehow even longer and more spectacular than he remembered, and her black hair was blown out straight and silky, reaching to the middle of her back. Every time he looked at her, images of that night in Monte Carlo flooded his brain. His fingers fisting in that long black hair as he pulled her head back and licked that long pale neck . . . pushing his way between those long legs as he pressed her up against the wall and fucked her there . . . It was incredibly distracting to say the least.

And now she was here, at Pinnacle. This day just kept getting better and better.

Violet gave Rabia a nod. "We've already met."

"During this morning's rousing welcome speech," Rabia muttered, shooting a glance at Reece's back.

"Looks like they'll be a while," Leon said, indicating Reece and Oscar, "so why don't we take you over to the garage and introduce you around? The mechanics want to meet you."

"Sounds good," Chase replied. "I'd like to meet them, too."

Leon cracked a smile. "A driver who hangs with the mechanics. Knew I liked you."

"The mechanics always know where the good food is in every city on the circuit."

Leon chuckled. "Guilty as charged. Follow me."

As they followed Rabia and Leon down a hall lined with offices, he glanced over at Violet. She was watching Rabia and Leon, who were carrying on a conversation entirely in whispers.

Violet nudged his arm with her elbow. "Keep an eye on these two," she murmured under her breath.

"Who? Rabia and Leon? Why?"

"I guarantee you, if you need something done around this place, it's these two you need to talk to."

"And Oscar?"

"Useless," Violet said dismissively. "These two are the brains of the operation. Trust me. If you need help with the car, you go to them."

"I'll keep that in mind, I guess?"

"Okay," Rabia said, swiping her ID at another door. "Here's the car in all its glory. Don't get your hopes up."

The race bay was significantly smaller than the one back at Hansbach, and missing a lot of the high-tech bells and whistles, but he wasn't under any illusions about Pinnacle.

"Your timing is good," Leon said. "The body's on. Yesterday it was in pieces all over the factory."

One of Pinnacle's cars was nearly fully assembled in the middle of the race bay, and Chase's eyes traced over it, assessing. The floor edge looked like a straight line—unlike those of the top teams, but he wouldn't know how it would play out until he got behind the wheel.

"When can I get in the sim and try it out?"

"When the engineers finally sort out which setups they want to start with in Austria," Rabia said. "They've been bickering about it for days."

"Hansbach's got software that runs all the possible variables and determines the optimal—"

"Yeah, well, we don't." Rabia sighed. "One of the many upgrades Oscar has decided isn't worth the time and money. So they do it by hand, one variable at a time. Then you test them out and they decide on the next one. Hope you're ready to spend a lot of time in the simulator."

"I'm happy to do whatever it takes," Chase said, and he meant it.

Rabia scoffed. "Then get comfortable in that sim, kid. You'll still be in it when you're my age."

3

Her first day at Pinnacle had been an utter shit show, and every day after looked like it was going to be just as bad. This was why, as soon as Violet escaped the factory, she headed to the nearest pub.

Eldham was grim—a featureless British town where the most cutting-edge fashion was whatever Marks & Spencer carried, and the "local" was just another bloody Wetherspoons.

But Wetherspoons served vodka. And it was close enough to her new flat that she could just stagger home on foot once she was sufficiently drunk.

Her phone buzzed with an incoming call just as she reached the door. The call was coming from someone in Hammond Holdings. If that fucker Reece was calling her now . . .

"Hello?"

"Violet Harper?" a woman asked.

"Yes?"

"Please hold for Carter Hammond."

She was shunted to hold before she could even process that. Carter fucking Hammond was calling *her*? Now? *Why?* She huddled up against the front of the pub and stuck a finger in her free ear, trying to block out the street sounds while she waited to be connected.

She'd done a little hurried research on Carter Hammond this afternoon. American, richer than God, CEO of Hammond Holdings, which was an umbrella corporation for dozens of other companies. He had his fingers in everything: hotels, restaurants, cable networks, several manufacturing companies, and a handful of online businesses. Not much of a European presence, but a real mover and shaker in the States. And now he wanted to talk to *her.*

The line clicked. "Ms. Harper," he said, telling her, not asking her.

Since he didn't need confirmation, she didn't offer it. "What can I do for you, Mr. Hammond?" She trotted out her best work voice, smoothing out the rough edges of her Essex accent.

"I trust you've gotten up to speed with the Pinnacle sale."

Again, telling her, not asking her. In a weird way, she appreciated it, the assumption she was prepared for this call, even though she wasn't. At all.

"I have."

"Then you should know, Pinnacle came as part of a larger package of acquisitions. It is, on its own, not of much worth to me. My goal with Pinnacle is to keep the situation stable so that its value improves."

While she respected Carter Hammond's directness, she still wasn't clear why he'd called her.

"Can I ask what you see my role as in this transition?"

"As you know, I've put my son Reece in charge."

"Yes."

Carter paused for a moment, a pause that spoke volumes. "You've met him?"

She paused, too, letting it speak for her in the same way. "Yes."

"Pinnacle seems like it will . . . keep him occupied."

Ah. Reece was the Fail Son, and Carter Hammond absolutely knew it. He'd been stuck at Pinnacle because there didn't seem to be much more that could go wrong there.

"I see."

"I understand the sudden sale of Pinnacle will lead to a great deal of negative speculation about the team. My expectation is that you can settle that down in the coming weeks."

"That's my job," she said, keeping her voice as neutral as possible. Yes, she knew very well what her task would be in the coming weeks. That was why she was on her way to a bar to get utterly fucking obliterated.

"I very much hope there is no additional negative press about the team going forward."

Ah, there it was. He was telling her it was her job to keep his idiot son from fucking things up. Add corporate childminder to her job description, then.

"Understood," she said at last.

"I took the liberty of doing a bit of research on you, Ms. Harper. You handled that mess at Lennox Motorsport quite well."

It was Mira's story, but Violet had been the one to get the information about Brody McKnight out there, making sure the world knew Brody had taken advantage of a vulnerable girl and then thrown her to the wolves to save his own skin. And she'd helmed the resulting flood of additional negative press about Brody just as carefully. His racing career was in shambles now, something Violet was extremely proud of.

"Thank you."

"I have every confidence you'll do as well this season at Pinnacle." Translation: Make sure none of Reece's nonsense spreads around.

"I will," she said, even though she wasn't at all confident about that.

"Enjoy your evening."

He didn't wait for her reply before ending the call.

"Fuck," Violet muttered to no one. She needed that vodka now more than ever.

Inside it was all wood paneling and old-fashioned lamps hanging over the booths, carefully manufactured "olde English pub" vibes. The booths were full, so she chose a stool at the mostly empty bar and ordered a vodka on the rocks. When she'd taken a long, steadying sip, she pulled out her phone to call Mira.

In retrospect, Violet wasn't even sure how she'd become friends with Mira, the daughter of and assistant to Lennox Motorsport's team principal. In the beginning, it was because they were two young women in a male-dominated world, so forming an alliance seemed smart. Then there was that ridiculous chemistry between Mira and Will, Lennox's star driver and resident fuckboy. She'd stuck around to watch Will get taken to his knees by Mira, because that was always fun.

And after that? Honestly it was just nice to have someone to talk to, someone who didn't see her as competition or a sexual conquest. And then all that shit with Brody McKnight went down, a stark reminder of why women in a male-dominated world needed to have each other's backs.

Once they'd come out the other side of it all, Mira had unexpectedly become her friend. She didn't have many female friends. None, really. And not many male ones, either. That probably said something not great about her personality, something she didn't want to think about right now.

Taking a deep breath, she hit call on Mira's name.

“Okay, here’s what I’m thinking,” Mira said as soon as she answered. “We now work for rival teams, which means there’s a whole lot of work stuff we probably shouldn’t discuss.”

Violet sighed. “Right.” Perfect. Now in addition to having the shittiest job on earth, she couldn’t even bitch about it.

“So I propose that if we really need to vent, we speak in a cone of silence. Nothing we hear comes with us to work. Deal?”

“Deal. How do we enter this cone of silence?”

“Um, I don’t know. Maybe we have a word we use. When one of us says it, we’re in the cone.”

Violet sniggered. “Mira, are you suggesting we have a safe word?”

“You know what I mean.”

“Okay, okay.” Her eyes scanned the bar, looking for inspiration. “How about ‘maraschino cherry’?”

“Ah, I see. It’s bad enough that you’re already drinking.”

“Maraschino cherry.”

“Got it. Cone of silence engaged. Proceed.”

She glanced around the bar to make sure no one was within earshot. “Mira, you have no idea. Reece Hammond is such a fucking idiot,” she groaned. “And Pinnacle is so dysfunctional. Everyone hates everyone else. This place is a disaster.”

Pausing, she closed her eyes, biting back the wave of anxiety rippling through her chest. Generally, she never let other people see her uncertainty. Always look confident, even if you were just faking it. But Mira had been brave enough to turn to Violet when she needed support, and, as she had to constantly remind herself, friendship was a two-way street.

“Mira, I’m not sure I can do this,” she whispered.

“Do what?” Mira asked.

"This *job.* It's too much. I should have stayed at Lennox. I knew what I was doing there. This . . ." She lifted her hand and let it drop. "I don't even know where to start."

"Hey. You are brilliant at this. I've been watching you up close for a year, so I know."

"I was just an assistant, though."

Mira scoffed. "*Just* an assistant. You and I both know assistants keep these companies running. Violet, I don't know anybody tougher or braver than you. You can do this."

Violet sniffed and took a swig of her vodka. Fuck. Enough of being scared. It didn't suit her. "Yeah, it's just going to be a fuckton of work."

"How's your staff? Can they help lighten the load?"

She laughed bitterly, remembering the introduction to the rest of the PR department that day. "One's called Maisie. She looks about sixteen, but I'm told she's actually twenty-one. She works on 'online engagement.' Today she said not one word beyond 'hi.' I'm not exaggerating. Not a single word. The other one is called Horace. He's forty-five, has all the charm of a rubbish heap, and immediately informed me that his contractual duties cover drafting press releases and no more."

"Yikes. Poor you."

"And then there's the Oscar Davies issue—"

"Notorious, I'm afraid," Mira muttered.

"Yes, I know. Stuck in the nineties. Sexist. Open about it. Uninterested in innovations of any sort. A brilliant quality in your chief technical officer. And then, on top of all of that, Joren quit and—" She cut herself off before she spilled that other piece of bad news.

Mira chuckled. "You mean your new driver? The word's already out. Sorry, I know he gets on your nerves."

She pressed her forehead against her palm. "It's just a bit . . . awkward."

Mira was silent for a beat. "Violet. You didn't."

She sighed in defeat. This was the problem with friends. They knew you really well. "Sleep with him? Yes, I did."

Mira let out a shocked laugh. "You don't even like him!"

"Who said anything about liking him? I just fucked him." And fucked him, and fucked him, and fucked him again. All night long.

"What . . . how . . . *when*?"

"It was Monaco, the Hansbach party. The one *you* were supposed to come with me to."

"I told you, it was an emergency—"

"It's fine. Anyway, I was on my own, and . . . there he was."

"And you just decided to *sleep* with him?"

"There weren't any better prospects. And he *is* ridiculously fit. The body is—"

"Okay, that's enough about *that* mess. Tell me about Reece. What's he like?"

Violet laughed without humor, but she felt better, talking about all of this with Mira. "Have you got time? This might take all night."

4

As soon as Chase was away from the Pinnacle factory, he made the call he'd been dying to make all day. His father picked up almost immediately.

"Chase? What is it? Are you all right?" Dad's Spanish accent always got thicker when he was caught off guard.

"I'm fine, Dad. Are you at work? I have some news."

"Your mother and I both work from home on Mondays now. What is it?"

He had to force the words out around the tightness in his throat. "Dad, I did it. Formula One. I'm driving for Pinnacle for the rest of the season."

Through the phone, he heard his father inhale sharply. "What . . . how?"

He gave his father the short version, ending with his arrival at Pinnacle this morning. "So that's it. I'm in. Thirteen races left in the season."

"My boy! I'm so proud of you!" He could hear the tears in his father's voice, and it made his throat get tight again. He blinked away the burning in his eyes. "I told you, Chase. Didn't I tell you

you'd make it to Formula One one day? You were born to drive! I'm so happy!"

He chuckled. "You did, Dad. Every day since I was four."

His love of racing had come straight from his dad. His earliest memories involved sitting on Dad's lap watching Formula One online as he explained the intricacies of the sport and the cars. He'd grown up worshiping Michael Schumacher and Ayrton Senna the way other Chicago kids worshiped Michael Jordan.

"Nic!" his father called away from the phone. "Come talk to Chase. He has news."

"No, Dad, don't bother her if she's working—" Chase protested, but it was too late.

He listened to the familiar sounds from back home—his mom calling down from the upstairs landing, the thud of her bare feet on the stairs, his parents' brief discussion as Dad passed off the phone—and felt a tug in his chest.

His parents were devoted to each other. He'd grown up believing that one day, inevitably, he'd find a relationship like his parents', and at one point, he'd thought he had. Something real and honest when every other relationship around him seemed cynically transactional.

But he'd been wrong. Not only was his relationship transactional, but he'd been traded in for a more valuable player. That was the first time his instinctive trust in others had been abused, but it wouldn't be the last. So he'd sworn off hunting for The One. Maybe that shit only happened once in a millennium, and his parents were the lucky two.

As long as he was racing, he didn't have the time or energy for dating anyway. For now, transactional relationships suited him just fine. A little fun, a lot of pleasure for both parties, then everybody goes their separate ways with no hard feelings. It worked for him.

Dad put Mom on the phone and he related his news all over again. Mom was thrilled, of course, but not like Dad had been. His dad was the one with the love of racing, a passion he'd passed on to all three Navarro kids. Mom was supportive, but she joked that racing had stolen her family, which wasn't entirely untrue.

"I'm going to call Sam and Tyler," Dad said when he got back on the phone. "They're going to be so excited. And your grandmother. And my sisters."

"Dad, it's late here. I'll call them all tomorrow. I promised to meet some of the guys from Engineering for a drink. I gotta go."

"You go," Dad said. "Have fun and celebrate. Chase, we're so proud of you. We love you, my boy."

Those words were more meaningful than the call from Pinnacle. "I couldn't have done this without you guys. Love you too."

When he got off the phone with his parents, he pocketed his phone and headed into Wetherspoons. Leon had asked him to join him and some of the engineers for a drink after work and he'd jumped at the chance to get to know the crew better. Leon was right. He'd always preferred hanging out with the mechanics.

He paused inside the door, scanning the room for Leon. He saw him and the rest of the group in a booth on the far side of the room, but then he also saw *her*... Violet, sitting alone at the bar with a tumbler of vodka.

For a beat, he hesitated. He could head straight over to Leon's table and ignore her. That's probably what she'd prefer. But there was something so dejected about her hunched shoulders, a kind of weary defeat that he'd never seen in Violet before. And instead of celebrating her new job and getting to know her new coworkers like he was, she was drinking alone.

Some stupid instinct told him he should check on her. She'd probably just hand him his ass, but at least he'd know he'd made the attempt.

He waved at Leon and held up a finger, then headed over to join her. When he slid onto the barstool next to her, she turned her head and scoffed when she saw him.

"Of course," she muttered.

"Nice to see you, too, Violet."

The bartender stopped in front of him. "What can I get you?"

"I'll have a Guinness. And another for the lady."

"I buy my own drinks," she snapped.

"Come on, just one. Celebrate with me."

She swirled the ice cubes in her empty glass. "To be honest, Chase, I'm not seeing much worth celebrating right now."

He looked at her curiously. "Are you kidding? Do you know how long I've worked for this? I moved to Spain to live with my grandma when I was *fifteen*, just so I could race."

That caught her attention, and she cast him a curious glance. "You did?"

"I did. All for a shot at this, and now it's here. I've made it." He smiled at her. She did not return it.

The bartender set their drinks down in front of them, and Violet scowled at hers, but she still picked it up and took a sip.

"Look," he conceded, "I know this team's not the best on the grid—"

"They're the *worst*."

"Right *now* they're the worst. But we can turn this around. I have to believe that. If I stopped believing I could do that, I'd have quit years ago. I'd be . . ." He waved a hand in the air. "I don't know. Running a go-kart track back in Chicago, boring all the kids with stories about how I almost made it to Formula One. But I didn't quit. I stuck it out. And now I'm here."

"Look, I'm super glad that all your dreams have come true. Just don't go looking for miracles."

"You really don't think we can turn it around?"

She half pivoted on her stool to look at him. "Did you see what I saw on that tour today? Oscar Davies hasn't had an original idea in two decades and is probably a nightmare to work for, because Rabia and Leon seem to be running a shadow government in that place. The new team principal is a clueless knob, and his assistant is too busy bursting into tears to keep control of him. The dysfunction in that factory would keep them from staging a successful fire drill, never mind a successful Formula One season. So, no, I do not think we can turn it around. My plan is to stay here just long enough to make it count on my CV and then get the hell out."

She turned away and took a long swig of her drink. He considered her for a moment, wondering when this young, gorgeous girl had gotten so angry and jaded. Her face was surprisingly delicate for such a spiky thing, with big eyes that were so dark blue they were almost the color of her namesake flower. She probably thought her dramatic dark eye makeup made her look tougher, but to him, she just looked mysterious and sexy. Her full lips were still stained with the remnants of the blood-red lipstick she favored. It occurred to him suddenly that he hadn't kissed her that night in Monaco. Well, not on her mouth, anyway.

"Yeah, I saw all that. But here's what I know, Violet." When he said her name, she turned her head to look at him again. "Not one of those people got into this sport because it was just some job to pay the bills. Every one of them got into racing because they *love* it. They love the cars and the tracks and the technology and the strategy and the *speed.* They loved all of that enough to try for it, even though everybody tries and almost no one makes it." He folded his arms on the bar in front of him. "And, yeah, we're last on the grid. But we're *on* it. I'm going to do my damnedest to turn this around. And I guarantee you, every other person here will fight to turn it around, too. Because we're all here for the same reason. Because we all fucking *love* racing."

Violet blinked, then turned away and tossed back some of her vodka. "Are you always like this?"

"Like what?"

She waved her hand in his general direction. "The can-do spirit, the plucky optimism."

He chuckled and took a swig of his beer. "I guess I don't like conceding defeat before I've even started. I'd rather pitch in with the team and try."

She let out a soft huff of laughter. "See? Can-do spirit."

Bringing up Monaco was probably the last thing he should do at the moment, but he couldn't resist teasing her about it a little bit.

Nudging her elbow with his, he murmured, "My can-do spirit worked pretty well for you in Monaco."

She kept her eyes fixed forward, but her lips parted slightly and she let out a breath.

"All things considered, I think we'd better forget Monaco ever happened."

He paused for a beat, then leaned closer. "You sure? I'm pretty sure we could improve your mood. No strings attached."

He knew that's what Violet preferred. And yes, what he preferred, too.

She turned her head to glance at him. Their eyes locked and his teasing smile faded. Attraction crackled between them, as clear as a lightning bolt in the night sky. Forget teasing. He was almost painfully invested in this, desperate to have a chance to touch her again, to kiss her finally. He could almost feel her lips against his, almost taste her tongue with his.

One corner of her lips curled up in a slight smile, then she threw back the rest of her drink in one go. For a split second, he thought she was game, and adrenaline flooded his body. *Yes.* God, yes.

But then she hopped off her barstool and clapped him on the shoulder. "Trust me, Chase, the last thing I'd ever expect of you is strings. But the answer is no. Have fun celebrating. I'm going home."

He watched her stride across the pub, that long sweep of black hair swaying from side to side, matching the movement of her hips. It took several long minutes for his body to unwind. Okay, he was bummed she'd turned him down. Bummed didn't begin to cover it. Right now, he'd crawl on his knees over broken glass to get her back into his bed. But she'd said no, and that was that. He took a sip of his beer and turned to join Leon and the rest of the crew.

5

The news of Pinnacle's sale and the new leadership had spread through the sport like wildfire. Everybody was desperate to get a glimpse of Pinnacle's inexperienced new head, Reece Hammond, so they could start ripping him to shreds.

So Violet had designed the Pinnacle press launch to prevent that from happening. There would be no access to Reece. Instead, she had invited a small group of *very* carefully chosen sports reporters to come to the factory to interview the drivers and Oscar Davies. Oscar was a pro with the press, much as she loathed him, and he'd been with Pinnacle his entire career, signaling stability. And to distract from the admin shake-up, she planned to feature their veteran driver Dieter Gruber, who had purportedly had extensive media training, whereas Chase had not.

Unfortunately, Dieter's training was nowhere to be found. Unenthusiastic didn't begin to encompass just what a black hole of charisma he was. She'd never seen anyone who could remain so steadfastly expressionless for so long. One-word answers, a dead-eyed stare that bordered on creepy, and not one hint of a smile in fifteen minutes.

Kathryn, one of the journalists, asked him her next question. "So, Dieter, are there any new challenges you foresee in the second half of the season?"

Dieter blinked slowly. "No."

Kathryn waited for him to expound on that, but apparently that was all Dieter had to say on the subject. Good lord, *who* had done his media training?

Violet turned to Maisie, her head of social media, who still hadn't managed to speak more than a handful of sentences out loud. Violet had checked out her work on the socials and she seemed to know what she was doing. Great graphics, punchy captions, posts that encouraged sharing and engagement.

"Whatever you do, don't put him on TikTok. He'll be deadly."

Maisie looked up from her phone, blinking her wide brown eyes rapidly from under her long, dark brown fringe, and nodded.

"Um, Violet?" Imogen was standing just inside the conference room door, clutching her iPad to her chest like a shield. "Reece wants to know what time his interviews start."

Oh, no. If the press got so much as five minutes of face time with Reece, Pinnacle would become a laughingstock overnight.

"We talked about this. He's not scheduled for interviews today."

"But he wants—"

"He can't. He's going to be talking with Kevin in Race Strategy, who will be bringing him up to speed for the next race, like we arranged."

"But he said he can do that any day and—"

"Imogen," she said gently, "I'm going to need your help here. Under no circumstances can Reece enter this room. I need you to keep that from happening."

Imogen's eyes went wide with anxiety. "How do I do that?"

Violet sighed. "Imogen, I'm going to tell you a secret. Reece isn't in charge here."

"Violet, he's my literal *boss.* His name is on the door—"

"Yes, but that's just a name, isn't it? Does he know anything about racing?"

Imogen shook her head.

"Do *you* know something about racing?"

Imogen nodded. "Been watching with my dad since I was little."

"I used to watch with my dad, too," Violet said, and even she could hear how her voice dipped into a snarl when she mentioned him.

"Really?"

"Yep. I've got my hands full with these guys, which means *you're* the one who's going to have to guide this ship. You're in charge of his schedule. *You* actually know what you're talking about. Are you up for it?"

Wide eyes. A tremulous nod. "If I have to?"

Violet suppressed a grin. "There you go. So take charge of him. And once he finishes with Kevin, I bet there are a thousand things that need to be signed off on all over the factory, yes? So lead him around and get him signing off. I'll handle this in here."

"If you think it's best . . ."

"Imogen, it's necessary. Now go."

As Imogen scurried back out, conversation from the other side of the room caught her attention. It was Chase, surrounded by reporters, even though she'd only slated him for five minutes at the end. He was dressed as he always was, like a careless university student who'd just rolled out of bed—jeans, a grotty gray T-shirt, and beat-up old trainers.

"And I'm telling you, this seagull came swooping in out of nowhere—"

"While you were in the car?"

"While I was in the car! And the bastard took a crap on my visor!"

The reporters burst into laughter. She looked from Chase to the reporters, two guys and a woman. They were hanging on every word of his dumb story. They *adored* him.

Chase's hands moved through the air with an innate physical grace as he continued the story. That bright white smile of his flashed like lightning between words. His overly long, glossy black hair managed to look both messy and perfect, falling across his forehead in a careless sweep until he unconsciously shook it back.

This was it. The key to generating positive press for Pinnacle—*Chase.*

Chase was beautiful, if a little rough around the edges, and he had *it*—charisma. That look-at-me factor you couldn't teach or train.

She'd been up close to this kind of star quality once before. Last time, she'd gotten badly burned. But she was much smarter now.

It gave her a little thrill, having a flash of inspiration about her work. To distract from Reece Hammond, she needed to make Chase Navarro a star.

6

"Honestly, I'm just excited to get behind the wheel and drive," Chase said to the bank of reporters with a shrug.

"We can't wait to see you do it," one of them—Kathryn—replied.

"You guys all coming to Spielberg next week?"

They all nodded enthusiastically.

"Great." He smiled. "Guess I'll see you then."

Violet stepped forward and angled herself in front of him. "That's all we have time for today. If any of you are interested in interviews after Spielberg, email me and we'll see what we can do."

Violet must be good at her job, because they all told her they wanted time with him in Austria. He'd never gotten this kind of press interest in F2.

"See you guys later." He waved. "And hey, Jon, don't forget what I told you about Ascari at Monza."

The middle-aged reporter he'd been talking to nodded enthusiastically. "Yeah, I'll check that out when we get there. Thanks, Chase."

As the reporters scattered and started packing up their equipment, Violet turned sharply to face him.

"Do you have a minute?" she asked.

There was a look in her eye he had never seen before . . . elation?

"You seem happy."

She promptly scowled.

"Ah, there she is."

She was wearing another one of those tight suits she liked, black this time, with a black satin bustier peeking out from under the jacket. Her hair was slicked back behind her ears, and her earrings were two ferocious-looking dangling silver spikes.

She let out an annoyed huff. "My office."

He followed her down the hall and into her office. It was small, with just one window looking out over the parking lot. It was also entirely bare.

"Where's your stuff?"

Her eyebrows furrowed. "What stuff?"

"You know . . . house plants, pictures of your family . . . stuff."

"I guess I don't do stuff."

He made a slow circuit of the room, opening drawers and thumbing through the folders on her desk. It had only been a couple of days since she'd started, but it was still so curiously empty it made him wonder what her home looked like. Did she like color or would she go for all white? Vintage or modern? Florals or skulls? Was it also this empty? Probably.

"Will you quit messing with my stuff?" she snapped.

"You just said you didn't have any. Aha!" Behind a box of files on the corner of her desk he spotted one picture frame. But when he pulled it out, it wasn't a picture of parents or siblings. It was her and Miranda Wentworth on the track, outside the Lennox mobile offices. They had their arms slung around each other's shoulders and were both grinning widely. Violet looked different, the way he remembered her from past seasons. Ripped jeans and a faded black Violent Femmes T-shirt. Her hair was a windblown riot, held off her face with a pair of sunglasses. He wasn't sure he'd ever seen her smile like that. Certainly not when he was around.

"You guys are really close, huh?"

She plucked the picture frame out of his hand and set it back on her desk. "She's my friend. Are you finished?"

He shrugged. "I guess. So what did you want to see me for?"

"Who's your PR person? We need to set up a meeting ASAP."

He turned to face her and leaned back on the edge of her desk, crossing his arms over his chest. "It's you, isn't it?"

"No, your personal PR person. You have one, don't you?"

"Of my own? No." A lot of guys did, but that always seemed like one of those luxuries you got when you ascended up the ranks, which had decidedly not happened to him, until now.

Her eyebrows drew together. "Who handles your media?"

He shrugged. "If someone wanted to talk to me, they went through Hansbach. Their PR person set it up. Didn't happen often enough to be an issue."

Violet sighed and pressed her fingers against her forehead. "Do you have someone coordinating your sponsorships for you?"

He scoffed. "There's not much to coordinate. My agent handles the contracts."

Violet glanced around the office as though looking for patience. "How have you survived this long?" she muttered.

"I've done just fine, Violet."

"Chase, you've been a bottom-feeder when you could have been a *star.*"

"What are you talking about?"

She stabbed a finger in the air, in the direction of the conference room down the hall. "That," she said. "Today. As much as it pains me to admit this, you were *brilliant.*"

"I was? I hardly said anything. You wouldn't let me."

"That's the thing. You spoke for two minutes and every person in that room was in love with you. Dieter was in there for two hours and I doubt any of them can remember a second of it."

"It's just press stuff."

Violet crossed her arms and he couldn't help glancing down at the swell of her breasts cresting over the edge of her bustier. That thing was just unfair.

"That 'press stuff' is fucking important. Look, Pinnacle's got a lot of liabilities. Oscar, who wouldn't recognize innovation if it bit him in the ass; Reece, who is a walking media disaster waiting to happen; Dieter, who is about as appealing as that fermented fish thing they eat in Sweden. Right now, we have one asset, and it's you."

"Look, I know I'm a good driver—"

"I'm not talking about your driving! I'm talking about *you.*" She waved a hand at him. "The face, the hair, the smile, the fucking American charm. We are making you a star."

"Violet, this is nice and everything, but I'm not into that stuff. I just want to drive."

"Do you really not get how this game is played? It's all the same thing. The press coverage leads to attention. Attention gets you sponsorships. Sponsorships mean next year the budget is bigger, and the car gets better. Sponsorships mean, Chase, that next season, you get re-signed to a Formula One team instead of getting bounced to Formula E or Rally Car or something. Press keeps you behind the wheel."

That caught his attention. He really wasn't interested in hawking watches and men's cologne or whatever, doing the promotional stuff he'd seen the big drivers do. But if this could keep him in the car . . .

"What do I have to do?"

"Whatever I say."

Despite the serious turn the conversation had taken, he couldn't help but grin. "Didn't know you were into that, but okay."

She huffed. "Will you pay attention?"

He laughed and held up his hands. "I am, I am. I promise. So you want me to, what . . . do some interviews?"

"I'm thinking bigger than interviews. I'm thinking photo shoots, publicity events, parties . . . Maybe we'll find you someone to date."

"Hey, I do *not* need help with that."

"Not *actually* date. Someone with a high profile. Someone who'll get attention, which would get *you* attention—"

"People *do* that?" Although he knew from firsthand experience how ruthless some people could be about relationships, so why was this a surprise?

"In my line of work it happens all the time. One thing at a time, though. First, we need to hire you a stylist and get that nightmare you call a wardrobe into shape."

"There's nothing wrong with my clothes." He gestured down at his favorite pair of jeans.

"You look like you sleep on your brother's sofa," Violet said flatly.

"Okay, but you just said I was hot."

"You *are* hot. I'm just going to make sure the whole world knows you're hot. This will work, but I need you on board. So?"

He considered it for a minute. It grated him, being told he had to dress up and maybe pretend to *date* somebody just to keep his spot behind the wheel. But on the other hand, since he was fifteen, he'd been willing to do whatever it took to race.

That was still true.

"Sure." He sighed. "Whatever you say."

"Great. I'll start making some phone calls." She pulled out her phone and started scrolling. "You can go."

He hesitated, watching her type out an email, her inky black lashes fanning out across the tops of her pale cheekbones. They'd had their fun once. He really should just move on. Repeats ran the risk of feelings, and that was something he was not about to wade into. Not again . . . not after last time, and certainly not with someone as . . . ruthless . . . as Violet.

But damn, every time he looked at her, he thought about it—that night in Monaco, her body under his . . . It was distracting to the point of obsession.

"Hey, Violet?" he said, his voice low and rough.

"Yeah?" she said without looking up.

"Know what I keep thinking about?"

"What's that?" she murmured, distracted.

"That night in Monaco, I never kissed you. I still think about it . . . a lot."

Her head snapped up, eyes zeroing in on his, and heat ricocheted through his body.

"Do you?" he asked. There was a pause and Chase realized with horror that he had accidentally expressed a vulnerability. To *Violet.*

But to his surprise, she didn't immediately tear him to pieces. She stared at him for a beat, then seemed to make up her mind about something.

"What the hell? It's after six. Let's go."

"Wait. Are you serious?"

Her hands went to her hips. "Why, are you changing your mind?"

"No, but you said you wanted to forget about it."

She shrugged. "Like you said, no strings, right?"

He nodded rapidly before *she* changed her mind. "No strings. I promise."

"So let's go. Let me guess, you still don't have your own place."

"I got hired last week. I'm still driving back to my apartment in East Luddleton. Plus, I have a roommate."

She sighed with deep disappointment. "You're lucky you're so hot. Follow me."

Violet watched from the entryway to her apartment building as Chase nimbly parallel parked his vintage Austin-Healey across the street. It was a beater, with faded paint and rust spots, but undeniably a great car underneath all that. Like Chase himself, she supposed.

He obviously knew how to handle a car, but it was hot just the same. And so was he, as he unfolded his long, fit body from inside the small car.

Sleeping with him would only complicate things if it mattered. This was simple and straightforward. They both knew what they wanted, and more importantly, what they *didn't* want. The last thing Chase Navarro would ever ask her for was a commitment.

Chase joined her on the sidewalk, looking up at the two-story building behind her. "This your place?"

"Upstairs."

She let them in and led the way up the narrow staircase to her flat.

"Just you in here?"

"Solicitors' offices below. Just me up here."

"I suppose I should have asked this sooner but . . . you live alone?"

She smiled at him over her shoulder. "Is that your way of asking if some burly boyfriend is going to come storming in to pummel you?"

"I can hold my own, but I'd rather not. Besides"—he shrugged—"I only have a few rules and that's one of them."

Funny, that was one of her only rules, too. No poaching other people's partners, not even if it was just for sex. "No," she finally said. "No boyfriend. *Absolutely* not."

As she paused on the landing to retrieve her keys, Chase stepped up behind her, settling his hands on her hips. He dipped his head and nipped at the side of her neck. Her body flushed warm with anticipation. Yep, this was definitely going to be fun.

"Why not?" he asked, pressing the length of his body against her back. She could feel the hard bulge of his cock against her ass.

She turned slightly, peering up at him. "Chase," she said.

"Mhmm?" His eyes dropped from her eyes to her mouth, drinking her in. It sent a thrill through her.

"We're not sharing." She fumbled with the keys and unlocked the door.

"Works for me." He walked her across the threshold as his hands slid around and up under her jacket, cupping her breasts through that hot as fuck bustier.

"This thing has been driving me crazy all day." He kicked the door closed behind him.

She pressed her ass against his hips. "Good." She wriggled out of her jacket and he helped peel it down her arms, tossing it off to the side.

"Bedroom?" he muttered against her ear as one of his hands slid down over her stomach and began working at the button of her trousers. "Or should I just bend you over that nice sofa and fuck you there?"

"Sofa is closer."

"Close is good."

She stepped out of her heels as they staggered toward it. He slid her trousers over her hips and she shimmied them down to her ankles before stepping out of those, too.

"You're killing me," he groaned, pressing himself again against her now-bare ass. She liked that he told her how much he wanted her. It felt delicious. They reached the couch, a long blood-red leather thing that had just been delivered, the first proper piece of furniture she'd ever bought. This seemed an auspicious way to christen it. Her hands slammed down on the back of it, fingers digging into the supple leather. Behind her, Chase briskly unbuttoned the fly of his jeans.

His wallet hit the couch in front of her and she heard the condom package rip open. She looked back over her shoulder just in time to watch him roll it on, because what a sight that was. His dick was very, very pretty.

"Ready?" He laid a hand between her shoulder blades, urging her forward. Two fingers reached between her thighs, sweeping her thong to one side. She moaned. Those same two fingers slid up inside her. "That's a yes," he ground out when he discovered how wet she was.

His fingers disappeared and then he filled her, suddenly, with one powerful thrust.

"Fuck," she murmured, gripping the back of the couch.

He groaned, a guttural, ragged sound that made her stomach twist with desire. His fingers curled into her hips. "You feel so good."

He pulled out and thrust in again, and this time they both groaned. His pace was brisk, which was good, because this wasn't going to take her long at all. As his hips snapped against her ass, she could already feel the tightening in her lower belly, and her thighs were starting to shake.

"Please tell me you're close," he said.

"Almost."

He slid a hand around in front of her and between her thighs, parting her. "This good?" His fingers found her clit and she moaned again.

It was all over after that. She came hard, gripping the couch to balance herself as her legs went boneless. He thrust twice more, his left hand digging into her hip hard enough to leave marks, before he let out another groan from deep in his chest. He slumped over her back as she panted.

Gradually his grip on her eased. "Bathroom?" he muttered.

She lifted a limp hand and pointed to the left. "Through that door."

He slipped out of her and disappeared to clean himself up. When her trembling legs could support her again, she stretched luxuriously, reveling in the aftermath of a really good orgasm, and walked back through the flat, retrieving her clothes and shoes from the floor. That was an excellent way to relieve stress. Maybe they could make it a semi-regular thing.

She ducked into her bedroom to dump her rumpled clothes on the bed. As she came back to the living room, sliding into her black silk robe, she found Chase across the room, examining her record collection.

"What are you doing?" Her voice sounded a little too hostile and accusatory. He was just looking. Still, having someone in her space poking through her stuff always made her twitchy. It's why she liked to go to the guy's place. Except that Chase was some eternal university student who didn't really have a place.

Typical Chase, he seemed unfazed. He glanced back over his shoulder and smiled. "I was right to be intimidated by you."

She scowled. "Intimidated?"

BEHIND HIM, VIOLET drifted closer as Chase flipped through a bunch of records. There was a whole bookshelf of vintage vinyl, rows and rows of it, mostly of bands he'd never heard of. There was all of Bowie's discography, which was familiar enough, but there was a lot more. The Misfits, Suicide, the Cramps, Urban Blight, the Slits, the New York Dolls . . . album after album. To the left, on another bookshelf, she had a pretty impressive stereo setup, with a turntable and massive speakers.

Up until now, if he'd been pressed to guess what Violet did in her free time, he'd have said "planning the invasion of a small island nation." Instead, she collected records—vintage vinyl, and judging from the stereo, she listened to all of it.

"You're intimidating because you're cool," he explained, sliding one record halfway out. "I've never even *heard* of the Stooges."

"Oh." Her scowl melted away. "They're a proto-punk band from America. Their first self-titled album came out in sixty-nine." She tapped the corner of an album. "But I prefer their third, *Raw Power*, from seventy-three. Iggy Pop was at his peak on this one." She ran her finger down the spine. "Williamson on guitar took them to a new level."

"Oh my god, forget it. You're not cool. You're a *nerd*." That was probably the most he'd ever heard her say about anything other than racing, and it was absolutely the most enthusiastic he'd ever heard her sound.

She scowled again. "I am not. I'm just a collector."

"Come on, Violet, this is extremely nerdy. I bet you've got them all cataloged in a spreadsheet. You do, don't you?"

She hiked one perfectly arched black eyebrow at him. "Do I look like a spreadsheet kind of person?" She paused for a beat, then shrugged in discomfort. "It's handwritten."

He chuckled, running a finger down the row of records, each one in a protective clear plastic sleeve. "Where did you find all these?"

"Some online. All my traveling helps. I find amazing stuff in Japan. Vinyl's huge there."

"Why vinyl?" Violet definitely struck him as an early adopter of technology. Her phone was never far from her hand. This whole collection was instantly available online. Why the vinyl and the record player?

"I like hearing it the way it was originally intended to be listened to. Nothing beats *Venus in Furs* by the Velvet Underground on vinyl. Digital just isn't the same. And . . ." She went quiet.

"What?"

She shook her head. "Never mind."

He nudged her elbow with his. "Say it."

"Well . . ." She pulled that Stooges album out enough to look at the cover. Some shirtless guy in goth makeup gripping a microphone. "This groundbreaking punk album barely sold. You could go see these guys play live whenever you wanted, at Max's Kansas City or Whisky a Go Go, or a million other shitty clubs. They were making magic and nobody even knew it at the time. The vinyl . . ." She sighed before sliding the record back into place. "It's the closest you can get to being there for the magic."

It was cute, actually—that she was so passionate about something so niche. "You must really love music, huh?"

She didn't answer right away, and when he glanced over at her, her eyes had gone a little flat and distracted. "Yeah," she finally said. "I do."

"Which one's your favorite?"

She let out a soft scoff. "That's an impossible question."

"Go on," he said, nudging her elbow. She'd changed into a silky black robe that made her pale skin look like velvet in contrast. He could imagine running his palm across the slick fabric and feeling the warmth of her body underneath it, but they'd just had sex, and she hadn't kicked him out yet, so he didn't press his luck. "Just pick one and put it on."

She cast him a suspicious glare. "Why? We're not hanging out."

He rolled his eyes. "Just pretend I'm not here. Put on what you want to listen to right now."

"Why do you care?"

"I'm curious. Humor me." Her apartment had turned out to be nearly as spare as her office, confirming that he'd been right on that point. Just that long red sofa he'd bent her over, and a coffee table. But there was *this*, these two shelves filled with her passion project. Now that he'd gotten a peek at off-hours Violet, he wanted to see more. What did she *do* when she wasn't barking orders at people?

She sighed and ran a red-tipped finger down the shelf, considering. Finally she slid one out.

"This isn't my favorite, because there's no such thing," she said, carefully sliding the album out of the paper sleeve. With her fingers bracing the edges, she flipped it over in a practiced—and very sexy—move, before settling it on the turntable. "But the Runaways are always a good choice."

She gently settled the needle on the record right between two tracks, and he swore he saw her shoulders relax infinitesimally the instant the hiss started pouring through the speakers.

Drums, wailing electric guitars, pulsing bass, and loud female voices shouting, "Take it or leave it!"

He smiled and nodded. "Now this is *you.*"

"You don't know me."

"Sure I do. And this song is you, Violet."

Her eyes met his for a split second, then she inhaled deeply and spun away. "Okay, this has been fun, but—"

He laughed despite himself. "Yeah, yeah, I'm going."

***GOOD*, VIOLET THOUGHT.** He'd already lingered here much longer than necessary, pawing through her record collection and asking uncomfortable questions. She didn't look at him as she walked back across the apartment to the front door.

"Guess there's no point asking if you want to go get a drink or something," he said, running a hand through his hair. He seemed . . . nervous, which was odd for Chase.

"Lucky for you, I'm not a wine-and-dine kind of girl. And you've got a long drive back to East Luddleton."

He paused for a moment as he tucked his wallet into his back pocket. "You know, there's something I keep forgetting to do."

She opened the front door for him. "What's that, Chase?"

He headed toward the door, but stopped abruptly when he got to her. Then his arm snaked out and grabbed her around the waist, as his other hand gripped the back of her neck and his mouth came down hard on hers. She was so caught off guard that for a moment, she just stood there, shock flooding through her. Then his mouth moved over hers and her blood started pumping again. It was a hard, hungry kiss, and he was *good* at it, just like he was at everything else. Her lips parted for him and before she was consciously aware of deciding to do it, she was kissing him back. Her hands found their way to his biceps and her fingers curled in. The Runaways were pulsing through the air, the vibrations of the music making her whole body tingle.

His tongue swept in and brushed hers and she had to bite back a moan. She felt that brush of his tongue all the way down between her legs. He was so *close.* She could feel the prickle of his stubble and the heat of his breath against her cheek. Funny, for all the sex they'd had, for all the ways he'd plundered her body so far—and there were a lot—this felt like the most intimate thing they'd done.

She wrenched her mouth away from his and took a step back. He let her go easily. That wicked smile that was becoming so familiar to her flashed bright white in the fading light of the day, and he reached up, touching his fingertip to the middle of her bottom lip. "Goodnight, Violet."

And then he was gone.

8

Spielberg, Austria

"See, now this is much better."

Violet waved her phone in his face as Chase zipped up his gray race suit. No, not gray—silver, because the Pinnacle livery colors were *silver and pewter.* They looked like light gray and dark gray to him, but what did he know?

He scowled at her phone, at a picture of himself at the press conference two days ago. "What's much better?"

"Your *clothes.* You look hot. I told you that stylist knew what she was doing."

That stylist had taken one look at the pile of clothes in his hotel room and declared it a total loss. Overnight, the closet had been repopulated with expensive jeans and jackets, fancy dress shirts, Italian shoes, and high-end suits. The T-shirts alone had probably cost more than his entire old wardrobe. He couldn't really see much difference, but Violet seemed to think the T-shirt and designer track jacket he'd worn to the press conference were a huge success.

"It's just clothes, Violet. All that really matters is what I'm about to do out there."

Qualifying was about to get underway, his first behind the wheel for Pinnacle. He wasn't quite sure how to identify what he was feeling. Excitement? Dread? Considering how quickly he'd come on board, no one in the Pinnacle garage expected much of him today. Show up and don't crash the car. But he'd set a personal goal for himself—do better than Dieter. Then everyone would know he wasn't there to keep the seat warm for the rest of the season. He was there to compete, and he'd do it to the limits the Pinnacle car would allow. So far, his simulator sessions hadn't been promising, but he'd do the best he could with the car he was driving, just like he always did.

"Just clothes," Violet scoffed. "Check out the comments."

"Violet—"

She pushed her phone into his chest. "Just *look.*"

He sighed and took it from her, scrolling down.

Who is this?? Where has he been all my life??

Chase Navarro is 🔥

I have a new favorite driver!

Social media was the worst.

"Great. Nice to know they're already fans before they've even seen me race."

"You have *got* to get better at this. Of course the racing is the most important part, but believe me, this part matters, too."

She took her phone back, scrolling through the comments and smiling to herself, so he took a moment to surreptitiously check her out as he secured the closures at his neck. Most of the staff in the paddock was wearing Pinnacle team gear—gray polos and T-shirts. Not Violet. Skin-tight black pants, black heels, and a black drapey shirt strategically fastened on her shoulders in a way that left her arms bare. Her only concession to the fact that they were spending the day in the sun was the big black sunglasses currently holding her hair off her face. She probably wouldn't be caught dead in a Pinnacle polo shirt. Which was fine, because she looked hot as fuck like this.

"What'd you do with Reece?" he asked, glancing around the garage. Everybody on the team was busy getting ready for his first qualifying stint, but their team principal was nowhere to be seen.

"He's over in hospitality getting loaded with some reps from Rally Fuel."

"Probably the best place for him," Chase muttered.

Violet glanced up at him. "I'll do my best to keep him corralled."

"Appreciate it. I have enough to deal with without that distraction."

"Hey, Chase."

He turned around. Speaking of fucking distractions . . .

"Hey, Liam."

They'd crossed paths plenty of times before now, but since Chase had been an F2 bottom-feeder and Liam had been a Formula One rising star, Liam usually pretended not to see him. Which was fine. It wasn't like he had anything to say to the fucker anyway.

"Congratulations on Pinnacle," Liam said in a flat, unreadable tone of voice.

"Thanks," Chase said, equally neutral.

Liam was suited up in his yellow Solaris race suit, sponsor logos splashed all over it. This was his third season in Formula One. He'd come in second overall in the driver's championship to Will Hawley last season, but Solaris had redesigned the car for this season, and it had hit the track full of gremlins they had yet to shake out, so Liam wasn't nearly as high in the rankings this year. Chase was petty enough to admit he was enjoying watching him struggle.

Beside him, Violet was looking from him to Liam and back again.

"Hi!" she finally interjected, sticking her hand out. "I'm Violet Harper. Pinnacle PR."

Liam smiled broadly at her and shook her hand. "Nice to meet you, Violet. I've seen you around, right?"

Fucker. That smile made his skin twitch, because he'd seen it before and he knew what it meant. And he held on to Violet's hand longer than he needed to.

"I was at Lennox until recently," she said.

"That's right." Liam's eyes cut to Chase. "Well, have fun at Pinnacle."

"I didn't know you guys knew each other," she said, eyes darting between him and Liam.

He shifted a step closer to her. "Oh yeah, me and Liam go way back," he said easily, locking eyes with him. "All the way back to Hansbach's young driver academy, right, Liam?"

Liam stared back at him. "That's right."

"How's Sophie?" he asked, reveling in the flare of heat in Liam's pale blue eyes.

Liam scoffed softly before answering, "She's great. Sophie's just great. So . . . guess I'll see you out there?"

"Guess you will."

"Okay, then. Good luck."

"You, too."

He watched Liam walk away and felt like kicking something.

Violet rounded on him. "What the fuck was *that* about?"

"What?"

"You, and the fact that you hate Liam O'Neill's guts. Pretty sure he loathes you, too. What's the story?"

He shrugged. "No story." At least, not one he had any interest in sharing.

Violet crossed her arms and narrowed her eyes at him. "Do you have any idea how good I am at digging up dirt?"

"Dig away," he muttered, fastening the straps of his suit around his wrists. There was nothing to find. Nothing official, anyway. Just a lot of personal shit that didn't even matter anymore. And a woman who left him for someone she thought was better.

He could feel her gaze still on him, but he kept his eyes fixed on the closures of his suit, even though he'd double- and triple-checked them all.

"You sure you're okay?" she said at last.

Now he did look up, shooting her a grin. "Don't tell me you're worried about me, Violet."

She scoffed and shoved at his arm. Then she blinked, her hand clamping down on his forearm. "Oh my god, there's Clive Pennington."

"Who?"

"He's . . . never mind. Just wait right here. I'm serious. *Don't move.*"

She darted away and inserted herself in front of some guy walking past in the pit lane. Fifties, salt-and-pepper hair, sports jacket. He watched, confused, as she chatted up this random stranger. Then she hooked her arm around his and led him back over to the Pinnacle garage.

"Chase, I want you to meet Clive Pennington, head of marketing at Arrow Beverages. Clive, this is Chase Navarro, Pinnacle's new driver."

Clive shook his hand. "Nice to meet you, Chase. Violet's been telling me your story."

He shot Violet a look. *What story?*

"Quite the thing, making it to Formula One like this."

"Ah, yeah, it's been a wild few weeks. But I'm excited to be here."

"Your new team principal is throwing a party on Sunday after the race, right?"

"I guess?"

"Come find me there. Let's have a drink."

Over Clive's shoulder, he could see Violet, eyes wide, nodding furiously. "Ahh, sure thing."

"I'll let you get back to qualifying. Good luck out there."

"Thanks."

Clive Pennington left and Chase turned to Violet. "What was that about?"

"That was me getting you a sponsorship deal."

"He didn't say anything about sponsorships," Chase said, sweeping his hair off his forehead in preparation for pulling on his balaclava.

"Of *course* he didn't. And he won't until you chat him up a little more."

He was more confused than ever, like Violet had heard an entirely different conversation than he had. "You think he really might be interested in sponsoring me?"

"I think he was intrigued by the story I pitched him."

"What story?"

"You know, plucky American kid from the hardscrabble streets of Chicago—"

"We lived in the suburbs."

"—moving to Europe as a teenager, living with his elderly grandma in the Spanish countryside, all to pursue racing—"

"My grandma lives in Madrid. She's a lawyer—"

"—driving reserve for half a dozen teams—"

"—three teams—"

"—before being plucked from obscurity and offered a seat in Formula One."

"Okay, that part is true. But Violet—"

She grasped his upper arms, staring into his eyes intently. Good god, her eyes were pretty. "Listen to me," she said. "I crafted a narrative that intrigued him. I baited the hook. At the party tomorrow night, you're going to reel him in. Got it?"

He chuckled. "You are so devious."

"I'm good at my job. So tomorrow?"

He saluted her. "Whatever you say, General."

She opened her mouth to complain, but just then Imogen popped up behind her. "Um, Mr. Navarro—"

"Imogen, I told you to call me Chase."

"Okay, Mr. Chase Navarro. Emil says you need to get ready."

He inhaled deeply. "Right. Let's go."

9

As Chase sat in the car, waiting for the go from his team, he did his best to clear his head. There would be no room for nerves or distractions out there.

The first qualifying session was always the worst. Nobody had been eliminated yet, so the track was crowded and, for a car like the one Chase was about to drive around the Red Bull Ring, even the slightest disturbance could bounce him down to the bottom in Q1, which meant starting in the hopeless zone on Sunday. The top-tier teams could manage the Q1 chaos without breaking a sweat and still make the cutoff for Q2, but for Chase, driving Pinnacle's car, it was going to take all his driving skill along with some luck just to make it to Q2.

His head mechanic waved him out of the garage. Time to go *now.* He navigated carefully around the messy turn in the pit lane and out onto the track. Here we go—keep the speed down until he was ready to start his hot lap, then drop the hammer as he made the entry to Turn Nine. *Hell yes.* He belted through Turn Ten with just a millimeter of tire keeping his lap legal, then he hit the DRS and started his hot lap.

Nothing about this track was easy. The engineers always wanted him to monitor a laundry list of information, but Chase was better off when he thought *less.* Tires and aerodynamics and strategy might keep him up at night, but once he was behind the wheel, he left all that in the garage. He trusted himself, his intuition, his focus. He just *knew* when he could take a turn slightly faster than reason said he should.

The roar of the engine filled his ears through Turns Four and Five. *God,* he loved this. Turn Six, and he was a few tenths of a second up on his expected time.

Up ahead, he saw Liam, cooling down on an in-lap. The fucker was absolutely ruining his entry to Turn Nine. Liam was right in the middle of his racing line—Chase *should* have been laser focused on the apex of the curve he needed to hit; instead, he was watching Liam, waiting for him to *move over.*

Chase surged forward, and Liam finally moved aside—but it was too late.

He'd hit the apex a bit too slow, turned out of it a bit too late.

He knew that asshole had purposely waited to the last second before sidling out of the way. But it was over now and he was through Turn Nine. As he barreled across the start/finish line, he looked down to see the dreaded red figures, half a tenth slower than his predicted lap time. Fuck.

He keyed the radio to talk to Emil, his race engineer.

"Would have done better except for that traffic blocking me into Turn Nine."

"Copy," Emil said. "I saw that. It's still not bad. Just a bit more than a tenth off Dieter. We'll discuss it in the pit."

Now he was pissed. He'd had Dieter dead to rights on that lap until Liam decided to fuck around.

They wheeled him into the garage to make adjustments for his second run. Chase scanned the telemetry Emil had just put up on his onboard screen.

"Liam was impeding, Emil," he growled. "How was that not a penalty?"

Emil sighed wearily. "Welcome to the big leagues, Chase. It's a game all drivers play. Learn to beat it or you will suffer."

"Seriously, Emil?"

"Now you know it's coming. Avoid it next time."

The mechanics dropped his car from the jacks and he fired up the power unit.

The radio crackled into life as he blended onto the track. "Okay, you've got traffic behind you."

"Copy."

He moved off the racing line as Liam blew past in his out lap.

See, asshole? That's how it's done.

Glancing at his mirror again, he spotted another oncoming car—Laurent Demarche for Hansbach. Up ahead, he noticed Liam was square in the middle of the racing line, just like last time.

Liam would have to slow down or swing way to the outside on Turn Three, otherwise he'd get a penalty. Knowing Liam, he was going to do the most dickish thing possible, so Chase decided it might be time to fuck with him just a little bit.

Laurent passed him and Chase slid neatly into his slipstream. Chase accelerated right along with him, inching ahead of Liam as he passed.

Emil's voice crackled in his ear. "Uh, tire and brake temps looking a bit high."

Chase chuckled. *I bet they are.*

"Good job with the positioning though," Emil continued. "You're in sync with Demarche and there shouldn't be any traffic in your way."

Liam was probably furious right now. *Pinnacle,* of all the teams, had backed him into a corner. Liam swerved from side to side behind him and then made a run right toward him. Chase nudged his car over to ensure Liam would have to go off track if he tried to pass.

Chase watched him fade and smirked. He was pulling ahead. Good. Turn Nine was approaching and Laurent, in Hansbach's far superior car, was long gone. That meant there was no traffic ahead of him to get in the way when he started his hot lap.

He mashed the accelerator and—there it was, that mind-blowing feeling of the bottom of the world dropping out as the car shot forward underneath him. He'd spent plenty of sim time in Formula One cars, but it was nothing compared to the real thing. Even in Pinnacle's shit car, this was, by far, the most sublime experience of his racing career.

He plunged through Turn Nine, down the hill, and through Turn Ten, into the start/finish straight to start his hot lap. He hung on to the tricky braking needed for Turn One, giving him some extra speed.

The car was a problem in complex turns, though. Chase kept it steady, but he had to wrestle it into line throughout the Turns Four-Five-Six complex. His tires felt right on the edge.

He was nearly there, but could sense his tires giving out.

Easy, Chase. He lined up the last entry and rolled onto the throttle. There was just enough left on the tires to carry him neatly through Turn Ten and across the start/finish line.

"Nice lap," Emil said. "You're currently P twelve and right on the bubble to move through to Q two."

His dash still looked green as he navigated through his cooldown lap. He was holding his breath as the rest of the times filtered in and drivers moved up and down the qualifying rankings accordingly.

"Brendecke is P thirteen . . . Nolan is P fourteen . . ." Emil read off the rankings as they settled into place. "And that's it. We're at P fifteen and no one else improving. You're through to Q two."

Chase blew out his breath, feeling almost lightheaded. He'd made the cut. Brand-new to F1, and in the worst car on the grid, and he'd made it through to round two. Considering . . . well, everything . . . that was nothing short of a miracle.

"Thanks, Emil." Then, trying to sound as uninterested as possible, he asked, "How did Dieter do?"

"P eighteen," Emil replied.

Once Chase was done shouting into his helmet, he keyed the mic and with his best attempt at sounding nonchalant replied, "Okay, let's see what we can do in the next session. Thanks, team."

10

Considering Pinnacle had finished seventeenth and nineteenth in Austria, Reece Hammond's massive post-race party seemed wildly over the top.

Then it became clear. The parties and VIP access were pretty much the only part of Formula One he had any real interest in.

The hotel ballroom was the tragic epitome of an uncool white guy's vision of a cool European party. Thumping bass, a bunch of low-tier spokesmodels in matching silver minidresses and blond wigs serving drinks, and a vodka bar with dry ice smoke pouring out of it. Despite that—or maybe because of it—the place was packed to the rafters. Reece saw it as evidence of his own personal magnetism, but Violet could see it for what it was. Everyone wanted to see what the deal was with the new Pinnacle.

Reece was up on a raised dance floor, dancing in that unspeakable way of his, surrounded by underpaid spokesmodels who looked like they'd rather be getting dental work. But he was confined and content for the moment, so Violet focused on the other, larger part of her job: turning Chase Navarro into a racing superstar, irrespective of his actual results on the track. Though he'd done fine. She supposed.

She found him hanging out in a corner, chatting with Rabia and Leon. Sigh. All that money on clothes to make him look his best, and he was hiding in a dark corner talking about *work.*

He looked amazing, she had to admit. The new charcoal-gray suit was fitted close to his body, showing off the wide shoulders, the long legs, the tight ass. They'd gotten him a haircut, too. Still long, but less "forgot to get a trim for three months" and more artful. She'd texted him and told him not to shave this morning. As a result, he was now sporting a shadow of dark stubble that outlined every dramatic angle of that gorgeous jawline.

She told herself that she was giving him a purely professional once-over, but come on . . . no one was *that* professional, especially not her. He looked *good*, and she sincerely hoped she'd get a chance to enjoy him one-on-one later.

"Here you are," she said as she strode over. "You're supposed to be chatting up Clive Pennington."

He turned and his eyes slowly skated down her body and back up. Oh, yes, she definitely wanted to get naked with him tonight.

"Who?"

"I introduced you to him before qualifying? Head of marketing at Arrow Beverages? He told you to come find him for a drink."

"Clive Pennington wanted to get a drink with you?" Leon asked.

"What are you still doing here?" Rabia added.

He looked around at the crowd awkwardly. "What, I'm just supposed to go up to the guy and start talking? What if he's not interested?"

Violet reached out and grasped him by the shoulders. "Chase, you're a Formula One driver now. *Everybody* wants to talk to you. So go have a drink with Clive. Show him how charming you can be, and how nicely you clean up. You need to sell yourself here. Why the hell did you think I dragged him over to introduce him to you?"

"You wanted me to make a new friend?" He grinned, that charming grin that he used to skate through life. Well, it was time to step up his game.

"I want you to make *money*. Arrow Beverages has half a dozen brands in their portfolio. Astro soft drinks, Essa coffee products, Jet Energy drinks . . . Your current sponsorships would pale in comparison to a deal with any of those. Now *go find him.*" She reached up and grabbed his jaw. "Smile. Make the most of this bloody gorgeous face. Be the charming bastard I know you can be, and land yourself a sponsorship deal."

He stared back at her for a beat, then he leaned in to whisper in her ear, "On one condition."

The heat of his breath washed over her cheek and she felt just a whisper of the scrape of his stubble. Her nipples got hard in response.

"What's that?"

She felt him take her hand and press something against her palm. "My hotel room. In two hours."

Her fingers curled around the key card and she caught her bottom lip in her teeth to hold back her grin. *Cool. Play it cool.* "Deal. Go land him."

He pulled back and the heat in his eyes made her ache between her legs. "See you soon."

She watched him weave his way through the crowded club, people stopping to stare at him as he passed. To her horror, she could feel her face was flushed. Fucking hormones. She needed to pull herself together. And keep him safely in his place.

"You think you can get him more sponsorship money?" Rabia asked.

She turned to Rabia and Leon, grateful for the distraction. "If I work this right, we could be flush with cash by next season."

Rabia sighed dramatically. "Wouldn't that be nice?" Rabia was dressed exactly the same as she'd been at the track earlier—gray Pinnacle shirt and black pants, which was very like her, Violet was learning. Unassuming, utterly without pretension, and she absolutely lived for her job.

"Money doesn't solve everything though," Leon grumbled. He'd changed into a sharply tailored black suit with a dark purple dress shirt and matching tie. Also very Leon. Not flashy or loud, but always on point.

Violet turned to face him. He was a real sleeper. Quiet, soft-spoken, but always around, always watching. People like him were usually the ones who knew absolutely everything. "Okay, honesty time," she said. "What are Pinnacle's biggest problems? In your opinion. I mean, I know the entire place is toxic right now. So how would you fix it?"

Leon held his hands up. "Oh, that's not for me to say—"

"The hell it's not. Spill." She turned to Rabia. "Both of you."

The two of them exchanged a telling look, which told her she was about to get the serious dirt.

"To be honest, it starts at the top," Rabia finally said.

"Reece? I know. I'm doing my best to neutralize him—"

"Not Reece," Leon said quickly. "I mean, yes, he's a disaster. But we're talking about . . ." He looked to Rabia again.

"Ah," Violet said. "Oscar Davies."

"He's just so . . . set in his ways," Rabia groaned.

"I was going to say 'utterly lacking in vision and completely incurious,'" Leon snarked, arching one eyebrow as he took a sip of his drink.

"Yes to all of that," Rabia replied. "Not to mention he's a pervert and a sexist."

"And a racist," Leon chimed in.

"He's positively allergic to innovation. If it was good enough for Pinnacle in the nineties, then it's good enough now."

"And racing technology has improved by leaps and bounds since then," Leon said. "It's an entirely different world. We're being left further behind every season."

Rabia nodded in agreement. "The lack of money is a big problem, but we could be doing better with what we have. I mean, I've got ideas, Leon's got ideas . . . but he doesn't want to hear them and anything we suggest just goes nowhere."

"Okay. Let me see what I can do."

Rabia laughed in disbelief. "About Oscar? Look, I like you, Violet. You're tough and kinda mean, which is fun. But what can you possibly do about Oscar?"

"You'd be amazed what I can accomplish when I'm motivated. Just ask Brody McKnight."

"That asshole driver who had a thing for underage girls? You did that?"

She shrugged. "He did it to himself. I just made sure everybody found out about it."

Rabia assessed her, clearly debating something with herself.

"Spit it out, Rabia. What are you thinking?"

Once again, she and Leon exchanged one of their *glances*. Honestly these two practically shared a brain. Put them in charge and Pinnacle would be unstoppable.

"No, seriously. For legal reasons, we can't talk about it."

"Come *on* . . ." she groaned.

Leon leaned in and whispered, "All I can say is that Oscar's employee file can tell some stories."

"Stories? Like stories that could get him shitcanned?"

Leon mimed locking his lips and throwing away the key.

"But Violet?" Rabia said. "If you can"—she cleared her throat pointedly—"do something about Oscar, you'd have my undying gratitude."

Leon raised his glass. "And mine. And the gratitude of every other person at Pinnacle."

"Okay, then. I'll try."

Rabia raised her glass, too, waiting for Violet to toast with them.

Part of her still fully believed what she'd said to Chase that first night—Pinnacle was a dead end, and any efforts to change that were doomed. But goddamn it, now that she was here, she couldn't just stand around and watch this place sink. There it was—her sheer, bloody-minded, obstinate determination.

She tapped her glass against Leon's and Rabia's. "Here's to Pinnacle."

11

Silverstone, England

Violet stopped in the middle of the paddock when she saw the name lighting up her phone.

"Sylvie! Hi. Thanks for getting back to me so fast."

"Hi, Violet. So this pitch you sent me. I'm intrigued."

Sylvie was an editor at *GQ*, and Violet wanted her to write a profile on Chase. It would put him on the map in a global way.

"I'm telling you, he oozes charisma. You'll love him."

Sylvie chuckled. "I'm looking at his pictures. You weren't exaggerating. He's gorgeous."

"And there's the racing angle. A lot to work with here."

"I agree, but no one outside of racing will have heard of him. I'm just not sure he's enough to build a profile around. Not yet, anyway. He needs to be recognizable."

Not what she wanted to hear, but she could work with it. "I just got off the phone with *Vanity Fair*. He's booked for a photo shoot with them in two weeks."

"*Vanity Fair*? Really?"

"Well, not just him," she conceded. "A photo spread of notable young Americans." She'd had to call in every favor anyone ever owed her, and hustle her ass off, and it still wasn't enough until she'd managed to get his photo in front of the editor at exactly the right moment. Nobody might know who Chase Navarro was—yet—but he was beautiful and American and an athlete. And when the baseball player they'd already booked had to pull out at the last minute, it had been enough to get him in the door. Honestly, it was more luck than hustle on her part, but she wasn't going to let anyone know that.

"If he's dropping in *Vanity Fair*, that might change the landscape with my bosses. Let me see what I can do."

"I'll send you a highlights reel of some of his racing and media appearances. Trust me, once they get a look at him, they'll say yes."

"Let's hope so. I'd love to make the piece happen. In the meantime, do what you can to get his name out there."

"Believe me, that's *all* I do."

She ended the call with Sylvie and pressed the corner of her phone against her chin as she considered her options. Chase needed to be recognizable. Outside of racing.

Chase needed a girlfriend, a famous one. She'd had the idea before. It could be a model or an actor or a pop singer. Someone who got an entirely different kind of media coverage. Someone eager for a little exposure.

If she were being honest with herself, it would be good for her, too. She rarely hooked up with anyone more than once, but this thing with Chase was becoming a little habitual. And the effect he had on her was becoming a little . . . unexpected. At the after-party in Austria, she'd been staring after him like a starry-eyed teenager, which was not her vibe *at all*.

She kept telling herself it was just all the great sex. But even so, seeing him with someone else, even if it was fake, would be a helpful reminder of that.

"Violet! Just who I was looking for!"

She spun around to see Reece advancing on her through the crowded paddock, Imogen hurrying in his wake. Her stomach sank. Reece literally never brought good news with him.

"I was just headed up to—"

He slung an arm around her shoulders and turned her around. "Walk with me."

She suppressed a shudder. "What can I do for you, Reece?"

"Now I heard that guy is here today. From that TV show? You know the one? Seems like that's the perfect person for me to do a big interview with. Why don't we track him down and set something up?"

"That is . . . a really interest—"

"Oh! I know!" Reece's eyes lit up with excitement. "Let's have him come to the garage during the race. He can watch me call all the shots."

Imogen was watching her with terrified eyes as Violet scrambled for a way to subvert disaster. The entire staff of Pinnacle conspired to keep Reece from *ever* calling the shots, especially during the race. And for Reece to play pretend strategy for the media? Absolutely not.

"You know," she said, reaching into the depths of her mind to come up with literally anything else for him to do, "as intriguing as all that sounds, I'm afraid we need you somewhere else today. The . . . the, um, director of marketing from Versa Communications is here and we really need you to work your magic. Can you meet him at hospitality? Show him a good time, talk us up, you know, that sort of thing."

Reece visibly puffed up with pride. "You know, at Hammond Holdings, my dad always sends me in for stuff like this. It's kind of my specialty. Dad calls me his secret weapon."

Violet was absolutely sure Carter Hammond had never called him any such thing, but whatever.

"I can totally see that," she said instead.

"At least half the deals Hammond has locked down were due to me." He waved a hand dismissively. "All those negotiations in the boardroom, all those numbers, it doesn't matter half as much as having a drink with someone."

"Absolutely." Sure, million-dollar corporate mergers had nothing to do with numbers and paperwork. It was all down to Reece Hammond spouting bullshit over scotch in the lounge. Honestly, what would it be like to walk through life with just half of his unearned confidence?

"Thank god we have you here at the helm. So can I count on you today? To entertain our very important friends from Versa?"

"Leave it to me."

Reece strode off in the direction of the hospitality center as Violet and Imogen both exhaled in relief.

"That was a close one," Imogen said.

"I'll have to send a gift basket or a really expensive bottle of scotch to Versa tomorrow as an apology, but at least Reece is sorted for the day."

She turned to Imogen. "I was actually about to come looking for you. I need a favor."

Imogen hooked her hair behind her ears. "What do you need?"

After a month of watching Imogen operate, Violet had revised her initial opinion of her. Yes, she was timid, but she was *smart.* She'd become quite adept at figuring out what was needed in the organization and then convincing Reece it was his idea to do it. And she hadn't cried once in two weeks.

"I need a tiny peek at Oscar Davies's personnel file," Violet said.

"His personnel file? Why?"

"I'm just looking to see if . . ." She scrambled to come up with a believable reason why the head of PR would need to see a staff member's personnel file.

"Oh, I suppose you need to know about the investigation," Imogen said knowingly.

Investigation?

Imogen leaned closer.

"I'm not sure because it happened before I started. But Richard said it was good that the whole thing was just a misunderstanding, because otherwise the press coverage would have been really bad. I suppose that's why *you* need to see it. Because of the press."

Violet blinked. "Yes. Yes, that's exactly why I need to see it. I need to know what I'm dealing with so I can get out in front of it, if need be. Can you help me out?"

"I'll see what I can do."

"You're the best, Imogen."

Okay, Reece was sorted for the day, and Imogen was on the Oscar case. She checked the time on her phone. If she hurried, she could get to the garage and tell Chase about the *Vanity Fair* shoot before the race. As she headed in that direction, she told herself this fluttery feeling in her stomach was all due to scoring *VF.* She was excited about her *job.* These flutters had absolutely nothing to do with seeing Chase.

12

Chase was just about to put his helmet on when Violet came sweeping into the Pinnacle garage, a vision in skinny striped pants and a red silk blouse.

"Clear your schedule after Budapest," she said without preamble. "We're going to Paris."

"Paris? Why?"

"Because *I* have gotten you a photo shoot with *Vanity Fair. I* did that. Me. I just got the official confirmation. You're welcome."

"A photo shoot with who?"

She rolled her eyes. "Honestly, Chase. *Vanity Fair.* This is *huge.* I had to hustle so hard to make it happen."

"Isn't that a fashion magazine? What do they want to do with a driver?"

She bypassed the question and poked him in the chest. "Hey, what happened with Clive Pennington?"

Okay, she had a point there. He'd found Clive at the afterparty in Spielberg. They'd chatted about what seemed to him to be a whole lot of nothing, but then, just before Clive took off, he said they should discuss a sponsorship deal. It wasn't a done deal, but the conversation was happening, just like Violet said it would.

She'd even introduced him to Jeff Corbett, a marketing agent she knew. He was one of the guys who worked the kind of deals that could propel a driver to a whole new level in the sport. And now he was working for Chase, trying to pull in new sponsors for him, starting with Jet Energy. That could change everything for him. Violet had been right so far, so he should probably just keep following her lead.

"You really think this photo shoot will make a difference?" he asked.

"Not all by itself, but it'll put you in front of the world's eyeballs. It'll help. So Paris. We leave straight from Budapest, yes?"

He saluted her. "Yes, sir." She *almost* laughed, which was a pretty big deal for Violet. He entertained himself sometimes figuring out what he could say or do to get her to crack.

"I'll email you the details. And we'll need to squeeze in some time to do some media training with you."

"You said I was a natural."

"Even a natural needs work. You have to be prepared for anything they might ask you. I'll work up some interview questions and we'll practice."

She started to turn away, her attention already on her phone, but he snagged her elbow. "Hey. My room tonight? You can play reporter and *grill* me."

"You are such a freak." She sighed, but she was smiling—again. He loved it. "Fine. Come find me after the reception."

He was still smiling to himself as he put his helmet on and got his HANS device in place, watching her walk away.

A couple of days in Paris with Violet. That wouldn't be so bad.

Violet cast a look around the half-empty Pinnacle post-race party, wondering how much longer she was professionally obligated to stick around. Everyone else had scoped out the new Pinnacle at Spielberg. Tonight was pretty much just Pinnacle staff and a few corporate sponsors who didn't have better invites.

The team's dismal nineteenth- and twentieth-place finishes today hadn't helped the vibes. Chase had been doing relatively well for the first half. But he'd had a disastrous pit stop and slid right back down the ranking.

Across the room, Reece was holding a loud conversation with Oscar Davies, the two of them in some competition to out-asshole each other. Oscar was more flushed and sweaty than usual, a sure sign he was drunk, and Reece was doing that squinty-eyed thing he did whenever he'd been snorting coke in the bathroom. Poor Imogen hovered behind Reece, visibly flinching every time his voice rang out through the room. Violet caught her eye and gave her an encouraging thumbs-up. Imogen waved back sadly.

"Hi."

She turned to face Chase. "Sorry about today. What happened out there?"

He winced and scrubbed his hands over his face. "Fucking Oscar," he groaned, spearing his fingers through his hair and fisting them. It took effort not to get distracted imagining her own fingers running through that silky black hair.

"What'd he do this time?"

He cast a quick glance around to make sure no one could overhear, then took a step closer, lowering his voice. "He decided to change up the tire organization when we got here, with no warning."

"Yikes." Pit crews drilled pit stops relentlessly. There was no time to wonder where something was. They had to know it in their bones so they could work on instinct. Changing things around at the last minute was a recipe for disaster.

"Yeah." Chase sighed. "When I came in for my pit stop, I ended up with three hard tires and one medium, because one guy messed up and went to the old rack location. It was like wrestling a whale. I can't even blame him. This is all on Oscar. I went into that stop in fourteenth and I finished the race in nineteenth."

"Fuck."

"Yeah, fuck. You were right, Violet. The biggest thing holding this team back is that guy." He glared at Oscar across the room, still grandstanding with Reece.

"I'm working on it."

He cracked a grin. "Then he doesn't stand a chance, does he?" He ran a hand across the back of his neck. "So I'm . . . uh, heading back to the hotel." He hiked one of his ridiculous eyebrows meaningfully. That was all it took for her body to start lighting up in anticipation.

Violet made a show of checking her phone. "Maybe I'll catch a ride with you." She shrugged. "You know, since there's a car for you and we're staying in the same hotel."

Chase shrugged playfully. "Well, that makes total *professional* sense. Maybe we can even get a jump on that media training on the ride back."

"I'll meet you out front in ten."

When she made her way outside, a black sedan was idling at the curb with the back door open. Chase was already waiting inside, suit jacket off, tie long gone, and his dress shirt unbuttoned at the neck. His long legs splayed out as he lounged back on the leather seat. Her pulse accelerated just at the sight of him.

God, she wanted to climb on him and do filthy things.

"Okay, so media training," she began as she joined him in the car.

He blinked. "I was joking. You really want to do media training now?"

"Well, *I* wasn't. Let's go."

He sighed. "What do I need to know?"

"The most important thing is to develop your talking points and keep them in mind. I'll help you with that in advance."

"Talking points?"

"What you should talk about with press."

"Oh." He visibly relaxed. "I just want to talk about driving."

"Yes, I *know* that. And we'll practice what to say about the team and the car. But if I do my job right, they'll also want to know about *you*. You need to be ready for the unexpected personal questions."

"Like what?"

Violet shifted to face him on the seat and crossed her legs, tracking his gaze as it traced up her legs to the hem of her dress. "Are you seeing anyone, Chase?"

His voice dropped to a low rumble. "You know I'm not—"

She sighed. "No, I'm a reporter right now. Are you seeing anyone?"

"Ah, right." He took a beat to rearrange his expression and sat up a little straighter. "Haven't met the right girl yet, I guess."

"No need to lay it on too thick."

"No, I'm not seeing anyone right now. My time is pretty committed to the sport."

"Better."

"However, I am sleeping with this hot chick on the side." His hand landed on her bare knee.

Her lips twitched as she tried to suppress a smile. "That's exactly the sort of thing you *don't* mention to the media."

His hand slid up the inside of her thigh. "Really? You mean I shouldn't talk about the sound you make when you—"

She reached out and slapped her hand over his mouth, tipping her head to indicate the driver.

He nodded, then licked her palm. This time she couldn't hold back a muffled burst of laughter.

"Because I'm sure reporters get bored hearing all about race strategy," he continued conversationally. "They'd probably be much more interested in hearing me talk about . . . something more personal." His fingers reached the apex of her thighs and brushed against her. This time she slapped a hand over her own mouth to keep from moaning.

Her eyes met his.

He slid her thong to the side in a movement he was becoming quite adept at, and slipped two fingers through her wet slickness. His mouth dropped open, and his eyelids drooped.

"The press is always going to want to catch you out saying something outrageous." Her voice was a little strangled. "That's their job. But yours is to keep your head on straight and keep on message, no matter what happens."

He slid two fingers inside her and hooked them forward. Her eyes fluttered closed and she rocked against his hand. He was so fucking good at this.

"I'd imagine that's hard," he murmured. "Staying on message when someone's really trying to distract you."

"You have no idea." This time her words were definitely a little breathy. His thumb brushed across her clit and her whole body shuddered. Motherfucker. If he made her come right now, in the back of this car . . .

Just as suddenly, he pulled his hand away from her. "Looks like we're here," he said, looking out the window.

She exhaled hard. When she climbed out of the car, she wasn't entirely sure her legs would support her.

"Maybe we should head inside so we can finish this . . . interview," he murmured once he'd crossed around the car and joined her.

"Yeah, sounds good."

Her whole body was throbbing with need as she pushed through the revolving glass doors. When she got him upstairs to his room, she was going to shove him down on the bed, climb on top of him, and—

"Sunshine?"

It was like a bucket of ice-cold water washing over her. The sound of that voice, and that nickname—after all this time.

She had to be imagining it . . . but when she spun around to look, there he was, unfolding his long, angular body from one of the leather club chairs in the lobby.

"Ian." His name left her on an exhale. "What are you doing here?"

What was he doing here? In Buckingham? In her hotel? In her *world*?

He crossed the lobby toward her in that long-legged, rangy stride of his. He still had the same square jaw and full, sculptural lips, and smudged black eyeliner that made his icy-blue eyes look even paler. But there were changes since she'd last seen him. His hair was longer, nearly to his shoulders, and the light ash brown was streaked with blond now. He was wearing a pin-striped blazer without a shirt, and she noticed a new tattoo on his left pec.

"Astrid said you were staying here," he said, a lazy smile tugging at his mouth.

"Astrid? How did Astrid know? Astrid hates me."

He shrugged, with all that sensual ease she remembered. "She doesn't hate you. She found you . . . challenging. And she follows you on Insta. You posted a selfie from here."

Violet closed her eyes and shook her head. "What the fuck. I don't care if Astrid follows me on Insta. *What are you doing here, Ian?*"

"Violet?" Chase asked quietly behind her. "Is everything okay?"

She felt a bubble of hysterical laughter threatening to burst out and fought it back. *Okay?* The one and only guy she'd ever loved, the one and only guy who'd ever broken her heart had tracked her down at her hotel.

No, she wasn't okay.

But he was here, and now she had no choice but to deal with him.

"I'm fine," she said over her shoulder to Chase, her tone dismissive. "Thanks for the ride back."

■

CHASE WATCHED IN silent shock as Violet stared down this guy—*Ian.*

Who *was* this asshole? Tall and rangy, with long dark blond hair, wearing skintight black pants, black boots, a jacket with the sleeves rolled up, and no shirt, tattoos all down his forearms and scattered across his torso. He was tricked out in a ton of silver rings and necklaces, and his eyes were smeared with black. Nobody dressed like that unless they were a pirate or a rock star, and since piracy was rare here in central England, he was guessing rock star. At least, he *wanted* to be a rock star.

The minute Violet laid eyes on him, she'd frozen like a deer in headlights.

Whoever the hell he was, he mattered to her. Which should have been fine, because she wasn't supposed to matter to *him.* That was their deal. But as he eyed this Ian asshole, clocking the greedy once-over the motherfucker was giving Violet, something suspiciously like jealousy started simmering in his gut.

He felt possessive and twitchy, fighting back a purely primal urge to step in between the two of them and assert himself. Violet would absolutely murder him if he tried that shit, though, without a doubt. And besides, it wasn't his place. She wasn't with him. Still, *he'd* been the one about to make her come in the back of the car not five minutes ago, and now he was being fucking *dismissed* for this asshole?

"Seriously, Violet?" he muttered.

She shot him one brief look, and her expression shut him right the fuck up. Violet—fierce, fearless Violet—was freaked out, caught off guard and shaken. He'd never seen that look on her face before. And fuck this guy for putting it there.

"I need to deal with this," she said quietly.

"Am I interrupting something?" Ian said with a lazy shit-eating grin. He had the same subtle inflections in his British accent as Violet did, like they came from the same place.

"Yes," Chase said at the same time Violet said no.

He scoffed. Yeah, fuck this guy. "Guess I'll go then," Chase said sarcastically. He didn't want to go. He wanted to stand there and glower at Ian until he shriveled up in fear and slunk back out the way he'd come in. But he reminded himself—again—that it wasn't his place.

"See you in Hungary," Violet said without looking back at him.

"Your room?" Ian asked her, eyebrows lifting. If she took this asshole up to her room right now—

"The bar," she snapped, pushing past Ian and heading into the hotel bar off the lobby.

Ian rocked back on his heels. Then he looked at Chase and smiled again. "Better luck next time, mate."

"Motherfucker," he muttered under his breath as Ian turned and followed Violet into the bar.

"What the fuck?" he said out loud, to no one.

Violet clearly had a history with Ian. And he'd promised her no strings, which meant if she wanted to head off with Ian, all he could do was stay out of her way and let her.

But fuck, he was mad. He didn't like the guy on sight.

Running a hand through his hair, he tried to shake off this feeling. He felt . . . forgotten, irrelevant, small. As much as he hated to admit it, he felt *intimidated.* He knew he was good-looking. He'd heard it often enough in his life, even from Violet herself as recently as this morning. But he wasn't . . . *that,* whatever that was. He wasn't tight pants and tats, silver jewelry and guyliner. And if that's what Violet wanted . . .

Fuck. It didn't matter. Who cared what she wanted? This wasn't . . . they weren't anything. They were just fucking. No strings. He didn't care what she did or who she did it with. Except he was still standing there, alone in the lobby, staring off in the direction she'd gone, and he realized he cared a lot more than he wanted to.

Jesus. He hated this feeling. He'd been here once before, and he'd promised himself afterward that he never would be again.

"Fuck," he muttered to the empty lobby. Then he turned and headed up to his hotel room alone.

14

Violet dropped into a chair at a small table for two in the corner by the window, and crossed her arms. Ian sat down across from her, all splayed limbs and easy confidence.

God, she'd forgotten this . . . the magnetism he radiated without trying. He could own a room just walking in the door. It was his own personal magic.

A server stopped by their table, her eyes roaming eagerly over Ian. "Can I get you something?"

"Whiskey on the rocks," Ian said, smiling up at her. "And vodka tonic for my friend. Is it still vodka tonics for you, Vi?"

"It's whatever gets me drunk the fastest," she muttered.

"I'll get that right out to you," the waitress purred, never casting a single glance in Violet's direction. Oh, she remembered this part, too. The problem with being in the presence of the glowing bright sun was that he threw everyone around him into the shadows.

"You look good, Sunshine." Ian's eyes roamed over her. "Different. You've gone lux."

God, that fucking name. It had been his term of endearment for her, their own little inside joke. *Sunshine,* because that was the literal opposite of who she was. His teasing her with that nickname used to make her feel *seen,* like she'd found someone who appreciated her enough to crack jokes about it. But it had never meant what she'd thought it had. None of it had.

She smoothed the hem of her blood-red satin sheath dress as she crossed her legs. Back when she'd been . . . when she'd known Ian, she'd been all shredded jeans and leather jackets, a tough little rocker girl. She'd kept that look when she started working at Lennox, and Simone, bless her, had never said a word about it, as long as she cleaned herself up for press events. She hated stuffing herself into conservative black skirt suits and pearls, but when she got this job at Pinnacle, she'd upgraded her wardrobe and found her own way to do it. She still wore suits for press events, but less Calvin Klein, and more Vivienne Westwood.

"I have a real job now."

"So Astrid says. Formula One. That's . . . different."

"I've always loved racing. You know that."

Ian's eyebrows lifted. "I remember. Never my thing."

And typical of Ian, if it didn't center around him, he had no interest. She'd followed racing on her own when they'd been together. Music had always been her first love, but when she and Ian ended, her life in music had, too. She'd turned to racing desperate to give herself something new to focus on, something that had nothing to do with Ian and his world. And she'd built a new life for herself here, one only she controlled.

The waitress returned, depositing drinks in front of them.

"Do you need anything else?" she asked Ian.

"We're brilliant, thanks," Violet answered for him.

When the waitress had gone, Violet took a deep swig of her drink. "So why's Astrid keeping tabs on me?"

"I think she misses you."

Violet scoffed. "Bullshit. She hates me." Astrid was Ian's bandmate and sister.

"Maybe she knows *I* miss you." He looked up at her with those ice-blue eyes that used to give her butterflies.

She'd spent a lot of sleepless nights longing to hear those words from him.

"Bullshit," she snapped again, but deep inside, her stomach turned over in slow motion. Not exactly butterflies, but unsettling just the same. She'd thought she was all done, immune to Ian and immune to all those old feelings. It was embarrassing, realizing he still had this effect on her, even after everything.

"It's true, Sunshine."

"How's . . . what's her name? Emma."

"Emily."

"Right."

Ian shrugged. "Long gone. That was nothing."

Nothing. She gritted her teeth to keep her reaction from showing on her face. He broke her heart over some girl he now dismissed as "nothing." Was that supposed to make it better or worse?

Ian sat forward, resting his elbows on his knees, and fixing her with a pleading stare. "Look, do you want to hear me say I fucked up, Violet? Because I fucked up. I know that now."

"Oh, for god's sake. Please don't tell me you've been pining for me. We both know better." She would bet there had been a lengthy line of girls filling his bed in her absence.

"But you were the best part of me. The truest part of me."

Violet picked at the red polish flaking off one nail. "Did Astrid write that for you?"

"Come on, Sunshine. You can't tell me we weren't good together."

She sat in silence, staring at the ice slowly melting in her drink. Good together? Meeting Ian had felt like unlocking a door to a whole new world, a world where she finally fit in, where she mattered. She'd willingly built her life around him—his music and his magic—because when she was with him, it felt like she was a part of the magic, too.

But he'd thrown it away for "nothing." That's when she'd discovered her place in that world was conditional.

Always on his terms.

So she'd quit being devastated. She'd also quit giving men enough room to devastate her. She built her life around *herself* now, and if she made magic, it was hers to keep.

She watched the ice cubes swirl in her glass to avoid meeting Ian's eyes. "I can't believe you don't remember this about me, Ian."

"What?"

She tossed back the rest of her drink and stood up. "I don't believe in looking back."

Ian shot to his feet and reached for her, but she jerked back, out of his reach. It had been a long time, but she wasn't about to let him touch her. She didn't want to test herself that way, not after everything she'd gone through.

"I'm not giving up, Violet. I know what matters now, and it's you."

She laughed without humor. "Ian, knock yourself out. I'm going to bed. And tomorrow I'm going to Hungary. Have a nice night."

As she made her way out of the bar, he called out behind her. "You'll see me again, Violet."

With a sinking sensation, she knew she probably would. This—the grand gesture, the abject groveling—appealed to

Ian's sense of drama. Fucking fine. Let him follow her around prostrating himself at her feet. It might do him good.

Because he still didn't understand the damage he'd done.

It wasn't about some idiot groupie who sucked his dick and made him feel like a hero. It was more than that.

She *made* him. Ian and Astrid and their stupid band would still be playing crap gigs in the shittiest bars in Essex if not for her. She'd put them on the path to greatness. And if they hadn't quite made it there yet? Well, she wasn't around anymore, was she?

Turned out there was exactly one magical ingredient in Revenant Saints, and it wasn't their golden god lead singer. It was *her.*

15

Budapest, Hungary

"So what'd he say?" Violet asked before taking a bite of over-cooked pasta. She'd spent the morning with her phone glued to her ear, hustling to get more press coverage for Chase. But in between calls, she'd finally had a second to grab lunch in the commissary.

Leon, sitting across from her and picking at a salad, sighed. "Nothing. Because I didn't say anything."

"Leon."

"I know, I know." He held his hands up in defense. "I'm a coward."

Leon had been secretly hooking up with the team physiotherapist for Optima Racing for most of the season, except he'd gone and caught feelings and wanted to make it official. He hadn't yet managed to say that out loud to anyone other than Violet, though.

"You have to tell him what you want."

"And if he doesn't want that? Then it's over."

Violet set down her fork and leaned forward on her elbows. "Leon, if you want a relationship but he just wants hookups, then it's already over. You just don't know it yet."

Leon blinked. "Harsh. Harsh but true."

She shrugged. "I call it like I see it."

"So when are *you* having the big talk?"

"What talk? With who?"

Leon gave her a bored glance. "You and Chase."

She swallowed around a bite of rigatoni that had suddenly turned to glue in her throat. "Umm, how did you know about that?"

"It's kind of hard to miss the way you two look at each other."

That was slightly alarming. It was fine if people knew they were hooking up. She didn't much care. But the idea that the way they looked at each other betrayed feelings . . . well, that certainly bothered her.

"No talk to have. Unlike you, I'm good with just hookups."

"Really?"

"Really. I'm not a commitment kind of girl."

"What if Chase is a commitment kind of guy?"

She let out a burst of laughter. "Trust me, he's not."

Leon's eyebrows hiked up as he made a show of cutting a piece of lettuce into tiny pieces. "Just be careful. Feelings have a way of sneaking in no matter what you intended—just look at me."

"I promise, I've got this under control."

If only she felt as confident as she sounded. She was always charging in, giving other people relationship advice, arrogantly thinking she had her own shit all figured out.

But now fucking *Ian* had taken to texting her. She never replied, but she also hadn't blocked him yet. She'd always imagined that if he ever reached out again, she'd shut him down in a heartbeat. Instead, she let every sappy fucking text glow on her screen and told herself that next time, for sure, she'd block him.

And then there was Chase. She should probably put an end to that, just to keep things clean. But just like she couldn't seem to block Ian, she couldn't seem to stay out of bed with Chase.

As soon as she'd arrived in Hungary, she'd texted him to come over.

Honestly, someone needed to give *her* the tough talk.

Behind Leon, Violet saw Imogen slip into the commissary and head in their direction.

"Please tell me Reece isn't already drunk," she said when Imogen reached their table.

Imogen waved her hand. "No, he's fine. He's watching from the garage today. Emil's got someone sitting with him to explain how qualifying works. I think he's really learning."

Imogen, bless her optimistic heart, had decided Reece wasn't beyond redemption, if only he understood the sport better. Thank god the world contained starry-eyed dreamers like her or there would be no hope for humanity.

"Speaking of quali," Leon said, pushing back from the table, "I'd better get back to my actual job. Toss that for you?"

Violet handed him her tray. "Thanks. And remember what I said."

"I will, I will. I promise."

Imogen watched Leon depart, then turned back to Violet. "I have something for you." She held out a fat manila file.

"Is this—"

"Yes." Imogen locked eyes with her. "It's worse than I thought."

And then she was gone. That Imogen. Underestimate her at your own peril.

Violet hurried back to the tiny mobile office in the Pinnacle portable headquarters. It was basically a wide hallway, set up for hot-desking. She usually had to jockey for space alongside the engineers and strategists. Thankfully nearly everyone was down in the garage watching qualifying on the monitors, so she had a minute to dig through the file.

Oscar Davies's personnel file.

The first thing she encountered was "the incident" Imogen had heard about, and it was exactly, horrifically, what she'd expected. Oscar had made repeated sexual advances to a woman working in the aerodynamics department.

Turned out, the FIA, the sport's governing body, got involved because it was only the latest in a long line of complaints from other women, one after the other, going back as long as Oscar had been at Pinnacle. Most had been handled in-house and declared "unsubstantiated." But not even one of those women still worked at Pinnacle, and she didn't recognize their names from other teams' rosters either.

By the time she got to the end of his file, she was livid. This asshole absolutely had it coming.

All these women, their careers derailed by Oscar because he saw them as no more than potential fuck buddies. And because he went so far back in the sport and had made friends with all the right people over the years, it had been swept under the rug, again and again.

She wasn't going to feel a single bit of guilt for crushing this guy's career.

She pulled out her phone and scrolled to Carter Hammond's number.

"Carter Hammond's office," his receptionist answered crisply.

"This is Violet Harper, head of PR at Pinnacle Motorsport. I need to speak with Mr. Hammond immediately."

"I'm afraid he's unavailable—"

Violet cut her off. "Tell him it's me. Tell him it's an emergency. He'll take the call."

The woman paused for a bit. "Please hold."

Two minutes later, the line clicked. "What's he done now?" Carter Hammond sighed.

"It's not Reece. I've just become aware of some extremely unsettling information about a member of Pinnacle's upper management. I've also become aware that this information is in danger of becoming public at any moment."

Because she would be the one to make it public, but only if Carter didn't want to play ball.

"What's the issue?"

She gave Carter a brief rundown of Oscar's many, many indiscretions. "So you see, I'm extremely worried that this news would cast Pinnacle in a terrible light. The careers of numerous women derailed in order to protect one man. I'm sure you see my point."

"Thank you for informing me, Ms. Harper. I'll deal with it immediately."

Violet ended the call. Now, to see just how fast he dealt with it. She had no doubt it would be swift. Up until now, Oscar had only dealt with other members of Formula One's Old Boys' Club, willing to do whatever was necessary to protect one of their own.

But Carter wasn't a member of that club. He was an outsider.

Now, all there was left to do was wait.

Thirty minutes later, Imogen texted her.

Reece's dad just called him. He left to talk to him.

I'll be right there, she texted back.

Chase was back in the garage when she got there, finished with qualifying.

"How'd you do out there?"

"Made it through to Q two. P fourteen."

"Very good."

"What's going on? Everybody's gone."

Usually the car would be swarmed with mechanics working on it. But right now, the pit crew were milling around uneasily, murmuring to each other in hushed tones. No one from upper management was there.

She shrugged. "No idea."

He eyed her narrowly. "What did you do, Violet?"

"If I've played my cards right, I'm getting you a functional team."

Just then Rabia came down from the mobile offices over the garage. She looked shell-shocked. Leon was right behind her, grinning like it was Christmas morning.

"What's going on?" Violet asked her, faking confusion.

Rabia looked at her, stunned. "Reece just fired Oscar. I'm interim chief technical officer."

Well, that turned out even better than she'd hoped. She knew she could get rid of Oscar, but getting Rabia a promotion was an unexpected and very welcome bonus. "Congratulations, Rabia. You deserve this."

Rabia shook her head in amusement. "I don't know how you did it, Violet, but I'm grateful. The whole team is going to be grateful."

"I just do what's best for the team."

Leon put his arm around Rabia's shoulders and squeezed her in encouragement. "And what's best for this team is you, Rab. You're going to crush it."

Rabia turned toward the pit crew and raised her voice. "Gather around, folks. I've got an announcement to make."

Chase lowered his voice and bumped his shoulders to hers. "Violet, did you just do something unselfish for this team?"

"Don't be a numpty. I was just being practical. Oscar was in the way."

"Admit it. You feel the tiniest bit of team spirit right now."

"I feel like a ruthless professional, which is what I am."

Chase chuckled and leaned in, whispering in Violet's ear: "You are terrifying. Sexy and terrifying."

Yeah, she should probably shut him down, but as she felt a smile spread across her own face, she knew very well she wasn't going to do that.

"See you later tonight?" she murmured.

The look he gave her—direct, heated, and ridiculously intimate—made her toes curl. Leon was right. There was no missing this. They were both practically lit up in neon. "Can't wait," he said with a wicked smile.

And fuck it, neither could she.

16

Paris, France

The Square du Vert-Galant at the very tip of the Île de la Cité had been taken over entirely by *Vanity Fair*'s production team. Behind them, at the base of the Pont Neuf, tents housed dressing rooms and hair and makeup. PAs hustled back and forth, rolling in racks of couture clothes, or ushering the photo shoot attendees into place up at the tip of the island.

Violet watched the whole glamorous event unfolding before her, squeezing her hands together to dispel her nerves. She still couldn't believe she'd managed to land this for Chase. This was all so *perfect*, and she desperately needed it to go well.

The spread was called "Young Americans in Paris," and it featured American notables twenty-five and under from across the spectrum of arts, entertainment, politics, and sports. Right now, Zuri Clark, the Olympic gymnast, was getting final touches to her hair as a PA spread the skirt of her navy blue dress on the grass around her. Dev Ahmed, Hollywood's newest action hero, was standing next to her, getting the bow tie of his tux tweaked. There was Katrina Howard, prima ballerina; Anson Fitzpatrick, the young novelist; Madison Mitchell, the up-and-coming hot new thing in movies; and Julia Rodriguez, a political activist from Texas. And in the middle of all this would be Chase Navarro, America's homegrown Formula One star.

"Hey."

She turned to look at Chase, just emerged from hair and makeup, and she had to swallow down a little gasp. They'd put him in a tux, but unlike Dev, they'd left his bow hanging loose, and the collar of his shirt was unbuttoned. The tux—Italian, expensive—fit him flawlessly. They'd leaned into the scruff, grooming it, but leaving it there to add shadows to his remarkable jawline. And the product in his hair had it doing that stand-up-and-flop-over thing that was just . . . damn.

"You look good," she murmured. That was a staggering understatement. He was *spectacularly* hot. For just a second, Violet felt slightly intimidated by *him*, which was a wild new sensation. What had she created when she turned her sights on Chase Navarro?

"I feel—" He reached for his hair.

"Don't touch it. It's perfect."

He finally cracked a small smile. "Thanks. This is some spectacle, huh?" His eyes swept over the park, the Seine streaming past them on either side, and the banks of Paris. And just like that, he was just Chase again, all unpretentious, casual charm.

"Paris is great," she said when she'd found her voice again. "One of my favorite cities."

"Ah . . . this is my first time here."

She turned to gape at him. "What? You've been living in Spain since you were fifteen and you've never been to Paris? How is that possible?"

"Hey, I'm not one of these jet-setting Formula One stars. I'm a scrapper. I go where the races take me. And they've just never brought me to Paris."

"That's . . ." She shook her head. "Honestly, that's tragic, Chase. What do you think so far?"

He grinned. "It's great. I can see the Eiffel Tower from my hotel room." He started to stuff his hands in his pockets. It was wildly endearing.

"Take your hands out of your pockets," she said instead, "you'll wrinkle."

"Bossy." But he did as she commanded, then his expression turned a little devious. "Hey, maybe tonight," he murmured in a voice so low nobody but her would hear it, "I'll press you up against the window, so you can look at the Eiffel Tower while I fuck you."

In an instant, her body was on fire for him.

"You sound awfully confident."

He chuckled, a low rumble that did something to her deep in her belly. "You gonna come over?"

She hesitated. Her conversation with Leon flashed through her mind. But just imagining him putting his hands on her, imagining him doing what he'd just described, set her on fire. She couldn't resist that temptation. "Yes."

"I'm looking forward to it."

God help her, so was she.

"Mr. Navarro?" one of the PAs called. "We're ready for you."

He leaned in so he could whisper in her ear, "Keep thinking about it."

There was little chance of her doing anything else. "Get out of here. Go be pretty."

He chuckled. "See you tonight, Violet."

IT TOOK A few hours, but they finished the big group shot that would be the two-pager kicking off the spread, and now they'd moved on to pairings. Chase was with Madison Mitchell.

They had Chase leaning against a tree while Madison reclined against his chest as they both stared at the camera, a picture of sexy rumpled couture. Madison was beautiful, with huge Bambi eyes, long golden hair, and a killer body. Her pale pink gown surrounded her like a cloud. They were amazing together, so much combined gorgeousness they were almost hard to look at.

Madison Mitchell. She was popping off right now, too. One of those young actors who suddenly seemed to be everywhere. She'd played somebody's sister on some cop procedural for a couple of seasons, until she broke out into leading roles a couple of years ago, with a Netflix rom-com followed by a couple of major theatrical releases. She could be perfect for Chase. Just what Violet had been looking for.

She watched them together for another minute, Chase's hands on Madison's waist, her golden hair spilling across his chest, and imagined them as a couple.

It gave her an uncomfortable feeling in her chest . . . jealousy?

No, no. This was not good.

She smoothed her hair out of her face. She was supposed to get Chase in the spotlight. Well, Madison was the key to that.

With a quick survey of the crowd, she spotted Madison's PR person, watching the shoot from a few feet away, and casually made her way over to him. She'd told Chase this sort of thing happened all the time in celebrity circles, and while that was true, she'd never actually set one up herself. Did you just bring it up directly, or was it all done in coded language, like buying drugs?

"They look fantastic," she said, keeping her eyes on Chase and Madison.

"They do," he agreed.

"Hi." She turned to him and extended her hand. "Violet Harper. PR for Chase Navarro."

"Cam Medeiros. I'm with Madison."

She decided on circumspection. "Madison's having a great year."

"She is." Cam's eyes narrowed as he watched the photographer arrange Madison's hand, placing it so her fingertips brushed Chase's jaw. "We're trying to make the most of it." Cam hesitated. "Chase is a Formula One driver?"

Violet kept her eyes on Chase, even as her excitement spiked. This felt like the opening of a deal. "He is. Do you follow the sport?"

"No."

"Very cosmopolitan. Very glamorous. Races all over the world. Wealthy patrons, high-end sponsors. The parties get a lot of attention." She paused, then glanced at him. "You should come to a race sometime. I'd be happy to set something up."

Cam rubbed a finger under his chin. Violet could feel his interest. "Thanks. Chase is quite an asset. He's gorgeous."

"He is." She paused briefly before saying, with a slight emphasis, "We're working on raising his profile."

"Is that so?"

Almost there. Maybe she should just go for it. Usually she just went for it, and somehow made it work out. Turning to face Cam, she said, "We should think about working on something together."

Cam nodded. "That could be promising. Let me AirDrop you my contact info."

Violet pulled out her phone, smiling. Cam's contact popped up and she saved it, then sent back a message. "Now you've got me, too. Let's see what we can put together."

"I like the sound of that. Nice to meet you, Violet."

She pocketed her phone with nothing but cool professionalism, like she did this shit every day, ignoring the twinge in her gut. "Same."

"I can't feel my feet anymore," Madison grumbled under her breath. "These shoes are a size too small."

"I think my back is fused to this tree trunk," Chase murmured in return.

"Hang on!" the photographer shouted. "We need to reposition that light."

He and Madison both broke their pose and stretched. "I had no idea this would be so hard."

"Try making a movie," she groaned, rubbing her neck under her hair. A PA brought them both bottles of water. "Thanks," Madison said, before carefully sipping at hers. At least he didn't have to worry about smudging his lipstick. "So where are you from, fellow American in Paris?" she asked as someone ran a comb over her hair.

"I grew up in Chicago."

Madison perked up. "No kidding! Me too! What neighborhood?"

"My parents live in Elmwood Park."

She clapped a hand to her chest. "Montclare! We were practically neighbors! Favorite pizza place?"

"Martin's."

"Aww, now we're solid. If you'd said Clyde's, we couldn't be friends anymore."

Chase made a face. "Clyde's is garbage."

"See, I knew I liked you."

She was fun and way more down-to-earth than he'd have expected. Today had been tedious and uncomfortable, but she'd made it bearable. "Do you miss it?" he asked.

"Martin's? I mean, you can't get better garlic knots."

He laughed. "Chicago."

"Sometimes. I mean, I wouldn't give up my career for anything, but when I was still a kid in Chicago, everything was just . . ." She looked out over the Seine. "Simple. Everything was so much simpler. People were easier. You didn't have to wonder about everyone's secret motivations."

"I hear you. People in Chicago love to tell you exactly what they're thinking."

She chuckled. "Yeah, I actually miss that. LA is . . . not like that."

As he knew all too well, auto racing wasn't like that, either.

The PA returned. "Okay, the photographer's decided she's gotten enough of you two. She wants to move on to Dev and Zuri before we lose the light. Let's get you changed."

"Gladly." Chase groaned as he stood up and stretched his back. "Okay, up you go, Cinderella." He reached a hand down to Madison, in the middle of her pink cloud of a dress, and pulled her up to her feet. "Time to go find some shoes that fit."

"Gladly. Hey, this was fun."

"Yeah, it was."

"Good luck with . . . everything."

"You, too."

Violet was waiting outside the tent when Chase finally emerged, back in jeans and a T-shirt, although his hair wouldn't recover from the product without a long, hot shower.

"You did well," she said, falling into step beside him. "What did you think of Madison?" There was something off about the way she said it.

"She's cool. Did you know she's from Chicago? We were practically neighbors growing up. Can you believe that?"

"Adorable. I might be able to set something up with her publicist."

"Like what?"

"Like . . . dating."

He tried to ignore the sinking feeling in his chest.

"Remind me again why you think this would be a good idea?"

Violet looked exasperated with him, which was a face he was becoming well acquainted with. "So you get covered in *her* media outlets. She gets covered in *your* media outlets. Exposure. Everybody wins." She paused. "Look, if I manage to make this happen, it's a big deal. You should be happy."

"It just seems weird. And what about you?"

"What about me?"

"Like, we're going to keep—"

She threw up a hand to cut him off. "Listen, nothing that happens between us matters. We agreed, right?"

As much as he hated to admit it, that bullshit back in Silverstone with Ian was still eating away at him. He had no idea how it had resolved. As soon as she got to Budapest, things between them had carried on as if nothing had happened. She hadn't mentioned him again and he didn't feel like he could ask. So he guessed everything was cool? Although how would he know?

"Sure," he finally said. "You're the professional. Whatever you think is best."

"Great, so let's get out of here."

He looked around, taking in the scene.

"Sorry, but I'm not budging until I eat something. I'm starving."

"Okay, text me when you're back at your hotel or whatev—Hey!"

She yelped when he took her by the arm and propelled her down the cobbled path next to him. "You might as well come with me."

"But—"

"Quit being weird, Violet. We both need to eat. We might as well do it together. So." He looked around. "I've never been here before. Where should we go?"

She heaved a sigh, then shifted her bag farther up on her shoulder. "I know a place on the Left Bank."

12

Ten minutes later they were seated at a table next to the sidewalk, overlooking the river, with people streaming past.

"This place is so . . . pretty. The people, the architecture, the *food.*" He gestured at the table next to them, where someone was dining on the most delicious-looking steak he'd ever seen. His stomach grumbled.

"Yeah, I love Paris."

"So you said. You spend a lot of time here?"

She fidgeted in her seat. "It doesn't—"

"Violet, are you a spy or something? Why can't you ever talk about yourself?"

She smiled slightly and looked away, that closed-off, edgy thing she did when she was uncomfortable. "You're not the first person to say that. Mira and Will like to say that I might be an international assassin."

He nodded. "That tracks."

"Guess I give off big murder energy."

"Only when you're hangry." He nudged the bread basket toward her and she laughed. He was in good form today. He'd made her laugh twice.

He started again. "So."

She plucked a piece of bread from the basket and tore it in two. "So."

The waiter had left a carafe of red wine on the table so he filled a glass and slid it across the table to her. "Paris."

She swiped it off the table and took a sip. "Ian. The, um . . . guy you met."

"At Silverstone. Yeah, I remember." Like it hadn't been running in a loop in his imagination ever since.

"He's in a band. Revenant Saints."

Of course he was. Nothing had ever been more obvious. "Never heard of them," he said, taking some petty pleasure in the fact that at least Ian wasn't a *successful* rock star.

"They're not really your scene."

"I've seen your record collection. I figured. Guess they're not that well-known?"

"Promising, but still mid-level. No movie soundtracks and stadium tours. Not yet."

"So, this band . . . Ian . . ." he prompted again.

"He and I dated."

"I figured that part out, too."

"You're so clever." She shrugged dismissively as she tore her bread into increasingly tiny pieces. "I was on the road with them for a few years. Three years, more or less. I met him when I was eighteen. And then I started with Lennox when I was twenty-one. So between the two." Her face clouded over.

"I feel like you're leaving a lot out."

"I am." She gave him a quick, challenging look that he was starting to think of as pure Violet. "Anyway, they did pretty well in France. We came through Paris a few times." She let out a sudden huff of laughter, like she'd just been surprised by a memory. "Kiz fell into the Seine right over there. I forgot about that. Kiz was the drummer. He was drunk. Well, we all were. And we were lost, but Kiz swore he knew the way back to the van. And Astrid was arguing with him, because she said it was in the other direction, and she grabbed his arm and he lost his footing and, boom. Straight over into the Seine. They had to call the gendarmes to fish him out." Her whole face softened—he could picture her, younger and edgier, drunk and laughing with her friends. "And Astrid was standing there on the bank yelling at him the whole time, while he splashed around and shouted back at her." She paused, staring off into the middle distance. "I haven't thought about that night in a long time."

Even her eyes had gone soft, and he wondered how much of that tough-girl armor was a recent thing for her. Maybe, back then with Ian's band, she'd been different. He doubted Violet had ever been cuddly, but she probably wasn't always sharp edges and glossy surfaces you could never get a grip on.

"Sounds like you guys had some good times."

Violet inhaled and just like that, the wall came back down hard. "Yeah, well, it was a long time ago and it doesn't really matter anymore."

He didn't call her on it, but that was one big fucking lie. Outside of Mira, she'd never mentioned friends . . . a group that she was a part of. But it sounded like she'd had that once.

His jealousy turned to anger. It seemed like that asshole Ian was the one who'd stolen that away from her.

The waiter arrived and slid their plates in front of them.

"So what happened?"

"I thought you were starving. Eat."

"I can multitask." He cut into his white fish, no sauce. There'd been a lot more interesting stuff on the menu, but his diet during the season was uncompromising. He was already pretty tall for a driver. He couldn't afford an extra ounce behind the wheel.

"Uh-uh. Your turn."

"What do you want to know? Unlike you, I'm an open book, Violet."

"So you said you moved to Spain when you were fifteen."

"To live with my grandmother, so I could compete in European open-wheel racing."

"Your family is Spanish?"

"My dad is. He came to the US for college. Met my mom and stayed. His family is all back in Spain."

"So do you speak Spanish?"

He looked up and locked eyes with her. "Eres el postre perfecto despues de cena."

Violet blinked, her lips parting slightly, and he grinned. That one always worked.

"Making a mental note of *that*," she murmured. "Your parents were okay with that? You quitting school to race?"

"Mom made me get my GED online, but yeah. My whole family races."

"There are more of you?"

"My sister, Samantha, and my brother, Tyler. Both younger."

Violet set her fork down with a clatter. "You have a *sister* who races cars?"

He nodded. "Sam is driving in the European Le Mans Series right now. Tyler's just getting started in IndyCar back home. He's only nineteen."

"*GQ* is going to love you," she murmured.

"So how'd *you* get into racing? Was it after the band?"

She kept her eyes on her plate as she pushed a green bean around with her fork. "Um, no. I've always been into racing."

"Really? Since you were a kid?"

"I, um, used to watch with my father."

He grinned. "Just like me."

Her eyes flicked up to his but she didn't return the smile. Apparently she didn't have the same sentimental feelings about those days.

"So what's your family like?"

She shrugged, eyes back on her plate as she cut that green bean into increasingly tiny pieces. "You know. Family."

"You're doing it again, Violet. International woman of mystery. Do you have brothers and sisters?"

"Nope, it's just me." There was something behind those words.

"And your parents didn't mind you running off to tour with Ian's band?"

She stabbed a potato with more force than necessary. "The sperm donor was too busy raising his new family, and my mother was too busy obsessing over him to notice or care what I did."

"Wow. That sounds—"

"It is what it is. Eat your fish."

Chase hesitated, but she'd turned to her own plate, one of those delicious-looking steaks, and taken a huge bite. Family conversation over.

"We're on the other side of the river," Violet said, directing him toward a pedestrian bridge over the water. It was a warm summer night, and it seemed like the whole world was out walking around Paris. The pedestrian bridge was filled with people. Some were camped out playing music, or talking. Others were lining up for the perfect selfie with the river behind them. Here and there, couples kissed or cuddled, looking out at the lights on the water.

"That's where we were this afternoon, right?" He stopped at the railing to look.

"The Île de la Cité. Yeah. And that's the Notre-Dame."

"I recognize it from pictures, but it's different being here, seeing it in person."

She leaned on the railing beside him, looking down at the river. The breeze ruffled her hair, and the lights reflecting off the water made her pale skin glow. For a second he glimpsed that younger Violet, before she'd strapped on all this armor.

"Hey, can I ask you something?"

She shrugged, eyes on the river below. "Sure."

"Why did you hate me so much last season?"

"I didn't hate you."

"Uh, yeah, you did. You hated me until that night in Monaco. And for a while after that, if we're being honest."

Violet was silent for a minute, considering. "Do you remember two years ago in Budapest?"

"What about it?"

"Compendium Banking's after-party. We were both there. I was talking to Caroline Hayes and you interrupted."

He remembered the night now. It was a flashy F1 party, but he'd scored an invite from one of the Hansbach engineers. He'd gone mostly because there was free alcohol. He remembered seeing Violet on the other side of the room chatting up some girl. He'd recognized her from around the track, of course, but that night had been different. She'd been in a tight black dress and heels and she'd looked . . . amazing.

"Caroline's a big sports influencer. I was pitching her, trying to get her to spend a weekend in the Lennox garage posting content. Then you sailed in and started flirting with her. You blew the whole thing."

He shook his head, laughing. "You and I remember Budapest very differently."

Violet turned her head to stare at him. "Did you just quote *The Avengers* to me?"

"It was a joke. I didn't realize Caroline was a work thing."

She rolled her eyes. "Yeah, I know. You were just thinking about getting laid and Caroline was pretty."

"Not her. You."

She swiveled to look at him again. "Excuse me?"

That night he'd looked up and seen Violet across the room, and before he knew it, he was heading straight for her, like she was a magnet.

"I went over there for you. I wanted you."

"You did not," she scoffed, but there was a blush creeping up her cheeks.

"I *did.* But you looked at me like I was something you'd just scraped off your shoe—"

"Because I was in the middle of a work thing!"

"I know that now. But then? I just figured you weren't interested. So I started talking to Caroline. She was nice."

"I'm sure she was."

"It all worked out in the end, right?" Without really thinking about it, he reached out and slid a hand up under her hair, squeezing the back of her neck.

"What are you doing?"

"Touching you."

"Why?" She froze.

He shrugged. "I like to. And it's not like I haven't done it before." He leaned in closer. "I'm pretty sure I've had my hands and mouth on every inch of your body at this point, Violet."

"That's different." But she didn't shrug him off, so they stayed like that, watching the Seine.

18

"They put us up in a good hotel," Violet remarked as they rode up in the elevator to Chase's room a couple of hours later. There were mirrors on all four sides, throwing back the reflection of the two of them standing side by side in tense silence.

There shouldn't be any nerves involved in this at all. They'd done this so many times.

She couldn't figure out why this felt different. Maybe she'd just spent too much time around him today, without a race to focus on, or Pinnacle to deal with. Just . . . them. Plus, she'd told him about Ian. She didn't tell *anybody* about Ian. She hadn't even told Mira about him, not in detail anyway. What had possessed her to tell Chase, of all people?

Maybe it was that Chase met Ian? And in some weird way, she felt like she owed him some small explanation. Which was absurd. You only owed explanations to people you were in relationships with.

The elevator dinged on his floor.

"After you," he murmured. "Room four twenty-six."

She walked out ahead of him, feeling his eyes on her back like a physical touch. Like earlier on the Pont des Arts, when he'd touched her, a casual, affectionate . . . *caress.*

Inside the room, it was dark, but the curtains were open, letting in a wash of city light.

"You're right, it's a good view," she murmured, dropping her bag inside the door.

She heard a rustle as he stepped up behind her. Then he put his hands on her hips and turned her around. Before she knew what he was doing, his hand had come up to the back of her neck, cradling her in that same spot, as his mouth came down on hers.

Part of her wanted to pull away. She was already feeling crowded and antsy and too close. But then his tongue was in her mouth and she just . . . forgot all that. He was honestly such a good kisser. And his tongue . . . it was wicked, what he could do with that tongue. She reached for his shoulders, sliding one hand up into his hair, that gorgeous hair she'd been staring at all day. His free hand slid down to her ass and grabbed her, pulling her hips in tight against his.

Then, as he held her in his tight grip, he began walking her backward across the room. He didn't stop until she felt the cool press of glass against her shoulder blades. He grasped her hips and spun her around. Paris lay out below her in glittering lights. Her palms spread out against the glass.

"I promised," he murmured in her ear. Then she felt the scrape of his teeth across the side of her neck.

Her head fell back against his shoulder and her eyes fluttered closed as one of his hands came up to cup her breast. Yes, this was what she wanted. She wanted to get lost in this mindless pleasure.

"Eyes open. What do you see?"

She did as he asked. "The Eiffel Tower," she whispered. His fingers slid up under the hem of her skirt.

She heard the rasp of his zipper lowering, the rustle of him retrieving a condom.

"And what do you want?" he asked.

"I want you to keep your promise and fuck me."

He shoved her skirt up over her ass and slid her thong to the side. At the first nudge of his cock, she moaned. Then he pressed forward, pressing her breasts against the glass as he filled her. He grunted in satisfaction.

"Can you see it?"

"Yes." She sighed, keeping her eyes on the glittering Eiffel Tower as he started to thrust into her. One of his hands gripped her hip, the other slid down her arm, covering her hand, and then he laced his fingers with hers against the glass. He'd never done that before.

"So good," he murmured. "You feel so good, baby."

Heat was building, sending her so out of her head that she didn't even react to his pet name. Somehow he had her on the edge of coming already. He released her hip and reached around in front until he found her clit.

"Is that good?"

"Yes," she whispered. It must have been the top of the hour, because just then, the Eiffel Tower began to shimmer, lights flickering all up and down the length of it. Her climax started low in her belly and flooded down through her shaking thighs and up through her chest and out through her arms, to where he still held her hand pressed to the glass. She moaned as it washed through her.

He thrust hard against her and then groaned, burying his face in her shoulder. She slumped against the glass, finally closing her eyes. Behind her, she heard Chase stripping off his clothes. Then his hands were on her, pulling her blouse up over her head, pushing her skirt and her thong down her legs.

She started to turn, to face him, but instead he crouched and lifted her.

"What—"

"Just quit fighting it so hard, Violet." He laid her on the bed and before she could move, he came down over her, his mouth on hers again.

She should probably leave now. She'd gotten what she came for. But his kiss was hard to quit, and he was relentless, kissing her deep and endless, as his hands stroked up and down her body. He knew what she liked, tugging on her nipples and rolling them until she was writhing and moaning under him. Her hands were grasping at him, shaping the hard curves of his shoulders, gripping his flexed biceps.

And then he was sliding down her body, pressing her legs apart. Before he even touched her, she was panting in anticipation. He gave her no time to get ready, and no time to build up to it. He just put his mouth on her and pinned her hips down when she would have bucked underneath him.

"Oh, god."

"That's it," he murmured against her, and the heat of his breath started her whole body shaking. "Come on, baby."

In moments she was coming again, gasping as it roared through her, harder and deeper than the first time. As she floated down from it, she felt him move up her body and sheathe himself again. He slid an arm under her shoulders and cradled her close as he pushed into her. His other arm came under her, holding her tightly against him.

Then . . . he kissed her. His hand came up to cup her face, a gesture that felt tender, personal, all the things they weren't supposed to be to each other.

He kept that hand on her face, ducking his head to whisper in her ear, "Violet . . ."

The intimacy of it all made her heart stutter. Was this panic? Or some other sensation she didn't dare put a name to? But then her body was responding to his again, winding up tighter and tighter as his did, too. And then her climax was rolling through her once again, and there was nothing more in her head but him. Just him.

Violet blinked against the light and cracked one eye. Bright morning sunlight flooded the room. Rumpled sheets, clothes on the floor. Through the window, rooftops and the Eiffel Tower. She lifted a hand to shield her face, and she felt the stirring in bed beside her.

With a start, her eyes flew all the way open. Chase. Sleeping next to her. Chase's bed. Chase's hotel room. Fuck, she fell asleep. *Fuck*, she spent the night.

She *never* spent the night.

His arm was slung across her waist as he slept on his stomach. His face was turned toward her, pressed against the pillow. She glanced briefly at him . . . at the wreck of his black hair against the white pillow, at his thick, black lashes against his tawny cheekbones, at the dark scruff shadowing his jaw, at his beautiful lips, slightly parted as he breathed slow and steady . . . Her eyes jerked away, back to the window . . . the window he'd pressed her against as he . . . Oh, god, she couldn't look at him in the bright light of morning. This was weird enough already.

Carefully, she slid out from under his arm, trying not to wake him.

Once she'd made it out of bed without waking him, she quietly snatched her clothes off the floor, retrieved her bag from where she'd left it by the door, and escaped into the bathroom.

One glance in the mirror brought the whole night back to her in vivid detail.

Last night . . . dinner, talking, walking through Paris, standing on the bloody Pont des Arts looking at the river . . . Had they just gone on a fucking *date*?

Hurriedly she pulled her clothes back on, splashed water on her face, and put her hair back in a ponytail. Then she grabbed her phone to check the time. The last thing they needed was to miss their flight to Milan. It was early still. Time enough for her to escape back to her room and shower off last night. If she stood under the hot water long enough, maybe it would wash her memories away, too.

Then she noticed a new message. It was from Cam.

Talked to Madison. She's on board. What does Chase think?

Her heart was pounding and her head felt thick, like a hangover although she'd barely drunk anything last night. She could still feel him all over her, touching her, holding her, kissing her.

Her hands were trembling as she typed out a reply to Cam.

Chase is on board, too. I'll call to work out the details.

Then, as quietly as possible, so she wouldn't wake him, she slipped out of Chase's room and fled.

19

Villa Reale, Monza, Italy

One of the biggest sponsors of the sport, Weatherfront Cloud Computing, was throwing a blowout party after Monza at the Villa Reale, an eighteenth-century Italian villa. Chase squeezed between clusters of party guests, holding his beer over his head to keep from spilling it. It felt like everybody who was anybody in the sport was currently stuffed into this ballroom.

"Rabia!" He finally found her in the corner with Leon and Violet and immediately caught her up in a bear hug. "You are my fucking *hero*!"

"Put me down, you idiot," she groused good-naturedly. "All I did was write a computer program. Well, I oversaw the writing of the program."

"Yeah, well, that program got me up to thirteenth place today. *Thirteenth!* We're practically fucking midfield."

Rabia had started making changes the second Oscar Davies had loaded his stuff into his car and driven away from the Pinnacle factory. And while there wasn't much she could do with the car itself—a car designed by Oscar—she was hard at work exploring every possible way they might maximize its performance.

The first thing she'd done was install software that could test every possible combination of suspension settings on the car, running thousands of simulated laps to find the best ones. Then she put the reserve drivers to work, trying out the promising ones in the simulator so she could pick the best starting point for Friday. It was something most of the other teams had been doing for a while, but Oscar had never wanted to devote the time and money to upgrading the system.

This weekend was the first time the car had started out much closer to its optimal setup, and the results were undeniable.

It was still not—and would never be—a *winning* car, but now it felt like it could be a *competitive* car.

Chase signaled to a passing waiter carrying a tray of full champagne flutes. The first he passed to Rabia. "If this is what you can do with just a couple of weeks, I can't wait to see what you do next season."

He passed a glass to Leon and, last, to Violet. She avoided meeting his gaze as she took the glass, the same way she'd been avoiding him since Paris. He suspected spending the night with him had freaked her out. He hadn't even been all that surprised to wake up that morning and find her gone. Pretty on-brand for her.

He'd figured that if he pursued her, she'd shut down even more, so he'd given her some space. She'd been texting and emailing about PR stuff and getting this weird Madison Mitchell thing going, but that was the extent of their connection since then. But she'd had a week to shake off her Paris weirdness, and he wasn't going to let her keep avoiding him.

"To Rabia," he said, raising his glass.

"To Rabia!" Leon said.

Violet was on edge, but she still toasted Rabia, giving a tight-lipped smile. When Chase touched his glass to hers, he tried to catch her eye, but she studiously glanced away, the Violet-is-uncomfortable move he knew so well.

"Everything okay?" Leon asked, glancing between him and her.

"I'm fine," Violet said, clipped and tight.

"Me, too," Chase replied. "I'm also totally fine. Been fine since I got back from Paris."

She finally looked at him, scowling with displeasure. "Chase."

"What?"

"Am I missing something?" Rabia asked.

"Nope. Absolutely nothing," Violet said, shooting him one last glare.

It was a start.

"Okay. So . . . speaking of next season," Rabia said, exchanging one of those speaking glances with Leon, "we're thinking of scrapping Oscar's design for next year and starting fresh. But if we do, it'll leave us really short of time."

"You absolutely should," Chase said. *Please.* Anything to shake Pinnacle out of its rut. And a car designed by Rabia had to be an improvement over Oscar's brick.

Rabia shook her head. "Leon's keen to have a go, but there are so many risks with an all-new design."

Leon held up a finger. "That gamble would be worth taking if we could get a new power unit."

Violet finally spoke up. "Okay, then get yourself a new power unit."

"But Oscar already committed us to Veben's power unit—"

"Oscar's gone," Leon said, "and that contract's not signed yet."

"So why not?" Chase interjected. "You know what you want. What you *need.*"

"I have the contacts, of course," Rabia said. "But then we'd need to get Reece to sign off on it."

Violet scoffed. "I'll talk to Imogen. She'll make it happen."

"You think so?"

"He does whatever Imogen tells him to do."

Rabia looked to Leon in question.

"It's impossible for us to get worse," Leon said to her. "What do we have to lose?"

"When you have nothing to lose, things get really interesting," Violet said with a wild grin. It had been a week since Chase had seen her smile . . . *really* smile . . . and he hadn't realized how much he'd missed it until just now. Missed *her.*

"This is crazy," Rabia muttered. "But if we're going to discuss it, we'd better do it somewhere more private. I'm pretty sure our rep from Veben is at this party."

"Let's go back to the hotel," Leon said. "Violet . . . you coming?"

"I, ah . . ." Violet looked around uncertainly. "I should—"

Rabia and Leon exchanged a glance. "We'll meet you there," she said, and Chase noticed Leon wink at Violet.

Once they were gone, he turned to her.

"Violet." At the sound of her name, she looked at him, really looked at him. "Quit avoiding me."

"I WASN'T!" VIOLET protested, which was a big fat lie, because she'd absolutely been avoiding him. What worried her was that he'd noticed. He wasn't supposed to notice. Or care.

"I haven't seen you in a week." His eyes caught hers significantly. "Not since Paris."

"I've been busy," she said, which was uninspired. What was wrong with her? Where were all her snappy comebacks? Gone. Lost in the tingling feeling that coursed through her the minute he showed up and swept Rabia into that hug.

After Paris she'd told herself she'd quit this thing with him. She'd thought avoiding him all week might finally break the spell, but no luck. It was actually *worse* after being away from him all week.

"Busy flirting with Madison Mitchell on your behalf, by the way," she sniped. So far Chase and Madison had only "connected" on Instagram, liking and commenting on each other's posts. All of Chase's input had been her doing. "You're welcome to participate in that whenever you're ready."

He scoffed. "*You* wanted this. I'll show up to the date when you tell me to."

He took a step closer and leaned in. She could smell him, that expensive aftershave she'd given him when he'd gotten his makeover. She could feel him, the press of his fingertips on the sensitive skin inside her wrist, the warmth of his breath on the side of her neck.

And that was it. She was done trying to resist him. When he looked at her like that, she knew very well she wasn't going to stay away from him.

The two of them looked at each other, wordlessly. And then Chase smiled, and what was weirder, Violet smiled back.

"Okay, let's go," she said.

He reached out for her hand and she let him take it, just because she was so hungry to be touched by him. It was ridiculous, the effect he had on her.

As she followed in his wake through the throngs of guests, she thought it must be some sort of Pavlovian response. Every time she was alone with him, they had unbelievable sex, so now her body was primed to expect it whenever he got near. It wasn't personal. It was hormones.

They'd cleared the ballroom and were halfway across the atrium, where overflow guests stood chatting in groups, when he stopped abruptly in front of her.

"Chase, what's going on—"

"Hey, Chase." It was Liam O'Neill on his way in, his arm around a tall, willowy redhead who looked vaguely familiar.

Chase dropped her hand.

"Liam," Chase said, with that flat tone of voice she only heard him use when he spoke to Liam. Then his eyes slid over to the redhead. "Sophie."

Sophie. Hadn't he asked Liam about a Sophie back when they'd run into him in Spielberg?

"Hi, Chase," Sophie said, and something in the tone of her voice, the look in her eyes made the hair on the back of Violet's neck prickle. She knew him, and not just in passing. "How are you?" Sophie asked, in a bright, friendly tone completely at odds with the tension radiating off Liam and Chase.

"Fine," Chase replied. Mr. Nonstop Charm was suddenly reduced to one-word answers, with all the warmth of an iceberg.

Sophie's eyes cut to Violet, looking at her curiously. Chase noticed, and tipped his head in her direction. "Violet Harper, head of PR at Pinnacle. Sophie Kincaid. And you know Liam."

She shook hands with Sophie, determined to be polite, despite Chase and Liam snarling at each other like angry dogs. "Hi, Liam. Sophie, nice to meet you."

"I'm giving Violet a lift back to the hotel," Chase muttered. "We should go."

Seriously? She didn't necessarily want to broadcast the fact that they were sleeping with each other, but he didn't need to act like he barely knew her either.

"Have a nice night," Liam said as they passed. There was something nasty in his tone. Teasing? No, more like mocking.

Chase scoffed and shook his head.

She didn't know the backstory here, but she'd already figured out Liam was a fucking wanker.

When they were nearly to the bank of open doors leading to the terrace outside, Sophie called out again. "Chase!"

He stopped to look back at her, and something in his expression sent a shimmer of unease through Violet. He said nothing, he just stared at Sophie, his expression flat. It was weird, seeing Chase so closed off and unemotional. Usually she could read everything on his face.

"It really was nice seeing you. Good luck this season," Sophie said, her eyes a little beseeching.

"Jesus, Soph," Liam hissed. Then he took her hand and led her away.

Chase watched them go for a beat.

"So what was—"

She didn't get to finish that thought because he turned and left. Violet hurried after him, out onto the terrace and down the wide limestone steps to the drive. A group of black sedans waited there to ferry guests to the hotel, even though it was just outside the park and across the road.

Chase jerked open the back door of one, holding it for her as she slid inside.

He was silent for the short ride back to the hotel, and silent as they crossed the wood-paneled lobby hung with oil paintings and scattered with antiques.

When they got in the elevator, she looked at him in question. "Third floor," he mumbled. She stabbed the button. So he wasn't feeling chatty. That was usually exactly what she was after. Violet wasn't an idiot. It didn't take much to realize that Sophie was Chase's version of Ian. So why did she feel like she needed him to say something, explain something?

He tapped his key card to open the door and ushered her inside. There was a lamp on by the bed, casting the room in soft golden light. The bed looked like a palace, with an ornate carved, gilded headboard and swags of red brocade fabric to either side. It was covered in a luxurious red velvet duvet and a heap of tufted gold throw pillows.

She turned to Chase, smiling in anticipation, and his hands slowly went up to her hips. God, she'd missed this. It felt like forever since she'd been with him in Paris. Why had she been avoiding him when she knew he could make her feel like this?

She ran her hands up over his rock-hard chest to grasp the back of his neck. But just as she was about to tug his head down and kiss him, he turned his head a bit to the side, eyes closed.

What the fuck? He was usually the one kissing her. She rarely initiated. And now when she actually *wanted* to kiss him, he wasn't even looking at her. His warm body was still pressed up against hers, and his hands were still sliding down her body, but Chase himself felt a million miles away.

"Hey . . ."

His hands tightened on her hips, but his eyes were still closed. There was still this sense of wrongness she couldn't quite identify.

"Chase."

She pushed away from him and took a step back. Finally, he opened his eyes and looked at her, surprised.

"What's wrong?" he asked.

"I wanted to have sex with you. But I'm getting the feeling you don't really want to have sex with me right now."

He let out a humorless huff, eyes on the floor. "Don't be ridiculous, Violet. Of course I want to. I always want to."

"But you're not . . . here. With me, right now. You're a million miles away. With someone else."

And while she had very few scruples about who she had sex with and why, if she was going to have sex with someone, she wanted to be the only person in their head for the event.

"What? Who?"

"You tell me. But I'm guessing it's Sophie." She took a deep breath and did the thing she never did. She asked. "So, tell me, what happened there?"

20

"She's nobody," Chase said, a knee-jerk reaction.

Violet scoffed, crossing her arms over her chest. "Sure. Nobody. Her and Liam, two complete nobodies you can't manage to hold a normal conversation with."

He turned away, raking his hand through his hair. "It's ancient history."

"Doesn't feel that way right now."

He winced. That was bad, what had just happened between them. She wasn't wrong. He had not been thinking about Violet, and that was really shitty.

"I'm sorry, Violet. I was an ass."

He sat down on the edge of the bed and dropped his head into his hands. She was quiet for a beat, then he heard her cross the room and sit down next to him. "Tell me about her."

"It's not important."

"The fuck it's not. Tell me."

He drew a deep breath and raised his head. He kept his eyes on the far wall. "I told you I was in Hansbach's young driver program with Liam."

"Yeah."

“We were best friends back then.”

“Can’t quite picture that.”

He let out a grim chuckle, too. “Yeah, me neither. Not anymore.”

“And Sophie?”

“She was my girlfriend.”

“Yeah, that was my guess. How long?”

“Me and her? A year and a half.”

Violet let out a low whistle. “I didn’t think you did that sort of thing. Long-term.”

“I don’t,” he snapped. “Anymore.”

“So I’m guessing Sophie dumped you for Liam?”

“Eventually. But him and me . . . that started to go south before that, on the track.”

“What do you mean?”

“Everybody’s aggressive behind the wheel. We wouldn’t be here if we weren’t, right? But Liam . . . with him it was different. We were racing at Sachsenring, and it was that same bullshit he pulled in qualifying in Austria, moving in the braking zone, refusing to concede a pass . . . He didn’t just toe right up to the line, he crossed it, over and over, seeing what he could get away with, until he finally caught my rear tire and forced me into the fucking wall.”

“Yeah, some drivers can be assholes like that—”

“I was the only thing standing between him and first place. So he put me out of the fucking race. He did it two more times that season, and at the end of it, one of us had an offer to drive F3, and it wasn’t me, who crashed out of three races.”

Violet paused for a beat. “That sucks.”

“Yeah, well”—he shook his head—“it wasn’t just that. You know I’ve always had a problem with sponsorships and shit. Liam never had that problem. His family has money, so they hired someone to put together deals for him. And that's how it works, right?" He let out a bitter scoff. "Deals mean money, money means racing. For Liam, it meant he kept moving up."

"So where does Sophie fit in?"

"She followed the money."

"Are you serious?"

He shrugged. "He was a much better deal than I was. She was trying to make it as an influencer."

"I thought she looked familiar. I've seen her online. Famous but no one's really sure why."

"That's Soph. By then, I was hustling just to drive from week to week. Might be test-driving for a team one week, then a race in the Le Mans series the next. Unstable, and not exactly glamorous. Not all that surprising she bailed. Liam . . . the sponsorship deals he was getting, his race results . . . it seemed like it was just a matter of time before he landed in Formula One. So Sophie took that gamble. And it's worked out for her." He couldn't keep the sarcasm out of his voice. "It's been a lucrative partnership for both of them."

She looked at him with those blue eyes. And Chase had the unsettling feeling she was seeing through him. "So that explains you."

"In what way?"

"The manwhore thing. Now that I know you a little better, it doesn't exactly fit. But if you swore off relationships after her—"

"I didn't. Not consciously anyway. It was just . . ." He bit back what he was about to say, but Violet wasn't having it.

"What?"

He shook his head firmly. "Nothing."

"Tell me," she groaned theatrically.

Despite the heaviness of the conversation, he chuckled. "It's stupid. It's just . . . my parents have this great marriage, and for them, it was love at first sight. One look and they were together for life. It's dumb, but I guess I grew up just expecting that's how it worked. That's how it would happen for me."

"So you and Sophie . . . it was love at first sight?"

He shrugged. "For me? Maybe? At least, I thought it was. For her, I guess not so much."

Violet inhaled deeply, running her palms down her thighs. "Well, if it makes you feel any better, I get the sense she wishes she'd waited it out with you a little longer."

"Bullshit."

"I saw the way she looked at you. There was a vibe."

"Right. Because now *I'm* in Formula One."

"Liam might have been a strategic move. But you're a contender now." Violet paused for a beat. "She could have the whole package. The access she needs and the guy she really wants."

"No, she can't," he said firmly. It had never occurred to him that Sophie might regret what she'd done. But now that he considered it for a beat, he found it didn't much matter. Whatever he'd felt for her back then was long gone. It felt like a faded memory from someone else's life. So much for love at first sight.

"You wouldn't want to . . . I don't know . . . steal her back?"

He turned to look at Violet fully. Those dark-rimmed eyes were fixed on him, and that expression he knew so well was giving nothing away. His head told him she didn't care. He could tell Violet that the two of them were done right now—tonight—and she'd shrug and move on without a backward glance.

But something else—his gut—told him maybe that wasn't the case. That maybe there was something lurking in the depths of those dark blue eyes, some part of her that was hoping he wouldn't choose Sophie.

Maybe he was just fooling himself. Maybe he was the one who didn't want to let go. Maybe he was just *hoping* that he mattered to her—at least a little. Because, as much as he hated to admit it, she was starting to matter to him.

He raised a hand and cupped her cheek. The delicacy of her features always surprised him, so unexpected for someone who grabbed the world in her teeth the way she did. "No," he said quietly. "I don't want to be chosen for status. And I don't want her back."

Violet didn't move a muscle. No relieved smile, no flicker of happiness in her eyes. But she also hadn't gotten up and left yet, and the Violet he'd known three months ago would *not* have stayed. She wouldn't be sitting next to him listening to all of this. She wouldn't be . . . waiting.

Violet was too hardened to hope, or wish, or even want. Wanting anything—or anyone—was a weakness she wouldn't allow. He knew her well enough by now to know that much. But she'd left the door open for him, which was not nothing.

He set his other hand on her knee. Her eyelashes fluttered, just a whisper of a reaction. "I'm sorry about tonight. I let them get in my head when I was with you, and that was wrong."

"You don't owe me an apology."

"Yes, I do. Will you stay?"

She opened her mouth to reply, then hesitated.

"Stay and let me make it up to you."

He slid his hand to the back of her neck, holding her still so he could lean in and kiss a spot just below her ear.

He could feel it in the air when she made up her mind, a shift in the energy around her, an infinitesimal softening of her body.

She was staying.

21

Circuit Zandvoort, Netherlands

Violet leaned against the backside of the Pinnacle garage, scrolling Instagram, while beside her, Imogen was on her phone, patiently explaining to Reece, back at his hotel, how to work the faucet in his shower.

She checked in on Chase's account to see what kind of traction he was getting on the last thirst trap selfie Maisie had posted of him, shirtless in the gym. She'd had to badger him for days to get him to take the damned picture. The post had twenty thousand likes, which was huge engagement for Chase's account. One of the first comments was from Madison Mitchell: **melting**, and her reply was racking up engagement.

Madison had just posted a candid shot of herself from the Paris photo shoot, teasing her pink dress, and captioned it *Exciting stuff coming soon!*

She was about to log in to Chase's account so she could reply for him, something cute and flirty, when she caught sight of his handle in the comments.

How are you so gorgeous?

Maisie was currently helming an Instagram live event from the Pinnacle account, so that wasn't her. Chase must have done it himself, which was a surprise, since he hated social media.

As she watched, the likes on his comment rolled in. That should be a *success.* So why was she standing here, staring at his comment, her stomach feeling all weird and hollow?

Frustrated with herself, she swiped Instagram closed and pocketed her phone. The buzz about Madison and Chase, combined with the amazing highlights reel she'd sent Sylvie, had been what finally locked down the *GQ* profile. That was a *huge* win, and the Madison thing made it happen. There was absolutely no reason to suddenly start feeling weird about it. None.

"Is the water hot now?" Imogen was asking. "Great! Enjoy your shower. We'll see you soon."

Violet groaned. "Imogen, do me a favor. When Reece eventually gets here, can you keep him away from Chase? That journalist from *GQ* is coming to do a feature on him and all I need is Reece wandering in and saying something embarrassing."

"No problem," Imogen said. "He's watching the race from the office today. Cliff from Strategy is sitting with him to explain it all."

"I've got a few things to go over with Chase before *GQ* gets here. Thanks for managing Reece so well. I know he's a nightmare, but you're the team hero."

Imogen blushed, looking very pleased with herself. "No problem."

When Violet found Chase in the garage, he was half out of his gray race suit, with the sleeves hanging loose. His white Nomex undershirt hugged his upper body like a second skin. As she got closer, memories of last night . . . her hands all over that sculpted chest, those broad shoulders, those rock-hard biceps . . . flashed through her mind in lurid detail. He was talking with Leon, one hand absently fisted in his hair. Last night she'd had her hands fisted in that hair, too.

"Can I borrow you for a second?" she said, slightly surprised her voice came out so steady.

Leon smirked and started backing away. "That's my cue."

"Leon—"

He held his hands up and grinned. "He's all yours."

She shot him a dirty look as he left.

"What's up?" Chase asked, with the sort of smile she usually only saw when they were alone in a hotel room.

"This is business," she told him. "First, Hannah Lumley from *GQ* is arriving soon. They're writing a profile on you—"

"A profile?" He blinked in surprise. "In *GQ*?"

"Yes, I convinced freaking *GQ* to do an entire profile on you because I am a genius."

"That's . . . thank you, Violet. You're so good at this."

His compliment made something warm bloom in her chest. It certainly wasn't the first time she'd received a compliment about her work. Simone had constantly called Violet her secret weapon and her personal lifesaver. So why did it feel so different when Chase said it? Because Ian never had?

"Okay, Hannah's going to shadow you for the next couple of races and she'll come with us to Vegas. We're flying out tomorrow morning."

Chase scowled in confusion. "But the race in Vegas isn't for another month."

"The local promoter needs some drivers for promotional stuff in advance of the race. I managed to get you on it."

"I'm guessing I was the cheap option, right?"

"Yes, but it'll be *your* face on the ads all over Vegas. That's a win. Plus it's a chance to set up a face-to-face with you and Madison."

"A what?"

"An in-person event. I've already set it up with Cam. She's going to fly in from LA to see you."

"Why?"

"For a *date*, you numpty. You're supposed to be *dating*. This is part of it. It's just one night, Chase." But she couldn't maintain eye contact with him as she said it. Judging from that Insta comment, he could be genuinely into her.

"Are you sure I really have to do this?"

"This thing with Madison is what finally helped me land *GQ*."

He sighed deeply. "Fine. I'll do Vegas. But tonight I do you."

That made her look up. He was giving her that mischievous grin again, the one that should annoy the fuck out of her, but all it did was make her fight back her own smile.

"Hush. Now that you're getting serious with Madison, not a word about that where anyone can hear you."

"Relax, nobody cares."

"Did you just catch that with Leon?" She hooked a thumb over her shoulder. "If anyone outside the team gets wind of it, it'll embarrass Madison and make *you* look like a world-class asshole."

Chase's brow furrowed for a beat as he considered that. "You make a good point."

"So. Tomorrow Vegas."

"And tonight?"

"Yes, tonight."

He saluted her. "See you later then, General."

22

Las Vegas, Nevada

Chase was standing on a plaza in front of the Bellagio, in his race suit next to a Pinnacle car—one of last year's cars, since this year's cars were in pieces, packed into shipping containers, and on their way to Azerbaijan. Floodlights lit him up from multiple angles. Behind him, the famed Bellagio fountains were lit up against the Vegas skyline. A photographer circled him, snapping pictures. A crowd of tourists milled around, chatting and snapping photos on their phones, and probably uploading them all to social media.

Violet hung back, outside the ring of lights, and congratulated herself. Trying to generate positive news about Pinnacle was a daily uphill battle, but her project to turn Chase into a superstar was going perfectly. *Vanity Fair*, and now *GQ*. Hannah, the *GQ* reporter, had spent most of the flight to Vegas doing a deep-dive interview with Chase, pulling out details about his childhood in Chicago, his race-obsessed family, and his rough early years of training in Europe. His narrative couldn't be more appealing if Violet had written it herself.

So with all this professional success, she couldn't figure out why she was watching this photo shoot feeling so unsettled.

A calendar reminder pinged on her phone and she glanced at it on instinct.

7:30- Dinner- Chase & Madison- Picasso

It was their first in-person date, and judging from that comment he'd dropped on her Insta, Violet was anticipating the fake relationship could become a real hookup. They were two young, beautiful, unattached people. It was practically expected, and she absolutely refused to be bothered by it. It was all her idea, after all.

If that did happen, she wouldn't allow herself to give him another thought. They'd had their fun. It was never meant to go on this long.

Her phone buzzed again.

Goddamn it. Ian. *Again.*

She never responded, but that didn't seem to faze him. His texts kept showing up with a tedious regularity. Why hadn't she blocked him?

"Chase, turn to your right a little more."

She glanced up just as Chase angled his body as directed and flashed an absolutely devastating grin at the camera. At least, it devastated something somewhere deep down in her chest. Yeah, it would probably be a good thing if he moved on with Madison. Ian was something she understood, something she could control. This thing with Chase was starting to feel . . . uncontrollable.

So maybe that was why, for the first time, she texted Ian back.

What do you want?

Where are you?

Not an answer.

Nowhere near you. Silverstone was a blip. It was just a couple of hours north of London, so Ian hadn't had to exert much effort to pursue her there. For the rest of the season, she'd been much harder to reach.

I don't know why you're bothering me after all this time, but I'm at work.

Like I said, I miss you, Sunshine.

She let out a snort of laughter. Sure he did. She had to admit she was enjoying watching him fling himself at the glass. There was something deeply soothing about dangling him on a string for a while. He deserved it.

A flare of deeply petty spite heated her chest as she typed out a reply.

What do you miss most about me?

Three dots appeared, then vanished, then started again. Finally he replied.

I miss your electric eyes.

And your honeyed mouth.

And the taste of your skin, like a drug.

She left him on read while he typed out line after line of lame song lyrics. That should keep him busy for a while.

"Okay," the photographer finally called out. "I think I have what I need here, Chase. See you tomorrow."

She pocketed her phone, still vibrating with Ian's incoming texts, and went to join Chase.

He set down the prop helmet he'd been holding for an hour and stretched out his shoulders.

"That shit's harder than it looks," he groaned.

"The burden of beauty. Let's get moving. Your date's in half an hour."

Upstairs, she swiped them into Chase's suite. "Okay, you go get cleaned up and changed. I'll let Cam know what your ETA is."

She was typing out the text when she felt Chase slide an arm around her waist and dip his head to whisper in her ear.

"Or we do this first."

He brushed her hair aside and kissed the nape of her neck. Her knees went wobbly and just for a second, she sagged back against his chest, wanting nothing more than to fall into the sensual oblivion he was offering. But sleeping with him just minutes before he met up with Madison felt shady as hell, even to her.

"Come on, Chase." She pushed against the arm he'd banded around her waist. "You have a reservation."

"You said this was a professional arrangement." He slid his hand down to caress her hip. "Like a business meeting."

"Yeah, but—"

"So sometimes people are late to meetings."

"Do you know how hard it was to swing this reservation?"

"Violet, Madison's not gonna care—"

But I'm afraid I'm starting to, her mind whispered to her. Something like panic welled up in her throat and she shoved herself away from him.

"Violet—"

She put several feet between them before she turned to face him, then pulled her phone out so she could focus on that instead of meeting his confused gaze. "Picasso is just downstairs. If you hurry, you won't be late."

"But—"

"Just *go*, Chase."

He heaved a sigh and threw his hands in the air. "Fine. I'm going."

Once the bathroom door had closed behind him she shut her eyes and blew out the breath she'd been holding. Too close. He'd gotten entirely too close.

When she glanced down at her phone, Ian was still at it and had broken out a thesaurus.

I miss your incendiary passion.

I miss your cloistered sadness.

That didn't even make any sense. Then again, songwriting had never been his strength.

She'd planned to give Chase a once-over before he headed downstairs to make sure he was dream-date ready, but she wasn't sure she wanted to face him when he came out of the bathroom. So instead she forwarded Cam's text explaining where to meet Madison and she left.

The door of his suite closed behind her. That might possibly be the last time she was alone with him in that way.

As she headed back to her own room, on a different floor, she told herself over and over that it would be a good thing.

23

When Chase got downstairs to the restaurant, Madison was waiting for him just inside the door, half concealed by the shadows, right where Cam had said she would be.

"Hi, Chase." She stepped into the soft light by the hostess stand. She looked amazing in a tight gold dress, with her blond hair down.

"Hey. Nice to see you again." He hesitated for a moment, not really sure how to greet her. Then, remembering this was all for show and someone might be watching, he leaned in and kissed her cheek, setting a hand on her waist as he did it. It felt weird and too forward, but she gave his arm a squeeze as he did it, so he figured he'd judged correctly.

"So." He rocked back on his heels and stuffed his hands in his pockets. "How does this kind of thing go?"

He was pretty adept at charming women when he put his mind to it. But that was always real . . . at least real in the sense that he'd been interested in the woman. This . . . pretending . . . was a different ball game, and suddenly he didn't know what to say, or how to stand, or where to put his hands. He'd never felt so awkward in his life.

Madison seemed to pick up on that and smiled. "I'm an actor, remember? Just follow my lead. I got you."

He smiled back and relaxed a little, remembering how chill she was, and how easy it had been to talk to her at the photo shoot. "Okay, let's do this."

She held her hand out to him and he took it. Like a boyfriend would.

The hostess led them through the dining room and out to a small terrace overlooking the Bellagio fountains. The low lighting and intimate tables inside were probably better for a date, but that would have defeated the purpose of this event—to be seen. Out here, the eyes of thousands were on them.

He helped her into her chair before settling into his, across from her.

"The flowers," Madison murmured under her breath.

"What?"

She threw a significant glance at the glass vase of peach rosebuds on the table. "Offer me one."

"Oh. Right. Got it."

With a flourish, he took a rose from the bowl, leaned across the table, and held it out to her. Madison looked adorably flustered as she smiled and took it. She was a good actor. Then she laid her free hand across his palm. His fingers curled around hers.

"Well done," she said under her breath. "It's on."

For all of his resisting, dinner was actually fine. The prices were eye-watering, but the food was amazing, the setting was beautiful, and Madison was fun. The conversation hadn't dragged once all night.

They'd talked about growing up in Chicago, about her family, about his family. She'd told him stories from her tough start in LA, sleeping on friends' couches for months, running from one audition to another, taking every small role that came her way, trying to break in. He told her about his early days in racing, pretty much doing the same thing, hustling, just trying to stay afloat in a tough sport. They had a lot in common that way.

She was savvy and a little bit cutthroat in a way he'd never quite managed though. She cared about her work, but she was also aware of all the compromises her industry required of her for success, and she was willing to do whatever it took. He supposed that's why she'd just taken this arrangement in stride. His career might have had a different trajectory if he'd had half her street sense.

As they lingered over dessert, which Madison barely touched, she smiled across the table at him. "I think this was a huge success."

"I guess we'll see."

"Oh, I know. Have you really not clocked how many times we've been photographed tonight? We're blowing up the internet as we speak. We're going to be viral by midnight. So, well done."

He'd been absolutely unaware of that, and it blew his mind that she'd been tracking it all even as she chatted so casually with him. This all felt weird, the performance of a lie.

"Do you ever get used to it? Having to do this kind of stuff just to be able to do the thing you love?"

Madison tipped her head to the side, considering. "I guess I've never tried to separate them out. I knew how the game was played from the beginning. This is just another move on the board."

He envied her for her ability to see the whole game being played and to know what moves to make. It was the part he'd never been good at. But listening to her stories about LA, he could tell Madison could read people and their motivations and navigate situations to get the outcome she wanted. She was a lot like Violet in that way.

Violet was probably back in her hotel room, scrolling through the hashtags, watching every moment of tonight unfold online. The thought made his gut twist up. This might be just another move on the board, but it wasn't one he'd ever be comfortable with.

"Everything okay?" Madison asked. "You just dipped out."

He shook his head. "Sorry. My mind wandered for a second. I'm glad this worked out tonight. Thanks for making it so easy."

"No problem." She hesitated, her eyes dropping to the table. "We don't have to call it a night if you don't want to. I know we've been on display all night, but we could move somewhere more private. You know . . . just so we can relax a little."

He leaned back in his chair, absorbing that. It wasn't an outright invitation, but she was definitely leaving the door open. If he wanted to walk through it.

But much as he liked her, he couldn't summon up that kind of interest. Because his fucking head was somewhere else, with someone else. Instead of blond hair, he was seeing black. His hands didn't want to trace over Madison's golden curves, he wanted Violet's icy-pale skin.

"I'd better call it a night," he said with what he hoped was a casual shrug. "I've got an interview over breakfast and then I'm heading straight into more press events."

"No problem. Cam's got me on a six a.m. flight to Vancouver tomorrow morning."

"Ouch."

"I have to be on set by noon."

"So . . ."

She looked up and met his eyes. "I guess I'll see you next time they set something up."

"I guess so. This was fun."

Her smile was wide and genuine, so she didn't seem to be at all hurt that he hadn't taken her up on her offer. "It was."

"So . . . how do we do this? The exit?" He cleared his throat. "Since we're not . . . uh, leaving together."

"Well, we leave the restaurant together, then Cam escorts us through the service exit so we can get back to our hotel rooms separately."

"Cam's thought of everything."

"It's all very well-planned." Madison looked up at him again. "Everyone will think we went home together tonight."

He swallowed thickly. "That's good. Okay, I'm ready when you are."

After an enlightening fifteen-minute tour of the bowels of the Bellagio Hotel, Chase finally found himself looking down a hallway lined with rooms. He took a quick glance around to make sure no one was there before he exited the service elevator. He was supposed to be in Madison's room right now.

But no one was there to see him as he made his way to a different room. He knocked quietly at the door. A minute later it cracked open. Violet's pale face appeared out of the darkness. Her eyes were still rimmed in dark, although she'd undressed, wearing just her black silk robe, which she was holding closed at her neck.

"You're here," she murmured with surprise in her voice.

Without a word, he slipped inside and closed the door behind him.

24

Singapore

Singapore was always a hot one, Violet thought, fanning herself with a race program outside the tent where they were setting up the drivers' pre-race press conference. Storm clouds threatened off to the south, and the air felt absolutely drenched already.

The first panel of drivers was supposed to start in ten minutes and Chase still wasn't here. No surprise there. He made lateness into an art. He was lucky he was so charming when he finally showed up that everybody forgot he'd ever been late.

She fired off a quick text.

Starting soon. Hope you're almost here?

His typical one-letter reply came a moment later.

k

Rolling her eyes, she checked her email while she waited. There was a new one from her contact at *Vanity Fair*. The subject line was "Just went live."

She clicked on the link inside and let out a gasp. The photos were *gorgeous* . . . lavish, colorful, romantic. A two-page spread kicked it off, with the title in scrolling white letters, "Young Americans in Paris," contrasted against the green of the trees in the Square du Vert-Galant. They were all in that panoramic shot, beautifully dressed and groomed, Zuri Clark in that stunning navy dress, Dev in his tux, Madison in her pink cloud of a gown, Anson Fitzpatrick in a sharp charcoal suit . . . and there was Chase in the middle of all of it, his undone tux, sex hair, and stubble, like some Spanish god. It was better than she could have hoped. Clicking through, she found the shot of him and Madison, Chase cradling her as they leaned back on the tree, her fingertips on his jaw, his arms around her waist. So beautiful. Both of them.

She was firing off an effusive thank-you to her *VF* contact when the sleek red sports car some local race sponsor had provided for Chase pulled up beside the tent. As he unfolded himself from the small front seat, he absently ran a hand through his riotous hair. For all his complaining at the shoot, he'd kept the stubble and sex hair since then. It suited him. And thanks to her ruthless nagging, he made sure he was always well turned out in his new clothes. Not a grotty T-shirt in sight these days. Today he was in an Italian polo shirt, designer track pants, and trainers—casual, but clearly expensive.

"You owe me," she said as he approached.

He looked at her apprehensively. "What for now?"

She passed over her phone, watching his face as he flicked through the article. "Looks nice," he said, handing her phone back.

"Nice? Nice! This is like . . . gold-standard publicity. I can't believe I managed to pull this off for you. Look! Just look at yourself! You're going to be trending online within the hour."

Chase chuckled and shook his head. "I've never seen you like this, Violet. Are you feeling genuine enthusiasm about something?"

She tapped his chest until he looked up and met her eyes. "Marketing execs in offices around the world are seeing this right now and trying to figure out how to tie their company's name to you. This means sponsorships, Chase. This means *money*."

He looked her straight in the eye. "I'm grateful," he said quietly. "I truly am."

Suddenly her chest felt weirdly tight, even though what he said pleased her.

"Good," she said, then cleared her throat. "You'd better get in there. They're waiting for you."

"What do you want me to say?" he asked dutifully. She had to give it to him, he followed directions and respected her expertise. Which was also a welcome change.

She absently reached up to fix his hair, to make it a little more grabbable. "It doesn't much matter what I tell you to say, because they're all going to ask you about this." She waved her phone at him. "But yeah, do try to steer it back around to the racing. You've had better results since Rabia started upgrading the car. Mention her by name. We want everybody to know that Pinnacle's improvements are thanks to her."

"As you wish." He saluted her, that joking little gesture of his that she was secretly becoming very fond of.

Then he reached out and touched her bottom lip with his fingertip. It was a whisper of a touch, just his finger against her lip. Before she could open her mouth to ask him what he thought he was doing, he turned around and ducked into the tent.

She raised a hand to her mouth, still feeling the brush of his finger there. She swiped the back of her hand across her mouth to dispel any lingering tingles and followed him into the tent.

Inside, a PA was waiting to whisk him away and get him up on the dais next to Dieter, Olivier Lavoie, and, unfortunately, Liam O'Neill. Chase and Liam shot each other one brief, stone-faced glance and then went back to studiously ignoring each other. Honestly . . . *men.*

Violet stood at the back of the room, taking note of the increased rustling and murmuring as Chase entered the room. The moderator, some guy from *Auto Racing*, asked the usual softball intro question about what challenges they foresaw in Singapore, and each driver dutifully answered, citing the street track, the heat, the stuff they always said about Singapore. But Violet was really waiting to see the reaction when the *Auto Racing* guy turned it over to the press pool. Who would they direct most of their questions to?

The first reporter stood up. "Terry Carmichael, from World News. This is for Chase Navarro. Chase, you've moved up in the rankings from nineteenth to sixteenth overall, and Pinnacle has moved up as well, to ninth place in the Constructor's Championship. Can you talk a little bit about what's behind your improvement?"

From the instant the reporter mentioned Chase's name, Liam's expression got even stonier. As Chase sat forward and smiled, Liam crossed his arms tightly over his chest and slumped back in his chair.

"While I'd like to chalk it all up to my stellar driving, I have to give credit where credit is due. Rabia Dar is working miracles with the car. Every week we see improvement. She and Leon Franklin are constantly finding new ways to optimize the package. They make a great team, and it's an exciting time to be with Pinnacle."

Violet gave a tight nod of approval. Perfect. He really was quite good at this, for all his fussing and resisting.

Chase leaned into the mic. "Also, I *am* a hell of a driver. Make sure you write that part down." He cracked a smile and laughter rippled through the room.

And *that* was why he was magic. They fucking loved him. You could feel it in the air. The entire room of reporters practically let out a swoony sigh.

And she could see why. When you were with him, he made you feel like you were the most important person in the room, like he was hanging on every word you said. Or maybe that was just the way he made *her* feel.

She'd been so sure he'd end up with Madison in Vegas, but he hadn't. He'd come straight to her hotel room after their dinner. And she'd seen the look in his eyes, the expression on his face. She'd felt it in that fingertip on her lip just now. It wasn't about sex or pleasure in those moments. Those touches felt . . . tender. Those looks . . . they weren't about her body, they were about *her*. At some point, they'd crossed a line. Now it was complicated, and only getting more so.

But every time she thought about ending it, she got that weird hollow feeling in her stomach again. She'd never been one to shy away from difficult decisions, but she was shying away from this one. She kept putting it off. One more week, one more race. After Monza, after the Netherlands, after Azerbaijan, after Singapore . . . she just couldn't seem to pull the trigger on it, which was unlike her.

The next two questions from the pool of reporters were also directed at Chase—sending Liam into a full-on sulk. Chase was the man of the moment, and even Liam knew it.

Violet was reveling in her moment of success when her phone buzzed with an email. It had been blowing up with congratulatory texts from work contacts as the *Vanity Fair* piece got traction. It was an email from Sylvie at *GQ*, letting her know that they were moving Chase's profile up to the next issue, to seize on the excitement. *Yes.*

She was just typing her reply when her phone started buzzing with a phone call—an unknown number.

Considering *VF* had just dropped, it could be anybody. She ducked out to answer.

She swiped to answer the call. "Violet Harper here."

"You sound like a bloody corporate knob."

Her heart dropped at the sound of a voice she hadn't heard in years.

"Astrid," she said dryly. "This is a surprise. To what do I owe the honor?"

Astrid sighed wearily. That was Astrid, perpetually bored with the world and everyone in it. "Ian tells me you're actually *working* for a race team?"

"A Formula One team," Violet corrected with asperity. "I'm the head of PR."

"Huh."

Violet felt herself bristling. "What?"

Astrid sniffed, and Violet could picture her perfectly in her mind, her long tangled blond hair, the pale blue eyes so like her brother's, the weary, put-upon expression perennially on her face. "Sports . . . it's just so . . . sporty."

"It's a *business.* A multibillion-pound-a-year industry. And it's pretty bloody significant, me heading up PR for an entire team."

"I suppose," Astrid said dismissively. "Ian said you're dating some knobhead driver?"

Violet scoffed. "Knobhead. Ian wouldn't last a full minute on the track beside Chase. Do you have any idea how difficult driving in F1 is?"

"So it's true, then? You've got a boyfriend?"

Violet realized a beat too late she'd protested all the wrong things. "What? No, he's not . . . we're not . . ."

"Because Ian wants you back."

Violet rolled her eyes, even though Astrid couldn't see her. "Yeah, so he said. And I'll tell you what I told him. I don't look back."

"That girl was nothing. It barely lasted a month."

If she heard one more time that the event that had broken her heart was "nothing," she was going to bloody scream. If that girl was nothing, but worth breaking her heart for, then what did that make her?

"Why do you even care, Astrid? You don't like me."

"I never said—"

"Astrid."

Astrid sighed again. "Fine. You're not my favorite. But I'm not so thick that I'd deny you were important. When you were here, with the band, you . . . made us better."

"I don't—"

"We couldn't have done it without you," Astrid spit out, as if it pained her to admit it, which, undoubtedly, it did. "The touring, the album . . . none of that would have happened except for you."

Violet inhaled, very slightly mollified. It was nice to hear *someone* admit it, even if it was three years too late.

"Do you want me to say thank you?" she asked sarcastically.

"Wouldn't dream of it," Astrid replied, unable to keep up the uncharacteristic groveling for that long. "Just . . ."

"What?"

"Think about it. I know my brother can be an idiot, but he really does miss you."

It was an appealing, if unlikely, thought—Ian pining away for her. She couldn't deny that it soothed her ego, so damaged where he was concerned. “Look, I know he’s your brother, but there’s no way I’m taking his cheating ass back—”

“Then come back for us!” Astrid snapped. “Come back for the band. Without you, Ian’s taste in music is shit. You know that. All he listens to these days is bloody *Imagine Dragons*! You were important, Violet. In lots of ways. We all know it.”

All of a sudden she felt breathless, and slightly panicky. This call . . . it was too much.

“Astrid, I have to go.”

“Talk to you soon?”

“We’ll see.”

25

Everyone wanted to talk to Chase after the race in Singapore. Even with a security guard ushering him along, it took over twenty minutes to reach the after-party at Cé La Vi, the bar and nightclub at the top of the SkyPark. He'd finished twelfth, which was great for Pinnacle, but nothing special overall. Didn't seem to matter.

Violet wasn't kidding about the impact of that *Vanity Fair* shoot. In the three days that it had been out, he'd blown up online. He didn't pay much attention, but Violet had been monitoring it all closely, shoving her phone in his face whenever there was something particularly good she wanted him to see.

Just as he stepped out of the elevator, finally at the top of the SkyPark, his phone dinged with a text from Jeff Corbett, his sponsorship consultant.

Check your email.

He swiped over to it and clicked on Jeff's email. It was an official sponsorship proposal from Jet Energy drinks. There was an attached PDF with the details, but Jeff had bullet-pointed the deal in the email, ending with the monetary offer at the bottom. His stomach swooshed and he felt lightheaded, reading the numbers once, and then again. The money was . . . life-changing. Career-making.

Regardless of what happened with Pinnacle this season, that kind of sponsorship money attached to his name would mean some Formula One team would want him in their car next season, without a doubt. He had to call his dad. Call Tyler and Sam. Call his agent. But first, he had to find Violet. She had made this happen; she deserved to be the first person to know.

He'd made it all of ten steps closer to the club, close enough to hear the thumping base, to see the flashing purple lights and the sway of bodies, when his phone buzzed again. It was Madison. They'd been texting a lot in the few days since the *VF* thing had dropped. It was huge for her, too, and people online were apparently going ballistic about the two of them as a couple. It pained him, but it turned out Violet was right about that, too. All those zeroes at the end of Jet's offer were proof of that.

Assuming you've heard we're scheduled for a date in London next week?

Violet had just put it in his calendar. There was a two-week gap after Singapore, and Madison had a reading with a director in London. So Cam and Violet had scheduled another date.

Just heard, he replied.

Any preferences on what you want to do?

Did he and Madison have any say? He'd assumed Violet and Cam had already sorted it all out for maximum exposure.

Anything's good with me.

Great, she replied. *Then I'm taking you to my favorite place in London. I think you'll love it.*

So Madison was planning this one? That felt . . . personal. All of this felt more like a date than a business meeting, which is how he'd been thinking about it to get through. Except maybe it wasn't anymore? Or it didn't have to be, if he didn't want it to be? He remembered Madison's casual invite in Vegas, offering to move their date someplace more private. Apparently, that was still on the table.

He fired off one more text to her.

Sounds great.

About as noncommittal as it got.

Inside the nightclub, the room was glass-walled, with low, curved couches on the edges for table service. Groups of people—mostly drivers with their entourages—occupied most of those. The bar opened out onto a wide terrace on three sides, the "prow" and sides of the "ship" that made up the top of the SkyPark, which spanned the tops of three hotel towers. More people were out there, enjoying the stunning three-sixty views of the Singapore skyline at night. A DJ had been set up in one corner of the terrace, surrounded by a dance floor.

"Chase!"

He turned at the sound of his name. René Denis, one of the most famous former Formula One world champions, was sitting at one of the banquets, with a small group of people. René lifted his champagne glass to him. "Come have a drink with us?"

Six months ago René didn't even know Chase's name. Now, he wanted to hang with him.

Surreal.

He shook his head. "Maybe later. I'm looking for someone."

He made his way slowly through the crowd, people stopping him every couple of feet. He finally caught a glimpse of the jet-black swish of Violet's long hair in the cluster of people dancing. She was with Mira Wentworth. He'd met her once briefly last season in Melbourne. She'd been with Violet, he remembered now with some amusement. It was wild, how much had changed for him since then.

At the edge of the dance floor, he found a spot by the glass half wall ringing the terrace. Violet was in the middle of the crush of people out there, arms over her head, eyes closed, blood-red lips curved in a smile as she danced to the thumping techno beat. Her dress was the same blood-red as her lips. He watched her, smiling to himself. She'd probably groused about dancing, but she looked to be enjoying herself nonetheless.

As much as she tried to hide behind that steel-plated armor of hers, he knew her better than she could guess.

And he *liked* her.

She kept insisting it was just sex, but that was bullshit. He knew it even if she didn't. Even if she wouldn't admit it, to herself or to anyone else.

In his pocket his phone pinged with yet another text. He pulled it out and glanced at the screen. Madison again.

Really looking forward to seeing you in London. Have a great night.

As much as he liked Madison, he felt no anticipation about seeing her in London. You can't help who you're drawn to, who you like, who you want.

And he wanted someone else—he wanted Violet.

He pocketed his phone, leaving Madison on read.

Now he just had to convince Violet to want him back. And not just in bed. That part was easy. Having her for more? Having an actual relationship with her? That was a lot harder. And she was going to fight him like hell.

Why did he always do this to himself, choose the most difficult path out of every option available? But it was definitely a pattern with him. As a racing-obsessed teenager back home in Chicago, he could have set his sights on NASCAR and probably had a successful career in half the time with one-tenth of the struggle. But Formula One had always been his dream, so Formula One was the goal he had set for himself.

He could date Madison Mitchell, beautiful, fun, available, and a *legit movie star.* Instead he found himself fixated on this prickly, defensive porcupine of a woman, one who guarded her secrets and her heart like a dragon guarding his lair.

Good thing he was determined.

Out on the dance floor, Mira turned and said something in Violet's ear. Violet nodded and they started weaving their way through the crowd.

"Hi," he said to them as they approached. Violet was flushed from dancing, pink suffusing her pale skin, and he wanted nothing more than to kiss her in the middle of this crowded room.

"Nice to see you again, Mira."

"Same. Congrats. Nice race today."

"Thanks." Chase raised his hand to summon a passing waiter with a tray of champagne flutes. "Take one. We're celebrating."

"Thanks, but I have to go find my dad." Mira waved her phone. "Duty calls. Violet, dinner in London?"

"Absolutely. I'll text you."

Mira disappeared into the crowd.

"What are we celebrating?" Violet asked.

"Well, aside from my fucking astounding twelfth-place finish, how about this?"

He passed her his phone and watched her face as she skimmed the email. When she got to the bottom, her eyes went wide and her mouth dropped open. It was hard to shock Violet. He wished he had more ways to do it, because she was adorable.

She lifted her eyes to his. "Oh my god," she murmured. Then, to his surprise, she launched herself at him, flinging her arms around his neck. "We did it!"

"*You* did it," he murmured against her shoulder, squeezing her closer.

In a matter of seconds, she remembered herself and pulled away. "That's . . . it's . . ."

"It's going to change my entire career," he said quietly.

"You're going to be . . . Chase, this is *huge.* Not just for Pinnacle, for *you.*"

"I know."

"You're a star."

"And you made me. Thank you, Violet."

"I only saw the potential. You did the rest."

He scoffed. "Bullshit. None of this would have happened if not for you. Now what do you say we get out of here and celebrate it properly?"

"You really should work the room. Everybody wants a piece of you right now."

"I don't care about all of them." He caught her gaze and held it. He cast a quick glance around to make sure no one was watching them. The crush of bodies on the dance floor provided good cover, so he reached out for her hand, snagging her fingers with his. Slowly he rubbed his thumb across her knuckles. Her thick black lashes fluttered down to brush her cheekbones.

"I only want to celebrate with you."

26

London, England

Violet was back at a tiny bistro in Shoreditch to meet Will and Mira for dinner. They'd had dinner here together before, just after Mira started at Lennox. It was Will's favorite restaurant and near his place in Hackney. Although now, Violet supposed, it was *their* place, since Mira lived with him when they were in London.

She'd beaten them there, so she snagged a table near the back and ordered some wine. While she waited for them, she hopped on Insta and started scrolling hashtags. Chase was in London tonight, too, on a date with Madison. By now they should have been spotted and photographed.

It took no time at all to find the first photos, slightly grainy and poorly lit, but clearly Chase and Madison, in a cozy booth at some trendy Asian fusion place in Southwark. Madison looked great, in a gauzy white sundress and heels, her hair up in a messy twist that she pulled off effortlessly. And Chase . . . well, he looked as hot as he always did, in a black polo and expensive jeans, all sex hair and stubble. She'd texted him guidance on what to wear and was pleased he'd listened.

Their booth was a half circle, but they'd both scooted all the way to the middle, so they were cuddled up side by side. His right arm was draped across the back of the booth, behind Madison's shoulders. They were angled toward each other, smiling radiantly, eyes locked. They really knew how to sell it.

But what if they weren't selling it anymore? What if they were into each other now? Maybe tonight she'd go back to his hotel room with him, instead of Violet.

That was the wrong thing to imagine. There was that weird hollow feeling again. She felt twitchy and uneasy, like she wanted to get up and run, but to where and to do what? None of this was any of her business. Well, this part was . . . the online part, and how it was hitting. What they chose to do at the end of the night was none of her business.

"Violet! Hi!"

She jerked out of her doomscrolling and set her phone face down on the table. Mira had just arrived and was winding her way between tables to reach her. Violet could see Will outside on the sidewalk, on the phone.

Mira dropped into the chair across from her, looking flushed and excited. Her cascade of blond curls was especially wild tonight, and her green eyes were bright.

"I can't believe we finally made this happen."

"It's wild that we're both working for Formula One teams, we're both at all the same races, and yet we never see each other." Violet poured her a glass of wine.

"Here's to our rival teams," Mira said, lifting her glass.

Violet snorted, and tapped her glass against Mira's. "Pinnacle is hardly a rival to Lennox."

"Maraschino cherry," Mira said.

Violet nodded in understanding. "Cone of silence engaged."

Mira took a sip of her wine. "The last few races, you guys have definitely been making some moves. Rabia knows what she's doing."

"She does. If we can put together the money, she could design a truly competitive car next season."

"Chase looks good, too. With a decent car, he could really make a splash."

That was true, too. And it was the point of all of this, she reminded herself. The magazine spreads, the dates with Madison, it was all to rake in more sponsorship money. More money would pay for that better car Rabia was designing.

"He's a good driver," Violet said levelly, taking a sip of her wine.

Mira eyed her over the rim of her glass. "We're still in the cone. What about you two? Is that still a thing?"

"We're not a *thing*," Violet protested. "We just sleep together. When we feel like it."

Which was becoming nearly every night when they were in the same place. Most troubling of all, most of the time, he *actually* spent the night—sleeping and everything. How had *that* become a habit they'd fallen into? Sometimes she woke up in the morning and he was *cuddling* her.

Mira shook her head. "It seems messy to me. Isn't he dating that actor? Madison whatever?"

"Mitchell. And I told you, not really. I set that up."

Mira looked at her curiously. "I don't know how you do that, send him off to date some other woman. Even if he was just faking it, it would kill me to see Will like that."

"This is different. Chase isn't my boyfriend. It's just . . ." What? What were they? Friends with benefits? Were they actually friends? Colleagues who slept together? That felt wrong, too. "It's fine," she finally said, firmly. "Totally under control."

Mira smirked knowingly. "Whatever you say."

"It is," she insisted.

"I believe you."

"Hey, what did I miss?" Will slid into the chair beside Mira's and leaned in to kiss Mira's cheek. Will was the one guy who disproved Violet's theory that you could never reform a manwhore. Because Will had once been the king of them, and now he was utterly devoted to Mira. Honestly, it was revolting how besotted he was with her.

"Violet's just explaining that she isn't actually *dating* Chase Navarro," Mira said innocently.

"What happened to bloody maraschino cherry?" Violet protested.

Mira shrugged, completely without shame. "That only applies to racing. Personal stuff is fair game."

Will held up his hands. "Sorry, she tells me everything."

"Good to know." She shot a half-hearted glare at Mira, but honestly she didn't care if Will knew. He probably understood the situation better than Mira ever would, since he'd been the king of meaningless hookups back before he'd met Mira.

"Speaking of personal stuff . . ." Will looked at Mira, raising his eyebrow. "Did you tell her yet?"

"I was waiting for you," Mira said back, reaching for his hand.

"Tell me what?"

Mira pulled her left hand from her lap, and it was only now that Violet realized she'd been hiding it all this time. And it was obvious why.

The diamond on her third finger, flashing in the candlelight, was impossible to miss.

"We're engaged!" Mira said, her whole face lit up with joy. Will was smiling at her with the softest, dopiest expression on his handsome face. Honestly, the two of them . . .

"Oh." Violet scrambled to formulate the right response. "Congratulations! That's amazing!" She was happy for them. Of course she was. And really, it was no surprise they were taking this step. They were quite obviously in love with each other.

It was only that Violet had long ago convinced herself that true love was a myth. She hadn't believed anyone could really love you until they died. She'd felt that way once, and she'd believed with every molecule of her being that Ian had felt that way about her, too. He'd told her he did. The great love of his life, he'd called her. His muse, his reason for existing. But obviously it was all a load of bollocks. True love, that kind of love, was just a fantasy people got high on. Because if it really did exist, what did it mean that Ian had thrown hers away?

But it seemed to exist for some people. Mira and Will had found it together. If Violet hadn't managed it . . . well, she'd picked the wrong guy, the wrong guy had picked her. Or maybe it was just *her*.

Some people, like Mira, could love that way, and be loved in return. And others, like Violet, just . . . couldn't. No one in Violet's life ever stuck around to love her, not even her family. That was why she didn't go around hoping and expecting them to anymore. That was a surefire path to misery, and once in her life was plenty.

She took a minute to examine the ring and compliment Will's good taste in choosing it—all the things you're supposed to do when someone tells you they're getting married.

"There's something else," Mira said after a bit.

"What's that?"

"I'd like you to be my maid of honor."

Violet blinked. "Me?" she blurted. "Are you sure?"

Mira laughed. "Well, you're my best friend, so yes, I'm pretty sure. Do you . . . not want to?"

"No, not at all." Violet recovered herself, shaking her head and smiling. "I'd love to. That's really . . . nice. Only I've never done it." She waved a hand at herself. "Couldn't imagine anyone wanting me up there in their wedding pictures."

Mira scoffed. "You look amazing."

Lurking behind Mira's petite blond radiance, she imagined she'd look like the evil queen come to cast a curse on the happy couple. Then a terrible thought occurred to her. "Oh, god, you're not going to stuff me into some hideous bridesmaid dress, are you? Pink really isn't my color."

"Violet, I *do* know you, you know. I wouldn't dream of it. Wear what you want."

"So is there a date for this big event?"

"Next July, during the midseason break."

"You're going to plan a wedding while you're managing a Formula One season?"

"There's never a time when I'm *not* managing a Formula One season, either this one or the next one. I'll figure it out."

"I'll help, if you need it."

"You will?"

"'Course. I'm the maid of honor. Isn't that in the rules or something? Whatever I can do."

Mira reached across the table and squeezed her hand, gazing at her with those big Bambi eyes, overflowing with gratitude. No wonder Will was such a sucker for her. She was impossible to say no to. "Thank you. I don't know what I'd do without you, Violet."

A year ago, this kind of pronouncement, this kind of affection, would have made her twitchy with unease. To be honest, it still did a bit. But as unexpected as this friendship with Mira had been, it had become important to her. Maybe she didn't let men into her heart anymore, but Mira was different. She had one friend, and dammit, she was going to keep her.

"Lucky for you you'll never have to find out. So now fill me in on all the plans."

"Well, we think it'll be easiest to do it near London, so it's central for everybody—"

On the table beside her hand, Violet's phone vibrated. She flipped it over to see who it was.

It was a text. From *Chase.*

Probably done here by ten. Your room?

She blinked at her phone, confused. She'd been so sure he'd end up going home with Madison tonight. She was right there, beautiful and available. But here he was, still in the middle of their date, planning to come back to hers tonight.

She was feeling something again, but it wasn't that weird hollow feeling. It was warm, and bubbly, and absolutely fucking terrifying.

"Everything okay?" Mira asked.

She looked back up, forcing a smile. "Absolutely."

Mira eyed the phone still clutched in her hand. "You can bring a plus-one, you know. To the wedding."

Rolling her eyes, she scoffed. "Right. I'll just ring up Andrew Garfield and see if he's free."

Mira laughed, and Will groaned about being starving, so they all turned their attention to the menus. Violet held her phone in her lap as she typed out an answer.

See you tonight.

27

Austin, Texas

"Good lord," Violet groaned. "If it's this bloody hot in October I can't imagine what it's like here in the summer." She'd worn a slate-gray linen trouser suit, but she still felt like she was baking. She wasn't cut out for this climate.

"Well, this is Texas," Chase replied, leaning against the railing of the roof deck of the hospitality center, looking cool and unruffled in a deep burgundy short-sleeve dress shirt and jeans—nice, designer. She'd managed to banish those ratty old things he wore the first night they'd slept together to the waste bin. Funny that she could still remember so much of that night—a night that was meant to be forgettable—right down to what he'd worn.

"I thought this late in the day it would be nice for you to eat dinner outside," she said. "But if your family is too hot up here, just text me. I can arrange for some space downstairs."

Chase looked up from his phone. "Text you? Where are you going?"

She shrugged. "My office?"

He blinked. "My parents are coming. You're meeting them."

What?

"What?" she said out loud. She did not meet parents. No one *wanted* her to meet parents. She wasn't the sort of person people presented to their parents. When she was a kid, parents usually stepped in front of their children, instinctively assuming she might bite. Later, meeting parents had usually prompted them to turn to their sons and ask, *Whatever happened to that nice Claire girl? She was lovely.*

"Of course you're going to meet them," Chase said, as if it was the most obvious thing in the world. "They're going to love you."

She scoffed. "No, they will not."

She could be winning enough in small doses. Handshakes and smiles, professional small talk—she could manage all of that with ease. But with any prolonged exposure to her, his family was sure to see just how . . . *challenging* she was, to use Ian's description. He was a wanker, but he wasn't wrong.

"Trust me," he said with a grin. "They will."

Just then one of the track PAs opened the glass door leading to the rooftop lounge and ushered in what was obviously Chase's family.

"Hey, guys!" Chase's face lit up with happiness as he strode across the outdoor lounge to meet them.

His father met him first, catching him up in a bone-crushing, back-slapping embrace that lasted several beats.

"My boy!" the older man said. "We're so proud of you."

Chase got his dark good looks straight from his father. The older man was a little thicker through the midsection and silver had begun to sprinkle his jet-black hair, but the face was just an older version of Chase's. Same nearly black eyes, same golden skin, same killer cheekbones. He was wearing a pale blue button-down shirt and dark trousers with a linen blazer, still noticeably European despite his years in America.

When Chase managed to disentangle himself from his father, his mother was waiting there to hug him, too, having to stand on tiptoe to reach him. She was petite and trim, in a blue floral sundress and wedge sandals. She wore her dark brown hair in a long bob and her pale skin was lightly dusted with freckles. The only thing giving her age away was the pair of light laugh lines bracketing her eyes when she smiled, which she seemed to do often. When she pulled away from Chase, she reached up and took his face in her hands, smiling up at him with an affectionate warmth that was totally alien to Violet.

The younger brother—good god, there were *two* of them—was next to greet Chase. He had the same dark hair and eyes as his father and older brother, but with his mother's lighter complexion. If she remembered her notes correctly, he was only nineteen, but carried himself with an easy confidence that made him seem older. And beautiful, just like his brother. He gripped Chase's hand with one hand and thumped him hard on the back with the other.

"Dude," the younger Navarro said. "Look at you. Formula One. Now I'll never hear the end of it. 'Why can't you be like your brother?'"

"Gives you something to motivate you, kid."

His father protested that they were proud of all their kids while his mother jokingly begged Chase not to goad his little brother into taking even more risks behind the wheel.

Now that Violet had made sure they'd arrived and they were happily catching up, she'd planned to slip away and leave them to their dinner. Except Chase turned back and motioned for her to join them.

Oh, god, this was happening. *Why?* Why did he want her to meet his lovely, normal family? They were sure to wonder why their beloved son—and it was clear Chase was beloved—was hanging around with her. But she made her feet move, crossing the deck to join them.

"Guys, I want you to meet Violet Harper, the head of Pinnacle PR. Everything that's happened to me this season . . . the magazines, the interviews, the sponsorships . . . it's all her."

Chase's mother extended her hand first. "Violet, we're so happy to meet you. Chase has told us all about you."

She shot him an incredulous look. *He had?*

"Violet," Chase said, "this is my mom, Nicole; my dad, Javier; and my little brother, Tyler."

"Not so little, man," Tyler protested.

"Always will be to me," Chase replied, ruffling his hair. Tyler swatted his hand away and punched him in the bicep.

"Boys," Nicole admonished gently, like they were still small, but she was smiling as she said it.

"I'm sorry Sam couldn't make it," Chase said. "You'd love her, Violet. Tough as nails, just like you."

"Violet, I can't tell you how grateful we are for all you've done for our son," Javier said, shaking her hand enthusiastically. His Spanish accent reminded her of that night in Paris, when Chase had spoken Spanish to her and her whole body had nearly gone up in flames upon hearing his accent. She wasn't even sure what he'd said to her, but remembering the look in his eyes, she'd guessed it had been dirty.

"Oh, he does all the really hard work out on the track. I just make sure everyone's paying attention to him when he does it."

"You've worked a miracle," Nicole said. "Everybody we know has been calling us up to tell us they've seen his picture somewhere."

"What do you say to doing that for me?" Tyler said with a grin she was all too familiar with already. Guess they both got that from their father.

"Hey, hands to yourself," Chase said, shooting his brother a look that was only half teasing.

Tyler held up his hands in defense. "Wouldn't dream of it, big brother."

Was Chase staking some kind of claim on her? Here? In front of his whole family?

"Okay," she said, mustering the warmest smile she could manage. "You're all set up for dinner here at the roof lounge, but as I told Chase, if you're too warm outside, I'm happy to get you settled in the hospitality center downstairs—"

"Oh, but you're having dinner with us, aren't you?" Nicole protested.

"I—"

Suddenly Chase's hand landed on the small of her back, solid and warm. "Yes, she is." She looked over at him and he just smiled back. "Of course she is."

Then they were all happily talking over each other, filling each other in on news as Chase herded them to their table. There was no way for her to extricate herself without making a scene, so Violet let herself be herded along with them.

She was mostly quiet as they got settled and ordered. Nicole and Javier bickered gently when Javier declared he was ordering a steak and Nicole reminded him about his high cholesterol. Then Javier said she was being too American, and this was a special occasion. By the end of the argument, if you could even call it that, their hands were clasped on the table and they were grinning at each other, all twinkly-eyed and sweet.

She couldn't remember ever seeing her parents interact like that. Maybe it had happened briefly, years ago, before she'd come along. But as far back as she could remember, it was all frosty silences and passive-aggressive sniping, when it didn't descend into outright warfare.

Well, sitting here in silence wasn't going to make them think any better of her, so she busted out her best company manners. "How did you two meet? I don't think Chase ever said."

"Here we go," Tyler muttered with an eye roll.

Chase leaned into her. "All three of us kids can recite this story by heart."

"I was a freshman at University of Chicago," Nicole said.

"Who'd never left Minnesota," Chase and Tyler recited in unison.

Nicole swatted at Tyler's arm.

"It was just a few weeks into the semester, and I took the L into the Loop so I could buy my mother a birthday present at Marshall Field's. And as I'm leaving the store, just like that, the lights go out."

"What happened?" Violet asked.

"Blackout," Javier said. "The whole city, for hours."

"Here's the thing," Nicole continued. "I'd just started school, and I only knew how to get to campus on the L. I didn't know the streets, so I had no idea how to walk home. Now everybody's got maps on their phones, but we didn't have smartphones back then. So, I'm standing there on the sidewalk trying to decide what to do, when all of a sudden this boy asks me if I'm okay."

Javier leaned in and stage-whispered. "She looked nervous. I wanted to be sure she was all right."

Tyler eyed his father. "And?"

Javier shrugged with a smile. "And I thought she was beautiful."

"Awww," Tyler and Chase chorused together, like it was a line in a play. Violet could imagine them telling and retelling this story at every family gathering until everyone knew it by heart, but wanted to hear it again just the same. As much as she hated to admit it, it made something ache in her chest. What must it be like, to have this kind of love and support at your back, no matter what? She'd never known.

"So I explained that I'd just started at University of Chicago and I didn't know how to get back to campus."

"And I said that's no problem! I go to University of Chicago, too. I'll walk you home and show you the way."

"So we walked through Chicago, talking the whole way," Nicole said, looking at Javier with gentle affection.

Javier smiled back at her. "By the time we got back to campus, I knew I was going to marry her."

"And four years later, we were!" Tyler and Chase chorused again, and the whole family burst out in laughter.

"That's a great story." She was pretty sure her parents had just had a drunken hookup, and her mother had gotten knocked up. "It's great, the way you all tell it."

"Just wait until you meet Dad's side of the family," Chase said. "Reenacting family beefs going back hundreds of years." He took a swig of his beer, so he missed the shocked look she shot him. Did he realize he'd just said that?

Before any of his family could comment on it, their dinner arrived.

"Chase, how did you meet Violet?" Nicole asked, once they'd all started eating.

She glanced at Chase again, but he was leaning back in his chair, smiling easily, not the least bit thrown by the question. "Well, we work together. But we've been crossing paths on the circuit for a while now, right, Violet?"

"Sure. Everybody knows everybody on the circuit."

"So tell us about you, Violet," Javier said, topping up her wine. "I can hear from your accent that you're English."

"Got it in one," she replied, nudging her grilled zucchini around her plate with her fork. "I, um, grew up in Colchester.

That's in Essex. I spent some time working in music before switching to auto racing." Just the bullet points of her existence, no hint of the drama and heartbreak behind those facts.

"Music, huh? Which are harder to work with, musicians or drivers?"

She couldn't help flashing a quick, teasing smile in Chase's direction. "Oh, drivers for sure. Pure chaos."

"Don't I know it?" Nicole groaned as the rest of the table laughed. Chase and Tyler reached out to fist-bump each other.

Javier elbowed Chase. "She's got your number, doesn't she?"

Chase turned to smile at her, a smile that was way too intimate to show off in front of his family. "She sure does."

As they ate, Nicole and Javier passed along well-wishes from Chase's large extended family. In addition to Nicole's tangle of American relatives, Javier had four sisters in Spain, so Chase had an army of aunts, uncles, and cousins in Europe as well, and it sounded as if they all talked constantly with each other in some massive WhatsApp chat.

"Nervous about the track?" Javier asked Chase as their plates were cleared.

Dinner was over, but no one seemed in a hurry to leave. As the sun set, the sky lit up in a brilliant explosion of orange, magenta, and purple, and the string lights overhead flickered on.

Chase shrugged. "I've driven some F2 races here. It's not bad."

"The car's looking good," Javier said.

"That's all Rabia Dar," Violet interjected.

Chase nodded in agreement. "It's unbelievable what she's been able to accomplish with the car in just a few weeks. Next year's car could change everything for Pinnacle."

"You should see Chase's simulator times in the new car," Violet said to Javier.

"Good?" he asked his son.

"Best I've ever driven."

"Rabia's a genius," Violet added.

Nicole leaned forward to address Violet. "I'd apologize for all the car talk, Violet, but it's clear you're used to it."

"I am."

Nicole shook her head sadly. "Every single family meal, this is what it turns into with these four. Tire pressures and aerodynamics and engine power."

"It's nice you all have so much in common."

"Everything I know about racing is thanks to Dad," Chase said, smiling at his father.

Javier reached out to squeeze Chase's shoulder. "I can't believe my boy is driving in Formula One. I never dreamed . . ." He trailed off, choking up with emotion.

"Oh, here we go," Tyler said. "You made the old man cry again, Chase."

"He's crying with *pride*," Chase teased back. "Unlike his tears of frustration over you."

Tyler laughed and tossed his wadded-up napkin at Chase, who was laughing too as he ducked to the side. "Better watch out. I'll tell Sam about that time we went karting and you fucked with her carburetor when she wasn't looking."

They were . . . Jesus, they were fucking adorable. All of them. So affectionate and open. She didn't belong here, her with all her hard surfaces and razor-sharp edges.

Violet was getting that overwhelming urge to bolt, the way she always did when she got too close to human emotions that made her feel uncomfortable. It was only good manners that kept her rooted to her chair, smiling and responding in all the appropriate places.

It didn't help that Chase kept glancing over at her with that look in his eyes. That look that meant he was feeling things he shouldn't be feeling. And he shouldn't. He *really* shouldn't. Not for her, who didn't belong here, and never would.

Chase reached out and nudged her knee under the table. "Hey. Mom wants to go see some band she likes that's playing downtown tonight. Come with us."

She forced a smile and shook her head. "I can't."

"Are you sure?" Nicole asked, having heard him ask.

"I have a million things to catch up on in my office," she lied easily as she stood. "It's been really lovely. Enjoy your night and I'll see you at the race tomorrow. You'll be watching from the garage."

"Violet—" Chase protested, starting to stand up, but she put her hand on his shoulder to stop him.

"I really do have to go."

And then she fled, as fast as she could go without breaking into a full-out run. Anything to put distance between herself and this clawing feeling of unease eating away at her.

CHASE WATCHED VIOLET striding rapidly across the deck, her long black hair snapping behind her in the warm breeze, and something twisted in his gut. Everything had seemed fine. She was chatting with his family, and they clearly loved her. Then all of a sudden she got that hunted look on her face and bolted.

As she disappeared through the glass doors that led to the stairs down to hospitality, he told himself to forget it. His family was here for the race and that's all that mattered. But as Mom and Dad chatted, he kept looking back over at the door she'd disappeared through. Finally he couldn't stand it another minute.

He slid his chair away from the table. "Hey, there's something I forgot to ask Violet about. I'm going to run downstairs and catch her in hospitality. I'll be right back."

"No problem," Tyler said, but the slight smirk he threw at Chase said he'd clocked what was going on between them. Considering he was half obsessed with her, it was no wonder Tyler could see it on his face. He wasn't sure how the whole world couldn't see it.

Downstairs in the hospitality lounge things were relatively quiet. Pinnacle staffers were busy putting finishing touches on the space, but there were no guests. Violet was still there, across the room conferring with Liz from catering.

She finished up and turned, surprise in her expression when she saw him there.

"Oh, good. You're here," she recovered smoothly. "I just talked to Cam and Madison's managed to clear her schedule."

"What?"

"She's flying in for the race. She'll be in the garage with your parents."

His stomach dropped. "Why the hell is she going to be in the garage?"

Violet got that hard, obstinate look on her face as her eyes cut to the Pinnacle staffers still working in the room. "This way." She jerked her head to the hallway off the reception room. He followed her down it and into a small temporary office at the end. She shut the door and leaned back against it.

"Madison is supposed to be your girlfriend," she said patiently. "Your parents are here. It would seem weird if she *wasn't* here."

He raked a hand through his hair in frustration. "I just . . . I don't like involving my parents in this. This is my job, not theirs."

"Explain it to them. They can play along, right? I'm happy to give them some coaching—"

"No. I don't want you coaching my parents on how to behave around this stranger I'm pretending to date. It's fucked up."

"You don't need to be embarrassed about it. These sorts of things happen all the time." Her calmness was infuriating, like he was just one more item on her to-do list, one more public relations issue to be managed.

"Not to me. Not to them. I just don't want her here, in that part of my life."

"Well, it's already arranged. She's arriving tonight. We've put her at your hotel so—"

"Violet, no. If everybody thinks I'm there with her, then I can't come see you, and—"

"So don't come see me. You shouldn't anyway. Not when she's around. If you were seen—"

"Fuck that. I don't care."

"I do. It's my job to care."

"I'm not just a part of your fucking job!" He was only aware as the words were coming out of his mouth that he was shouting, the sound echoing in the tiny space.

Up until now, she'd maintained that expressionless professional face, refusing to even look directly at him. Now her eyes snapped up to his, blazing with anger.

"You *are* my job. I'm not going to forget that and neither should you."

There was a little alarm buzzing in his head, trying to warn him to shut up and stop pushing her, but he wouldn't be the driver he was if he listened to the caution warnings that held most people back.

He took a step closer, crowding her against the door. "This—what we do—this is not a part of your job, and don't you dare pretend otherwise." She opened her mouth to protest, but he barreled on. "Don't pretend like you don't want me. Don't pretend you don't care."

Her hands came up between them and she shoved hard against his shoulders. He stepped back out of her space as she pushed away from the door.

"Sex is just fucking, Chase. And don't *you* pretend otherwise. You want a nice girlfriend to introduce to your fucking happy family, call up Madison and leave me out of it."

Then she spun around, wrenched the door open, and stormed out. This time he didn't follow her.

28

Chase hurtled through a tricky turn complex, trying his best to clear his head and focus on the track in front of him. But his thoughts kept returning to that fight with Violet the night before, over and over again. Was that what that even was? Had he and Violet just had a fight? Could you have a fight with someone you weren't even technically dating?

He'd woken up mad today and honestly, he still was. Frustration welled up in his chest with nowhere to go but out on the track. Generally it was bad to let anything from the rest of your life get into your head during a race, but maybe the anger was working for him today. He'd been driving aggressively from the instant the lights had gone out and was sitting in eleventh place as a result, which was a minor miracle for Pinnacle.

He couldn't even bring himself to think about Madison watching *with his family* in the garage.

So he did what he did best: drove. He'd come into today expecting the usual fight for his life, but Rabia was beginning to tame the unpredictability that had plagued this car when he'd first climbed into it. Each update seemed small on its own, but they all came together out on the track. He could feel the balance coming back.

"Okay, Chase," Emil said into his ear. "We want you to push now."

Time for some really aggressive driving, which was fine. Today he felt like he had nothing but aggression, and for once, the car was responding to it. "You got it."

He flipped a switch, turned a rotary, and adjusted his brake balance as he headed for Turn One. He peeled another half a second off Elian's time up ahead. He was getting ready to launch it through Turn Fifteen again when Emil crackled in his ear.

"Box, box. Do the opposite of Elian."

Shit. That meant they were in serious contention to take tenth place, and Emil thought they might be able to undercut Elian if they did their pit stop now. He kept his eyes fixed on Elian's gearbox, bracing for the tiniest twitch to give away Elian's intention. At the last possible second, Elian sped past the pit lane exit.

"Okay, boxing!" he shouted as he entered the pit lane, smashing the brakes when he hit the white line. He nosed into position and they had him up on the jacks in the space of a heartbeat. Then they dropped him and dumped it into gear.

Hell yes. That *had* to be just over two seconds stationary. He sped out of the pits.

"Push, push!" Emil barked as he banged his way through the gearbox. "It's gonna be tight with traffic."

He could do this . . . he could do this . . .

Chase glanced in his mirrors and spotted a car coming for him up the hill. Rolando Castenada swooped around his outside.

"Motherfucker," he muttered under his breath. "You're not getting me that easy."

He managed to keep in Rolando's slipstream for half a lap, but he couldn't get around him. Turn Eleven was approaching, a wild hairpin that led to the longest straight on the track. That was his opening. He released the brakes and dove up the inside, forcing Rolando wide as they both fought to get the advantage down the straight.

But Chase's new tires, now fully warmed up, won out, and halfway down the straight Rolando dropped back.

There was no time to enjoy it, though.

"Elian's in the pit," Emil said. "Push to the pit lane exit."

Pushing through the tight Turn Twenty was going to be tough, and if this car was the same he'd been driving under Oscar, he wouldn't stand a chance. But now he could feel the car grip the track as he powered through the turn.

As he barreled down the straight, he caught a glimpse of aqua blue off to his left—Elian, accelerating through the pit lane. He had to get to the next turn ahead of him, otherwise Elias would be perfectly set up to overtake him.

"Push, push, push!" Emil shouted.

"I'm pushing!" he shouted back, spinning the throttle. He channeled all his simmering anger from that fight with Violet last night straight into his driving, practically screaming his frustration out loud as the roar of the engine built. This was it—he could feel it. When he gave it the last bit of acceleration, the car responded. Aqua blue receded in his mirrors. Elian, on cold tires, was unable to match his acceleration.

"That's it!" Emil shouted. "Elian fell back. You are now P ten."

P ten. Which meant points. Pinnacle hadn't seen points in four seasons.

"Congratulations," Emil said.

Chase smiled.

"Congratulate Rabia. It's her car that got us here."

■

Pinnacle had just had its best race finish in four years. Half an hour after the race had ended, people were still lingering in the Pinnacle garage, celebrating. Because Madison was there, there were media and photographers, too. Which was the point of her, Chase supposed. Media coverage. Just like Violet had said.

Violet.

Now that the race was over, there was no place for him to channel all this gnawing frustration, and he was feeling twitchy with it.

"You seen Violet?" he asked Tyler.

"Nope."

Chase cast another glance around the garage, which was pointless because he knew she wasn't here. Madison was chatting with Rabia and his parents, all of them casually trying to ignore the photographers capturing every second of the interaction. His parents had been surprisingly chill when he'd told them about the setup last night, and they'd been as welcoming and polite to her today as they were to everyone. Tyler had immediately started up with the jokes about Chase needing a rent-a-girlfriend, and he'd probably keep it up for the rest of their lives. Fucking brothers.

"Why don't you just go find her?" Tyler asked.

"Mom and Dad are here. And Madison."

"Look at them. They're fine."

"But Madison is supposed to be my girlfriend."

"She's *not*, though," Tyler said, raising his eyebrows. "Speaking of, if she's not actually your girlfriend—"

"Don't even think about it, Tyler," he warned. Tyler might be young, but where women were concerned, he was . . .

precocious. Chase had done his fair share of sleeping around, but Tyler was steadily decimating his record.

Tyler laughed. "Look, just quit looking like your dog died and go find your girl."

"She's not my girl."

"Seemed that way to me," Tyler said.

"Mom and Dad are here. I can't ditch them."

"I can handle riding herd on the parents, Chase."

Tyler was an adult now, he reminded himself. He might always seem like a kid to Chase, but when he'd been Tyler's age, he'd already been living in Spain for four years and was traveling solo constantly to race. And Madison had to leave soon anyway; she had to be on set tomorrow.

"Okay, tell them I'll see them at the hotel later."

"Go, get out of here."

Chase didn't waste any more time debating. He got out of there.

29

An hour later, he was knocking on Violet's hotel room door. He hadn't bothered to text her that he was on the way. She would have just told him not to come. She cracked the door and peered over the safety lock.

"What are you doing here?"

"Can I come in?"

She unlatched the door. She'd changed into that black silky robe he liked so much, and she was barefoot, leaving her several inches shorter than him.

"Where's your family? And Madison?"

"Madison's on the way back to LA. Tyler's with my parents so I could come talk to you."

She lifted one eyebrow, her fingers tracing the silky belt of her robe. "Talk?"

"We do that sometimes, you know."

She rolled her eyes, which he knew she employed to convince the world how unconcerned she was, but frankly, he found it kind of adorable, like a hissing kitten. But he'd never, ever tell her that.

"What do you want to talk about?"

"Dinner last night. Why you ran away."

"I didn't run away."

"Violet, you left skid marks."

Letting out a frustrated huff, she turned and crossed to the other side of the room. She swiped a glass filled with ice and vodka off the table and took a swig.

"My family freaked you out. Why?"

"They didn't. Your family is fine."

He moved up behind her. "So then what was it?"

"I'm not a 'meet the parents' kind of girl," she said quietly. "Parents usually hate me."

"Mine didn't."

She let out a soft huff of laughter, still not turning around to look at him. "Really? My own do."

Now they were getting to it. He reached out and took her glass from her hand, setting it on the table. Then he took her by the shoulders and turned her around. "Maybe you should tell me about them."

She scoffed again, keeping her head turned to the side and her eyes on the window, closed off and shut down. "There's nothing to tell."

"Bullshit. Tell me about the 'sperm donor.' That's what you called him, right? Was he not around?"

Her gaze dropped to her feet. "Oh, he was around. For a while at least. My parents divorced when I was twelve."

"What happened?"

"If you ask my mother, he cheated. Which is true. But they were miserable long before that. As long as I can remember. If they weren't outright fighting, they were giving each other the silent treatment or engaging in elaborate passive-aggressive sabotage. It was like growing up in a fucking psychological experiment. Nothing at all like that perfect couple you grew up with."

"No couple is perfect. But they're great parents. I'm sorry you didn't have that."

"It is what it is," she said with a nonchalance he could tell was forced. "Not sure it would have mattered if I'd had great parents. I was a hard kid to love."

He hated hearing her talk about herself that way. "Why do you say that?"

Her eyes flashed to his, a moment of vulnerability, then away again. "I wasn't exactly your typical little girl."

"What's typical? I'm guessing you were less Disney princess, more Wednesday Addams, right?"

She laughed softly, although it didn't lessen the tension radiating through her body. "A bit. Anyway, when my father finally started fucking his secretary and left Mum, she said it was because our family wasn't what he wanted. And by 'family,' she meant me. That wasn't exactly news. Kids can sense stuff like that. I mean, I started watching racing with him when I was six to try to make him feel better about having a daughter. But that didn't work. He barely tolerated me. After he left, Mum said I'd been a miserable disappointment."

Out of nowhere, fury flared up bright and hot in his chest. "Who the fuck would say that to a little kid?"

"Mum is . . . well, I suppose to use therapy speak, she's toxic. Not that he's absolved, but I don't exactly blame my father for leaving. I wouldn't want to be married to her either."

"What happened after he left?"

"She certainly didn't decide to become mother of the year, if that's what you're wondering. She got even more bitter, and quasi-obsessed with his new life, even though she hated the wanker. Gathering up every morsel she could about him and the new wife became her hobby. I honestly think she sometimes forgot I was still there."

“And what about your dad?” He very much feared the answer. It sounded like Violet had been set adrift by both of them, and left to parent herself.

“He had a baby with the new wife . . . a son . . . and basically forgot all about his old family.” Her voice was small and tight. Something like pain flashed through her expression, and to his shock, her eyes were glassy with tears. Jesus, Violet was about to cry.

He lifted his hands to reach for her. “Violet—”

She seemed to remember herself, shaking her head and drawing herself up before he could touch her. “I fucking hate him, but I can’t say I blame him much on that one, either. If I was a hard little kid to love, I was a rotten teenager. Of course he didn’t like me.”

“I’m sure he liked you. And if he didn’t, *he’s* the idiot. Not you. You were just a kid.”

She’d been as vulnerable with him as she was willing to get. He could see it in the sudden set of her jaw, and the flash of temper in her eyes. “Look, I know you’re used to those amazing parents of yours, providing all the love and support you needed to chase your dreams, or whatever, but a lot of people are born to a couple of selfish fuckups, and I’m one of them. My parents don’t like me. *Most* people don’t like me. I know that. I’m used to it. Fuck, I *like* that.”

Fuck her parents. What kind of people deliberately make their kid believe she’s unlikable? Violet was one of a kind. If she said it, she meant it. And she was a fighter. When Violet was on your side, you could take on the world.

“Hey.” He took a step closer to her. She shifted uneasily in response, still looking off to the side, down at the ground, anywhere but at him. He reached up and set his hands along the sides of her long, slender neck. “Violet.”

"What?"

He traced the angle of her jaw with his thumbs, urging her face up. Her eyes lifted to his, and he understood in a flash of clarity why she piled on so much steel-plated armor all the time. He could see the truth in her eyes. Because underneath it, she was as vulnerable as an exposed nerve. First her parents had effectively abandoned her, and refused to love her. Then, when she'd thought she'd found belonging with Ian and his band—a new family—she'd lost that, too.

"I like you."

VIOLET STARTED TO scoff again, her knee-jerk reaction to any human emotion that made her uncomfortable, but Chase cut her off.

"Hey."

She looked back to him, even though meeting his gaze made her feel horribly exposed.

"I know you pretty well," he said, rubbing his thumb along the edge of her jaw. "And I like you."

Goddamn it. Her stupid eyes were burning again. She would *not* cry. She *never* cried.

"That's your dick talking." It came out as a whisper, nowhere near as flippant and confident as she'd have liked.

He cracked a smile, still smoothing his thumbs along her jaw, massaging the nape of her neck with his fingertips. "Sure, my dick likes you. But so do I. Kind of a lot."

Then he held her face still as he leaned in and kissed her. They'd kissed a lot at this point. He'd explored every inch of her body with his hands and his mouth. But this felt different.

This felt tender and sweet and a whole bunch of things they weren't supposed to be to each other.

When he pulled back, the look in his eyes sent a spear of pure panic through her chest. Before he could give her some sort of declaration she wasn't ready for, or ask one from her in return, she pressed up on her toes and kissed him back, hard. This one wasn't tender and sweet. She opened her mouth over his and found his tongue with hers, pulling her body flush against his. Chase hesitated for a beat, then made a low sound of satisfaction in his throat and pulled her in tight against him.

Yes, this was what she wanted. This felt good and right. She pushed against him, keeping her mouth on his, and he stumbled back a few steps until he was in front of the armchair in the corner. She climbed into his lap even as he was sitting down. Her knees slotted in on either side of his hips and his hands landed first on her waist, and then slid down to grip her ass and drag her forward, until her sex was pressed against the fly of his jeans.

She broke the kiss and sat back slightly, keeping her eyes on his. Her hands went to the belt of her robe and tugged at the knot. It came free and she shrugged, sending the silky black fabric slithering down her arms. She was naked underneath it. Chase watched it slide down her body, his eyes hungry, then he reached for it, pulling it completely free and tossing it to the floor.

She reached for his hands and brought them to her bare breasts. The expression in his face shifted, that familiar hunger sparking in his eyes. It made the same hunger spark in her belly, and down lower, between her legs. When he kneaded her breasts and gave each nipple a hard twist just the way he knew she liked it, she sucked in a breath and her eyes fluttered closed. He did it again and this time she moaned.

"Tell me you like it, Violet," he murmured.

"I like it." Her voice was low and breathy.

"Tell me you want me."

"I want you," she panted as he twisted again. "So much." She put her hands over his as he kneaded her breasts. "I love it when you do that."

Maybe she wasn't ready to bare her heart to him just yet, but this much she could do. She could tell him she wanted him. More importantly, she could show him.

She put her hands on his shoulders and pushed back. He released her and fell back on the chair, watching her avidly. Then she reached down between them and hooked her fingers into the waistband of his jeans. His eyes dropped to watch her hands as she popped each button of the button fly. He was so hard already, the ridge of his cock, covered by the black knit of his boxer briefs, pushing up through the opening.

When she ran the flat of her palm down the length, he sucked in a breath. She ran her hand back up him, and up under the hem of his T-shirt, brushing against the hard ridges of his abdomen. His muscles twitched and flexed under her fingertips. Then she slipped her hand under the waistband of his briefs and down to grasp the warm, silky length of him.

"Violet . . ." he murmured.

"Shhh." She stroked him once, then again harder. He shifted in the chair, arching to give her better access. But this wasn't enough. Or, it wasn't what she really wanted. She gave him one more tug, pulling him free of his clothes, and then pushed herself off his lap.

His hooded dark eyes stared down at her as she knelt between his feet, stroking his cock with one hand while she tugged his jeans out of the way with the other.

His hand came up to brush against her cheekbone. "Baby . . ." he moaned. The term of endearment sent a tiny jolt through her body. It was the second time he'd called her that.

"Baby," he said again, rubbing his thumb across her bottom lip. "I want to feel your pretty mouth on me."

Maybe she wasn't ready to tell him what she was feeling, because she wasn't sure herself yet, but she could show him. She was good at showing. She leaned in, taking the head of his cock into her mouth.

"Ah . . ." The sound was wrenched out of him as she slid him farther in, as deep as she could take him. "Fuck, Violet."

She sucked hard, reveling at the sound he made, at the way his hard body arched up underneath her. His hand tangled into the hair at the back of her head, so gently at first, but gradually tightening into a fist as she worked him with long, slow strokes.

"You feel so fucking good," he muttered. "Baby, I'm going to come."

She tightened the hand she had braced on his thigh, to let him know that she wanted him to, and took him as deep as she could again. His hips flexed and a long, guttural groan ripped from his chest as he pressed his head against the back of the chair.

When he'd gone slack underneath her, she let him slide out of her mouth and she sat back, running a finger under her lips to clean up.

He lifted his head to look down at her. "That was fucking amazing."

Before she could reply, he stood up abruptly. She fell back, and he leaned down, his hands closing around her upper arms. He pulled her to her feet, turned them both around, and pushed her back into the chair he'd just left.

He grabbed her calves, spread her legs, and draped them over the arms of the chair. "Don't move," he ordered. Then he was the one dropping to his knees. She was already wet, but seeing him kneeling between her spread thighs sent heat licking through her.

He ran his palms from her knees up the insides of her thighs, the rough scrape of his skin setting every nerve ending along the way on fire.

"Eyes here," he ordered softly, and she looked back at him.

"So bossy," she murmured.

He cracked a smile, that wicked, crooked grin of his that had always been her secret weakness. "I know you like it."

That was her secret, too, one he'd figured out from the start. She *did* like it, but only for him. Only with him.

As she was busy getting lost in his dark eyes and inky long lashes, he slid two fingers into her, forcing a gasp out of her.

"So ready," he said, pumping gently. His other hand slid up over her stomach, cupping her breast and flicking her nipple.

"Mmmm," was all the reply she could manage. Her head tipped back against the back of the chair and her eyes started to close.

"Eyes on me," he reminded her.

It felt vulnerable, looking into his eyes as he did this to her. She usually avoided looking directly at him when they were together, she realized. In those moments when he was physically taking her apart, it felt like too much, to let him see in her eyes what he was doing to her.

It was still hard, still scary, but she made herself look back, even when he lowered his mouth to her. The second his tongue licked across her clit, she moaned and nearly closed her eyes again.

"Eyes open," he murmured, right against her, and she felt the vibration as much as she heard him. He put his mouth back on her, stroking and sucking, until her thighs started to tremble and her fingers were curling into claws, her nails cutting into the arms of the chair.

"Please," she murmured, almost mindless with the need to come. His dark eyes softened as he gazed up her body, never stopping what he was doing with his mouth, with his hands.

"Come on, baby," he whispered against her most sensitive skin. One more pass of his tongue was all it took. She came, her whole body shaking and trembling, and finally her eyes slid closed as the wave of pleasure rocketed through her. She slumped down in the chair, boneless with her release.

She felt him move, standing up, sliding her legs back together. She opened her eyes in time to see him whip his T-shirt off over his head, marveling in the gorgeous ripples of his abdomen as he turned and tossed it away. He bent down, sliding one arm under her knees and the other behind her back.

She reached for his broad, solid shoulders to steady herself. "What are you doing?"

"Taking you to bed so I can finish this," he said as he carried her across the room.

She wasn't sure what they were doing anymore, or how she felt about it, but as she rested her head against his shoulder, she knew she didn't want it to end.

30

Las Vegas, Nevada

Chase shifted uncomfortably from foot to foot. He stuffed his hands in the pockets of his suit pants, then took them back out. He'd been at his first major function as a "brand ambassador" for Jet Energy drinks, a huge post-race party in Vegas, for all of an hour and it already felt like an hour too long. This wasn't his kind of place or his kind of people.

Everybody was being nice enough. He'd been surrounded by Arrow Beverages corporate bigwigs since he'd walked in the door, and they all seemed delighted to have him there, but he still felt out of his depth. Violet was supposed to come with him tonight. She'd have made everything easier, whispering in his ear all night, letting him know who was who, why they were important, and what he should say to them.

But at the last minute she'd found out Reece was planning a private post-race party of his own, so she'd gone there to make sure he didn't embarrass himself or the team too much.

"How did you feel about the race today, Chase?" one guy asked. Tim? Tom? He couldn't remember. He was surrounded by a trio of nearly identical thirty-something guys in nearly identical gray suits, all of whom worked for Arrow. All of them were drunk, enjoying a party on the company's dime. This was part of what the corporations got out of sponsorships. He got money, they got VIP access to the races and one-on-one time with drivers.

"Oh, you know. There are some spots I felt I could have done better, but overall it wasn't bad."

"Has Pinnacle signed you for next season yet?" Ron? No, it was Rob.

"If they do, you'll be the first to know," Chase said with a grin. The whole little group of guys in suits laughed. Tom, Rob, and . . . He had no idea what the other guy's name was, and now it felt too late to ask.

"Must have been nice having your girlfriend at the race this weekend," Tom said.

For a second he was confused. She was there every weekend. Then he realized Tom wasn't asking him about Violet. He meant Madison.

"Oh . . ." He paused, searching for the right words. He should have practiced this one with Violet. "I'm always pretty focused on the race, you know? I can't afford to get distracted."

"She's a distraction, for sure," Rob said, and the other guys chuckled.

His phone buzzed in his pocket and he fished it out, hoping it was Violet telling him she was on her way to rescue him. Not Violet. Madison.

I have a movie premiere tomorrow in LA. Want to come?

It was the sort of public event Violet would go nuts for, but this felt different.

It hadn't come through Violet and Cam. Madison had asked him herself. Which meant this probably wasn't for a PR appearance. He got the sense Madison was asking him out. On a date.

Okay, this was officially too much. He'd been fine faking it as long as Madison had been faking it, too. Nobody was getting lied to except the press. But he'd felt uncomfortable introducing Madison to his family because now he was dragging his parents into the lie, too. And now it felt like Madison wanted this to be real.

He had one rule. He didn't sleep with other people's partners. And it went the other way, too. He didn't get entangled with women when he wasn't free, and while he and Violet hadn't put a name on it, he now considered himself involved. Wasn't that what they'd figured out after that fight in Austin? Not specifically, in words, but they were a thing now, right?

That meant he could not keep up this thing with Madison. It wouldn't be fair.

Tomorrow he'd tell Violet and Cam to come up with some clean and equitable end to the whole situation that would allow both of them to walk away looking good. And for tonight, he wouldn't answer Madison. He didn't want to lead her on with any possibility this was more than it was. If it was strictly business, he'd let the experts handle ending it.

"Gentlemen, do you mind if I join you?"

Chase looked up from his phone to see who it was. Eric Lenore, the team principal of Allegri.

Tom, Rob, and Other Guy greeted Eric with boozy familiarity, even though he was pretty sure none of them had met him before.

Eric reached out and shook his hand. "Chase. Good to see you again." He'd never directly spoken to Eric Lenore in his life.

"Eric. Nice to see you, too."

"You're looking very strong this season."

"Thank you. Allegri looks good, too."

Eric smiled and shrugged with a bit of false modesty, because come on, Allegri was number two on the grid, second only to Lennox. René Denis had won two world championships for Allegri, one as recently as two seasons ago.

"We've got a good car this season," Eric said simply. "And it's looking even better for next season."

"Is it?" Why was Eric Lenore telling this to him, of all people? Again, he wished Violet were here. She was so good at this stuff. She'd have seen Eric coming from twenty feet away, and instinctively known every hidden motivation and angle.

"Yes, next year's car is going to be really special," Eric went on. "Why don't you stop by the garage in Mexico City? Our head of design, Karl Aurbach, is eager to meet you."

"Me?"

Eric laughed, like he'd said the funniest thing, but Chase was still clueless.

"Sure. Swing by and let's talk."

"Okay? I mean, sure. Yeah, I'll stop by."

Eric shook his hand again. "Good talking to you. See you in Mexico."

"Right. See you."

Eric disappeared into the crowd. Chase watched him go in confusion.

Suddenly, Rob clapped Chase on the shoulder. "It's gonna be a blast bragging that I was here when it happened."

"What? When what happened?" He was more confused than ever.

"You moving over to Allegri next season."

"What? He didn't say anything about that."

Rob slung his arm across his shoulders and leaned in. "That, my friend, was a corporate opening salvo. He's poaching you."

Chase looked from Rob to Tom and Other Guy. They nodded in agreement.

"Shit. Seriously?"

The drunk trio seemed to find that hilarious and all three of them cracked up laughing.

He paused to absorb that. Allegri wanted him? Holy shit. He had to tell someone. Violet. He needed to relate this entire conversation to Violet so she could dissect every word and intonation. He pulled out his phone to text her, but that wasn't what he wanted. He wanted to see her. Alone.

31

Violet's heels rapped on the marble lobby floor of the boutique hotel Reece was staying in as she strode toward the elevators in a fury. Tonight was big for Chase. She should be at the Arrow Beverages party with him, helping him navigate his new reality. The *GQ* profile had just dropped to huge buzz. Crowds of fans now materialized at the track entrance every day of the race weekend, and they'd needed security guards to get him inside unscathed.

But no. Instead, she was here to babysit some *asshole.*

His own private party. Motherfucker. The fact that the guys in the garage were talking about it meant it was as private as the queen's bloody jubilee.

Beside the elevator, a sign on a silver stand indicated that the party was at the rooftop bar. Renting that place out had to be costing a fortune. She rode the elevator up to the roof, fuming. Carter Hammond could more effectively rein in his Fail Son if he cut off his allowance now and then. As soon as the elevator door slid open into the small lobby upstairs, Violet's stomach contracted with panic.

That song . . .

She knew it. She had been there when it was written. Fucking Ian had even told her it was about her, which was probably just another lie.

But this wasn't Spotify piped through the bar's sound system. This was *live.* Which meant . . .

She rounded the corner and the room opened up in front of her. Dark, half full of people, lots of purple neon light, and on the far side of the room, up on a stage, Revenant Saints was grinding out "Love Like a Drug."

Ian looked good. He always did when he was in his element, up onstage with every eye fixed on him. He gripped the mic with one hand while his other glided suggestively up and down the mic stand as he growled out the bridge, all performative angst. Behind him, Astrid wailed on the guitar, her face twisted up with tough girl rage. Ben was still on bass, and Kiz was there, too, on drums. Kiz had always been her favorite—gruff, no-nonsense, and thoroughly unsentimental, like her. He was the only one she'd stayed in nominal contact with after the breakup, at least until recently when Ian and Astrid had insisted on inserting themselves back into her life.

How the fuck had this happened? She found Reece up near the front, doing his embarrassing dance again. A couple of attractive women danced with him, and Violet wondered how on earth he'd convinced them to show up.

When she tapped him on the shoulder, he spun around, scotch sloshing out of the crystal highball glass he was gripping.

"Hey, it's Vi!" he half shouted, slurring slightly. God, she hated it when he called her "Vi." The squinty eyes and flushed face indicated he was already drunk and/or stoned.

"Reece, what the bloody hell are *they* doing here?" She hooked a thumb at the stage.

"Surprise!" He tried to do jazz hands but only succeeded in spilling more of his drink.

"It *is* a surprise. What did he—" She paused, squeezed her eyes shut for a moment, then regrouped. "How did this happen?"

"I met your boyfriend at Silverstone—"

"My boyfriend?"

Reece gestured at the stage. "He said he's your boyfriend."

The fucking nerve of him. "He's *not* my boyfriend." Had Ian been lurking around the race that day? She'd only seen him at the hotel, but if he'd crossed paths with Reece, he must have spent the whole fucking day trying to track her down.

"Anyway, he said they could play parties and I liked their stuff, so I thought I'd give them a chance."

She pressed her palm against her forehead in exasperation. Maybe Revenant Saints wasn't quite selling out stadiums, but she doubted they needed to play private parties for rich assholes to make ends meet. This was just Ian trying to insert himself into her life, pure and simple. Which meant she needed to put an end to this bullshit.

"I didn't know you were planning a party in Vegas," she said to Reece, once she'd gotten a handle on her temper. "You should have run it through the PR office."

"I tried. You said no. So I did it myself." He shrugged petulantly. "Besides, this party is better than anything Pinnacle would have thrown. I can do it my way." He turned to leer at the two women he'd been dancing with, who smiled back at him with far too much enthusiasm.

As Violet pieced it together, her stomach sank. Fuck. No wonder his party buddies seemed unaccountably thrilled to hang out with him.

"Reece," she hissed under her breath. "Did you *hire* these girls?"

He grinned, unashamed. "It's Vegas, baby. Everything's for sale here."

"Good lord, if word gets out that the Pinnacle team principal hired a couple of sex workers, we'll never hear the bloody end of it. If your *father* finds out—"

"Relax, Vi."

"I can't relax! I've got to clean up your mess, and then I have to deal with *that*!" She stabbed a finger at Ian, who'd just launched into "Bloodstream." If they hadn't changed up their set list too much, that meant they were going to take a break soon. And that meant she'd have to deal with Ian. But not until she'd dealt with this brand-new problem. "Give me your wallet."

Reece blinked blearily. "Why?"

"Because I don't carry cash! Just hand it over!"

Reece fished his wallet out. She snatched it away and rummaged through the contents. Thank god Reece's ego was fragile enough that flashing wads of cash was still important to him. She cleaned it out and thrust it back at him, just as his phone started ringing.

She waited impatiently as he fished it out. "It's Dad!"

Her stomach sank. Oh, god, not here, not now.

"Here, I'll put him on speaker so you guys can hear," Reece said.

Violet gestured wildly to stop him, but it was too late. Carter Hammond's voice boomed through the phone, audible even over the band and the crowd.

"Reece."

"Hi, Dad!"

"Hello, Mr. Hammond," Violet said quickly. "You're on speaker." Just in case Carter Hammond was poised to say something scathing to his son.

"Ms. Harper. Are you at a party?"

Violet glared at Reece. "Reece is just entertaining a few of our sponsors," she lied smoothly. Reece owed her so big for tonight.

"Did you watch the race today?" Reece asked. His desperate need for his father's approval was almost sad. "We didn't win, but we placed tenth and everybody here says that's really good."

"You know I didn't watch it," came Carter's brusque reply. "I'm calling about this *GQ* interview with one of our drivers."

"You saw that?" Reece's eyes shot apprehensively to Violet's. That little fucker. The article was fantastic, but if his father didn't approve of any part of it, she had no doubt Reece would fling her straight under the bus. Violet held her breath, ready to hear if she'd still have a job tomorrow.

"That was quite a coup. The team came off looking very good. And this driver . . . Chase Navarro . . . came off looking even better. It was well done." Violet got the distinct impression Carter Hammond rarely gave out praise and that was as close to it as he was liable to get.

Reece visibly relaxed. "You like that, huh? Let me tell you, I had to hustle to make it happen, but it was worth it."

Violet didn't betray her reaction with so much as an eyelash twitch. *She'd* hustled to make that profile happen. It should have been an impossible get, but she did it through sheer determination. Worse than getting thrown under the bus, the fucker had just stolen her hard-earned glory.

Reece was still talking as he started wandering off through the crowd, puffing up more and more, preening before his father's scant approval.

All she wanted to do was go slink away to some quiet bar and drink a very full glass of ice-cold vodka. Instead, she took a very deep breath.

She turned to the two women who were standing patiently to the side.

"Ladies, can I speak to you for a minute?"

She herded the two women back through the crowd and into the vestibule by the elevators.

"You can have all the cash in his wallet if I'm assured no one will ever hear a word about tonight. No one knows you were here. No one knows about this payment."

One woman, the dark-haired one, nodded quickly and held out her hand. "Deal."

"So . . ." the other one, a petite blond, said uncertainly. "You don't want us to stay?"

"I want you to go home, change into your pj's, spend the rest of the night watching Netflix on my dime, and forget this ever happened."

"You got it," the brunette said, folding the wad of cash up and stuffing it down her cleavage. "Come on, Brook. We'll split up the money in the car. Pleasure doing business with you," she said to Violet.

"But Savannah—" the little blond protested.

Savannah grabbed her arm. "You heard the lady. Let's go!"

Once Savannah and Brook had been packed into the elevator, Violet took a deep breath. Disaster number one dispatched. She turned back to the bar, where Revenant Saints were just finishing their set.

Now on to disaster number two.

■

As she made her way toward the stage, she noticed Kiz and Ben over at the bar. For a brief moment, Violet regretted not being able to join them. She missed those two, and hanging out to catch up over beers would have been nice. Instead she had to talk to Ian, who was chugging a beer onstage between sets.

"I need to speak to you," she said without preamble.

He turned toward her slowly, grinning with that seductive promise she remembered so well. "Hi, Sunshine."

"I'm going down to the lobby. You have five minutes to join me there, or I come back up here and we have this conversation in a really loud, public, embarrassing way. Your choice."

Before he could reply, she turned around and stormed back across the club.

In the elevator, she fired off a text to Maisie, directing her to scrub Reece's social media of any and all evidence of this party, and to double-check team members' accounts as well. Downstairs in the lobby, there was no sign of Savannah and Brook, and she prayed all evidence of their presence here had disappeared with them. Behind her, the elevator door dinged open to reveal Ian.

He'd arranged his expression into something approximating contrition, although she doubted he'd ever experienced that emotion in his life.

"Over here." She led him to a dark alcove off the lobby, where there was at least a chance of privacy. "What the hell are you doing here, Ian?"

"I wanted to surprise you," he said, smiling in that way he thought was charming.

She let out a scoff of laughter. "I sure was surprised. How *dare* you show up at my job like this?"

"But your boss loves us—"

"My boss is an idiot! This is my *work.* Putting me on the spot like this is an asshole move, and you know it."

"I'm trying to show you how important you are to me, Violet. I dragged the band all the way to bloody Vegas to play that wanker's party, just for a chance to show you—"

"Show me what?"

"That I love you. That I want you back."

The words sent a shock of clarity through her. "You don't love me, Ian. You don't really love anybody besides yourself. And maybe Astrid a little bit. On her good days."

Her rejection had rattled his confidence, she noted. The seductive smile had vanished as he ran a hand through his sweaty hair in agitation. "Yeah, I know I'm a mess. I'm broken, Sunshine, okay? Is that what you want to hear? I am. My soul is broken. But you . . ." He reached out and seized her hands, gripping hard. "You could fix me, Sunshine."

"No one can *fix* you, Ian." She tried freeing her hands, but he held on to her.

"You could, though," he said. "You can do anything. You're magic. When you were around, the band was magic. Don't you remember when *Rolling Stone* said we were the tip of the spear of the next British Invasion? They called us the next Oasis. Don't you miss being a part of that? I can get there, and you can be with me when I do. You can be a part of the music. A part of the magic."

She stared into those familiar ice-blue eyes, processing that. Processing *everything.* The thing was, she did miss the music. She missed those days when something as simple as a bridge in a song, or a thumping bass line, or a chord progression would burrow into her brain and heart and preoccupy her for weeks.

"I do remember that," she murmured.

Ian grinned, tugging her closer. "I knew you did. I remember everything, Sunshine. Every moment I spent with you. You remember us, too, don't you?"

"Oh, I remember."

He released her hands, sliding his palms up until he could grasp her upper arms. As he did it, he moved in even closer. She could smell the cigarettes he'd chain-smoked just before the set, and his sweat, tinged with that patchouli stuff he apparently still liked.

He was leaning in now, his face getting closer and closer to hers. She held still and let him come, watching his eyelids droop and his mouth soften as he got ready to kiss her. To her great relief, his nearness made her feel nothing. When he was just a breath away, she spoke again.

"I remember everything, too, Ian. That wasn't fucking magic." She braced her palms against his bare, sweaty chest and shoved hard. He stumbled back in surprise.

"That was muscle, Ian. Muscle and hard work. *My* muscle. *My* hard work. I'm not your manic pixie goth girl. I'm a talented professional. *Rolling* fucking *Stone* didn't say that about you. *I* said it. Then I convinced that reporter it was his idea, because that's what I do. I convince the world that something's brilliant and then I convince them that liking it was their idea all along."

A muscle ticked in his jaw, and she knew she'd hit him right where it hurt. Good. Ian's ego could use a stiff kick in the bollocks.

"Fine," he said at length. "You felt unappreciated. I guess I can see that. I suppose I can work on that. Making you feel like you're a part of things."

"Ian, you're not listening. Yes, I felt unappreciated, but that was a long time ago. Now I'm valued. My work is valued. And I *am* a part of things. I'm part of this team and maybe it's not easy, but what we're doing . . ." She cut herself off before she veered into the kind of impassioned pep talk that would have made Chase proud.

Chase.

"You can't be serious. This racing team can't matter more to you than the music. I know you, Sunshine."

That fucking name. How had she ever thought it was sweet? It was like he was mocking her every time he said it, diminishing her until she was small enough for him to manage.

"Believe it or not, Ian, you aren't the origin of all music. I still have music in my life even without you. We are *over.* I've already moved on. I'm seeing someone."

She hadn't meant to say that out loud. She hadn't even fully come to terms with it in her mind. But she'd gotten over Ian, and now someone else was in the spot that used to belong to him, the one that had stood empty ever since. The one she'd thought would stay empty forever.

Chase *valued* her, and not just for the sex. How many times had he thanked her for what she'd done for him? How many times had he turned to her for advice, for guidance? How many times had he made it clear he couldn't do it without her?

And these months with Pinnacle, she realized, mattered more to her than all the years she'd spent at Ian's side, working so hard for an ounce of appreciation—something she now received every day.

"You mean that knobhead driver?" Ian waved away the idea.

"Chase is worth a hundred of you," she said quietly. "A thousand. You'd better get back to finish your set. And tomorrow,

I want you to leave and don't look back. Because I won't be there."

He hesitated, watching her, and she could almost hear the wheels turning in his head as he assessed the situation, as he weighed pressing on or retreating. Finally, he smiled again. "Just think about it. Think about me."

He snagged her hand, squeezing her fingers, and she wrenched them from his grip. "I don't need to think about you. You do enough of that on your own. I now task you with the impossible: Get over yourself."

She turned on her heel and strode away.

She doubted he'd even wait an hour before finding some other girl to fill his bed. But that was no longer any concern of hers.

She walked across the lobby to an alcove and sank into one of the club chairs, dropping her head into her hands. It felt like she'd just surfaced after spending a long time . . . days and months and years . . . underwater. She hadn't even been aware of the weight of Ian and that old heartbreak until she'd shaken it off. In the aftermath, she felt light. She felt free. She felt shockingly *happy*.

And the first thing she wanted to do was to see Chase. That should probably terrify her, and maybe tomorrow it would, but tonight, she just wanted him.

He was probably itching to escape the Arrow Beverages event by now, so she fired off a text to him. *Heading back to my hotel. See you soon?*

By the time she got back to her hotel, he still hadn't answered. His text finally came as she was letting herself into her room.

Not tonight. Early flight tomorrow.

She blinked at his text, bewildered. They'd spent nights apart, when their travel schedules didn't line up, or one of them had an early morning.

So why did this night feel so wrong?

Finally, she made herself reply.

Okay. See you in Mexico City?

By the time she went to bed, he still hadn't replied.

32

Since Chase hadn't heard from Violet since she'd said she was heading to Reece's private party, he just decided to head there.

He'd been walking toward the elevator across the dimly lit lobby, some kind of electronica pounding in his ears, when he caught sight of a familiar flash of ivory skin and jet-black hair to his left, half hidden around a corner. *Violet.*

He'd taken all of a single step in her direction when he realized she wasn't alone. He went still as he registered who was with her.

Ian. Here in Las Vegas.

Violet and Ian had been standing close together, eyes on each other, so wrapped up in whatever was going on that they were oblivious to everything and everyone around them. Ian's hands had been on her, sliding up her bare arms, and Violet . . . she was just standing still, just staring at him. Then he had leaned in to kiss her—

Chase hadn't stayed to watch anymore. He'd seen enough.

He'd gone straight back out the way he'd come, not stopping until he'd caught up to his driver and slipped into the back seat.

Now his head was pounding and he felt ill, panicked. They'd seemed to have kind of a breakthrough the other night, but maybe it had only felt that way to him. They hadn't declared themselves exclusive. Not even close. He couldn't even get Violet to admit out loud that they were dating.

Maybe Ian had followed her here, but what if Violet had invited him?

He leaned his head against the leather seat, closing his eyes. Misery settled heavily in his gut. His chest felt tight, but he bitterly reminded himself that he had no right to be angry. She'd warned him. He just hadn't wanted to listen. She hadn't promised him anything. He knew her well enough to know she didn't believe in promising herself to anyone. Not even him, apparently.

And he suddenly felt tired of trying, if she didn't even really want him to.

His phone buzzed in his pocket, but he was past hope that it was Violet. Whatever she was doing right now, he was the last thing on her mind. When he looked, it was Madison again.

The premiere is a red carpet thing. Lots of press. I felt like I should warn you. I totally understand if that's not your scene.

He stared at his phone for a beat, rubbing his thumb over the rounded corner. Violet had told him he needed to get better at the game if he wanted to run in the big leagues. Okay, game on. Before he could talk himself out of it, he typed out a response.

Sounds fun. Email me the details. See you there.

33

Harry Reid International Airport,
Las Vegas, Nevada

Violet sat down in the business-class lounge at the airport and checked her phone for what felt like the thirtieth time in as many minutes. It was blowing up, as it always was these days. Texts and emails from the media, from sponsor reps, from upcoming race venues . . . all wanting a piece of Chase Navarro, Pinnacle's unexpected secret weapon.

But still nothing from Chase himself.

Telling herself she was checking in on him for purely professional reasons, she typed out a text.

> When do you arrive in Mexico? I've got scheduling stuff to discuss with you.

It wasn't untrue. Her inbox was overflowing with requests for face time with him.

It was ten minutes before he replied.

> Not until Thursday. I'm in LA.

LA? That's where he was heading off to early this morning? She didn't know every facet of his schedule, but since he hadn't yet hired his own personal PR person, she knew quite a lot of it. And she knew he didn't have any business reasons to be in LA right now.

That same uneasy wrongness from last night was still simmering in her gut. Out of habit, she opened Instagram and tapped through to his account. The first picture on his grid made that feeling in her gut harden into a knot as heavy as a stone.

It was a selfie Chase had taken with Madison, posted just a few minutes ago. They were both turned out, Chase in that amazing perfectly tailored tux the stylist had bought for him, and Madison in a sparkling green floor-length sheath dress. She could tell they were in LA from the bright afternoon sunlight and the top of a palm tree off in the upper-left corner. Behind them was a step-and-repeat splashed with the branding for some movie Madison had shot earlier this year.

Their faces were pressed close together and they were both mugging for the camera, Madison doing exaggerated duck lips while Chase had one dark eyebrow hiked to cartoonish heights. The caption was *We clean up pretty good*, along with the requisite hashtags for the movie.

Chase was with Madison at her premiere in LA.

They were *together.* And she and Cam hadn't set this up.

What the fuck? He'd come to her room and dragged that whole sorry story about her childhood out of her against her will. He'd stood in front of her, hands on her face, eyes overflowing with sincerity, telling her that he *liked* her.

Well, he might *like* her, but that clearly meant fuck all.

She'd thought something had changed.

This . . . finding out on his fucking socials . . . felt like a slap in the face. And worse, it *hurt.* Yeah, she was mad, but she also felt stupid. Like she'd fallen for a con once again. At the end of the day, men were just *men*; they were all the same, no matter how nice they seemed, or how well they treated you. All the caressing and earnest eyes and gentle kisses didn't mean shit. The second something more interesting tempted them, they were off like a shot. She'd learned that lesson with Ian, and now Chase had just served her a stone-cold reminder.

"You're heading to Mexico today, too?" Rabia's voice startled her and she nearly dropped her phone.

"Um, yeah." She hastily swiped Insta closed, banishing that taunting picture. "Want to sit down?"

Rabia dropped into the chair and parked her roll-aboard beside the table. "It's early for you to fly into a venue, isn't it?"

She lifted her coffee cup to her mouth and was dismayed to see her hand was shaking slightly. Fuck him for this. She felt like she'd been sucker punched in the middle of the goddamned airport.

"I have a lot of sponsor events to set up in Mexico City."

Right. Work. Hadn't she decided long ago that she was done pouring herself into relationships? You gave yourself completely and in the end, you got nothing back. Her career, on the other hand, didn't fuck off with some movie star to LA.

"Did Reece's party cause you too many headaches?" Rabia asked.

What? It took a moment to register the question.

"Oh! Um, no. Not a one. All sorted."

She'd been checking all the usual places and there hadn't been a single whisper about it, thank god.

She forced herself to ask a question, so she didn't sound as shaken as she felt.

"How's next season's design coming?"

"Good," Rabia said, nodding thoughtfully. "The wind tunnel tests are looking good. And Chase is laying down some impressive times in his simulator sessions. I hope we get to keep him next season. He'd be magic in this car."

Violet laughed softly. "Chase won't have any problems with funding for next season. We'll be able to sign him."

Rabia arched one eyebrow over her glasses. "That's not what I meant. I mean we're very likely to get outbid by another team. A better team."

"Has he got offers?" She was surprised—wouldn't he have told her?

Then again, it seemed like there were lots of things he wasn't telling her these days.

Rabia shrugged. "Nothing firm that I know of. But there's talk."

"What kind of talk?" Her voice was sharper than intended.

"Rumor has it that Eric Lenore was chatting him up at the Jet Energy party last night. Went there specifically to see him."

"Eric Lenore? Fuck."

"Yep," Rabia said, shifting in her seat. "Fuck. No way we could compete with Allegri, if they make him a serious offer. Hell, I'd sign that contract for him myself. He'd be a fool to turn it down."

Violet paused for a minute, digesting that piece of information. "Yes, he would be a fool to turn that down." To go from nearly being dropped from F2 to an offer from the second-best team on the F1 grid in a single season? It was a fucking fairy tale. One that seemed to be coming to life for Chase Navarro.

And she'd helped make it happen. So why was she so *angry*? At the end of the day, if he wanted to wrangle a better deal for himself, he was free to do it.

She'd already succeeded, regardless of what happened next.

She set her coffee down on the table, hard.

Let him fuck off to LA with Madison and to Allegri with Eric Lenore. Both she and Pinnacle could survive his departure.

"Where is he?"

Violet looked up in surprise. Rabia tilted her chin at Violet's phone. "Chase. Where is he right now?"

Violet glanced down. Without realizing it, she'd opened her phone again and started scrolling the hashtag for Madison's movie, looking for more photos of the two of them.

With a snort of disgust, she swiped it closed again. *Pull it together, Violet.* He's just some fucking guy.

"Um, LA. He's at the premiere for Madison Mitchell's new movie. That actor he's dating."

Rabia let out a snort of disbelief.

"What? He is."

"I'm sure he's in LA. But he's not dating that girl. He's dating *you.* Everybody knows that, Violet."

"He's not . . . I'm . . . we're not . . ." God, she never had a problem speaking off the cuff. She could bullshit an answer with the best of them.

Rabia shrugged. "I don't know what you young people call it these days, but whatever it is, you two are doing it."

She took a deep breath and cleared her head, so she could pick her way carefully through this. "We've been very casually involved in the past. But we're not dating."

"So you're sleeping with him." A statement, not a question.

"Yes, but—"

"But he's in LA with that girl?"

"It's fine. He's free to do whatever—"

Rabia shook her head. "It seems complicated. When I met Rajan, he just asked me to get a coffee after class. Then it was dinner. And a few months later we got married. Simple."

"You're *married*?" She'd known Rabia for months now and talked to her almost daily, and she'd had no idea there was a husband in the mix.

"Twenty-three years," she replied, turning her phone to show Violet. Her lock screen showed her and some man—the husband—sitting in the sun, at a wooden table outside a pub, both smiling and lifting pints to whoever had taken the picture. He looked friendly and unassuming—roughly Rabia's age, salt-and-pepper hair, also Southeast Asian. "Rajan Dar. He's a podiatrist."

"A podiatrist? And you work in racing? How does that work?"

She shrugged again. "We have our own interests. I respect his, he respects mine. It works because we want it to."

"And he doesn't mind you spending half the year on the road?"

"Nope. He gets the Netflix all to himself and I don't have to watch those Korean gangster dramas he loves so much." She chuckled softly. "He trusts me, if that's what you're asking. And I trust him."

"Wow. I can't imagine that." She hadn't been able to turn her back on Ian for a millisecond without some other girl moving in. And Chase had just run off to LA with a movie star, so she was sticking to type, apparently.

"When it's right . . . when you're *ready* for it to be right . . . it's easy. What you're doing?" Rabia's eyebrows hiked behind her glasses. "That sounds hard. Exhausting, really. Can I ask you something?"

"Sure."

"Do you like him?"

Violet opened her mouth to reply, but nothing came out. Such a simple question. Why couldn't she answer it?

Rabia leaned in and lowered her voice. "I've seen you with him. I think you do."

"But that doesn't mean . . . there are things . . . it's just complicated."

"Is it, or are you making it complicated?" Rabia waggled her phone in the air, that picture of her and Rajan still glowing on the screen. "I'm hitting the loo once more before boarding." She stood up, shouldered her bag, and gestured to Violet's phone. "If you want the advice of someone older and wiser, quit making it so hard. Not when it's the simplest thing in the world. See you at the track, Violet."

34

Los Angeles, California

A woman with a clipboard and a headset ushered Madison on to the next reporter, and Chase dutifully took his spot at her side, ready to smile politely and compliment her hard work in the movie, even though he hadn't seen it yet.

"Madison, it's a big night for you," the next reporter said. She was young, about their age, with short dark hair. They'd heard that half a dozen times already, but Madison lit up with a smile, as if her enthusiasm and delight were brand-new and one hundred percent genuine. Truly, only twenty percent of the acting work she did was caught on film. The rest was all out here.

"Working on this film was an honor, and a highlight of my career," she said. "I'm just thrilled to finally share it with the world."

She'd said some variation of that to the last six reporters they'd talked to, and somehow she'd had yet to repeat herself. It was a gift.

"How did you like your first Formula One race?" the reporter asked. "Was it exciting to watch Chase race from the garage?"

Madison flashed Chase a twinkling smile. "Oh, so exciting. No words for it, but it was such an adrenaline rush."

"Chase, how did it feel, having Madison there to cheer you on?"

His brain spun, trying to find something to say that would put her in the best light. "Honestly, anybody who has Madison Mitchell cheering them on is the luckiest person on earth."

Both Madison and the reporter nearly let out audible dreamy sighs. Madison gazed up at him with adoring eyes. He never could tell when she was acting and when it was real.

"Isn't he the sweetest?" Madison gushed to the reporter.

"The absolute sweetest! You're one lucky girl."

Madison squeezed his hand and leaned against his shoulder. "I sure am."

As they made their way through the slow-moving crowd entering the reception room, she leaned in to whisper to him.

"Sorry, but it's not much better inside. Just a different kind of grilling. But at least there's alcohol."

An hour later, he knew what she meant. The reception inside was an endless parade of industry small talk, all of it like thinly veiled negotiations. It reminded him of his conversation with Eric Lenore. Whenever they had a moment alone, Madison would fill him in. This producer was a potential investor in some project she was hoping to work on. That director was about to start casting his next movie.

She'd told him she saw it all as a strategic game, and watching her in action backed that up. Outwardly she was all smiles and bland chitchat, but inside her mind was working away, moving those pieces on a board, all to angle herself into a better position.

Violet would have been impressed.

And now he was thinking about Violet, in the middle of this fancy Hollywood party, when he was here as Madison's date. He'd come here to give things a go with Madison, since it was becoming clear Violet was never going to let him in. He owed it to Madison and himself to take it seriously.

Three hours later, after the reception and the screening of the movie (which wasn't half bad), they were free, at least momentarily. The official premiere was over, but the director was throwing an after-party at some nightclub, and since everything was about networking, Madison had to go.

They were in the back of her chauffeured SUV, crawling through LA traffic as she answered the blizzard of texts she'd gotten.

"You were great tonight," she said without looking up.

"I was? I barely said a word."

She glanced up, flashing him a smile. "You didn't have to say much. You're a natural, you know. Everybody loves you."

That's exactly what Violet had told him when this whole thing had started. His thoughts just kept circling back to her, like an itch he couldn't quite reach.

He forced himself to smile back at Madison, who was *great*, and deserved his full attention. "Glad I could help."

She set down her phone and turned to him. "I hope it was fun for you, too?"

"Sure. Oh yeah, tons of fun."

She chuckled. "You don't have to lay it on quite that thick." She paused and reached out for his hand, where it rested on his knee. He let her take it.

"Chase." Madison's eyelashes fluttered down as she considered something. "I asked you here to see if there was any possibility of this thing we're doing for show to become something real."

"Yeah, I picked up on that." He liked how open she was being, how up-front. But there was just so much hesitation inside him.

She shook her hair back over her shoulders. "See, it's kind of hard for me to casually date. I can't exactly go on Tinder. Dating costars is its own kind of hassle. And I'm not going to date randos who approach me in public."

"I see how that could feel impossible."

She smiled and shrugged. "But you're already 'vetted,' for want of a better word. I know you're safe. I know you'll be cool. You won't sell my salacious secrets or texts to TMZ or whatever."

He felt a little bit like one of her game pieces being moved into place. Not in a bad way. It was just . . . there was a calculation to it that he wasn't used to. Although seeing how she handled her career, he shouldn't be surprised she handled relationships in the same way.

"You're nice. We get along okay. You're *very* easy to look at. I figured it was worth a shot."

Chase swallowed over the sudden lump in his throat and smiled. "I, um . . . I've been thinking the same thing."

He *had* been thinking that, but now that he was here, he realized he couldn't be as calculated about it as Madison. All of those things were true, and he genuinely liked her. But that spark, that heat, just wasn't there. Not like it was with—

"Except I think you're already into someone else," Madison said, squeezing his hand briefly before releasing it.

He paused for a second, which made him feel shitty.

"I'm right, aren't I?"

Again, he hesitated. "I'm sorry if I've been distant. I was . . . kind of casually involved with someone, but it's not going anywhere, and so I thought I should . . . you know, move on."

"Violet, right?"

His eyes snapped up to hers. "How did you know that?"

She shrugged. "Chemistry? I noticed it between you two in Paris, and again in Austin. It's kind of like you with the press. It's just *there*, a natural occurrence."

"Okay, yeah." He exhaled. "It's her. But . . . I'm into her and I'm pretty sure she's never going to want that from me."

It was a relief to admit it out loud at last, even if it was to Madison. He wanted Violet. For real, officially, out loud. Not . . . whatever they'd been doing.

"Have you tried?"

He let out a frustrated huff of laughter. "I thought I had? Then she turned around and was with her ex in Las Vegas. She doesn't like to be pinned down. I know that about her. She's been very clear about what she wanted and what she didn't want. So if I'm the idiot who's hung up on her now, it's my own stupid fault."

"Well, I don't know anything about her ex, but the fact that he exists means she didn't mind being pinned down at some point. And as far as you and her? I noticed how you were around her, but I also noticed how she was around you. It goes both ways."

"She finds me attractive. That's not the issue. It's . . . the rest. Being in a relationship. God, I can't believe I'm saying this. I can't believe it's what I want. And I'm saying it all to you. I'm really sorry, Madison. I'm being a total dick right now."

Madison laid a hand over his again. "Relax, Chase. It's true that you'd have made a convenient option for me, but don't worry. I wasn't in love with you or anything."

Sure, Madison was calculated, but she was honest about it. What she wanted wasn't really all that different from what he and Violet had been in the beginning. In another universe, where Violet didn't exist, he might have given it a try with her.

But Violet did exist, and, however they'd started, now it had turned into something else. Something real.

"You're great, Madison. You know that, right?"

"I do, but thanks." She grinned widely at him. "For what it's worth, I don't think you should give up on her yet. Talk to her about it before you write her off."

Even hearing Madison say those words . . . write her off . . . made something go cold in his chest. God, he didn't want to do that.

"You're right. I will."

Madison reached out and gave him a gentle shove. "So what are you still doing in LA? Drop me off at this dumb party and go get her."

"That's not the way my mom raised me. I'm *not* ditching you. At least not until our publicists have broken us up properly."

"Okay, one more date for the media and then you and I are done *forever.*" The words were full of melodrama, but she was laughing as she delivered them. He and Madison weren't going to happen, but he was pretty sure they'd always be friends.

36

Mexico City

It was Wednesday night before he finally found himself outside Violet's hotel room. His agent had booked a full day of meetings with PR agencies while he was in LA—Violet had been on him to hire his own person. The wait had been agony. He couldn't think about anything else but talking to her.

But now that he was here, he wasn't sure what to say or how to say it. He hadn't actually *dated* anyone since Sophie, and he'd basically still been a kid then. This felt like entirely uncharted territory.

And he still didn't know what *she* wanted. So if he was hesitating about knocking on her door, maybe it was because he feared it might be the last time he ever did.

Finally, he told himself sternly to fucking man up and rapped on the door. She took her time answering it, eventually cracking it open just enough to see him over the security bar.

The surprise showed in her eyes. "What are you doing here? I thought you said you were flying in tomorrow."

She had music on inside, something angry and loud that he didn't recognize.

"I came early. Can I come in?"

Wordlessly, she closed the door enough to release the bar lock then swung it open. He was relieved she was alone. In the back of his mind, he'd been dreading finding Ian there.

Her room was dim, just a couple of lamps lit in corners. Violet was in her black silk robe, and barefoot. She'd washed her face, so the smoky black eyeliner and blood-red lipstick were gone. She looked much younger and almost vulnerable without them.

As he closed the door behind him, she crossed the room to a small bar under a mirror and hit pause on a portable Bluetooth speaker, plunging the room into sudden silence. She retrieved her half-empty glass of vodka and turned back to him, leaning against the bar, one arm wrapped around her midsection.

"How was LA?" Her voice was flat and uninterested.

He sat on the edge of the bed, across the room from her, and leaned forward, forearms braced on his knees. "Fine."

"And Madison?"

Her tone was the same, but he felt the chill emanating from her all the way over here.

"Also fine."

"The response on social media was great. People love you two together."

"We're not together," he replied automatically.

She'd been looking into her glass, down at her blood-red toenails, anywhere but at him, but now her eyes shot to his. But she said nothing, so he decided to prod the sore spot, just to find out once and for all what the deal was.

"How's Ian?"

Violet visibly startled. "Ian?"

"He was in Vegas, right?"

She paused before nodding slowly. “Reece hired the band to play his stupid party without telling me. He left me with multiple shit shows to clean up, as usual.”

He hadn’t even been aware of the tightness in his chest until it released.

“Reece hired him?”

“Did you think *I* invited him?”

“I wasn’t sure—”

“I didn’t.”

He looked down at the carpet and blew out a breath, trying to dispel his nerves so he could keep going. “I mean, I know you guys have a past, so—”

“Chase.”

He looked back at her. She’d set her glass back on the bar and was gripping the edges of it with both hands. “I didn’t invite him there. I didn’t even know he was there until I showed up. First I had to deal with the sex workers Reece hired and then I had to deal with *him*.”

“Sex workers?”

“Don’t ask. The whole night was a disaster.”

“Sorry.”

She shrugged dismissively. “It’s fine.”

Violet shifted her weight from one foot to the other, her arms still braced against the bar behind her, like she was afraid to let go of it. It was the closest to uncertain he’d ever seen her. “So LA. Cam and I didn’t set that up,” she said at last, eyes on the floor.

He rubbed his hand over the back of his neck. “She invited me.”

“So, is that—”

“No.”

Her eyes lifted to his again. “No?”

He shook his head. "No. I mean, she suggested it, but I said no."

She let out a soft huff of laughter. "You said no to a woman?"

"It has happened, you know."

She was smiling, even if it was slight, and he'd cracked a joke, so it felt like maybe there was something here, but he still didn't know. Finally, he just couldn't take it anymore. Whatever happened next, he just needed to know for sure. If this was going to end, then he'd end it. Like pulling off a Band-Aid, it was better done fast.

"Look, Violet, I gave it a shot with Madison because I thought you were with Ian last weekend."

"I didn't—"

"I know you didn't ask him there. It was stupid, and I should have just talked to you about it. But I thought you just might not care, and that would hurt . . . Except here's the thing." He kept his eyes on a patch of carpet between his feet so he could get through it. Then he took a deep breath and forced the unfamiliar words out. "I'm into you. *Really* into you. And if there's no chance of you feeling that way about me, I'd just like to know it, so I don't get in any deeper here than I already am."

VIOLET WAS GRIPPING the edge of the bar so hard her hands hurt. She still hadn't quite recovered from opening the door to find Chase there when she'd least expected him. She'd spent the entire flight to Mexico City imagining Chase with Madison.

It had been utterly humiliating, realizing that she *hated* imagining Chase with Madison. The mental images of the two of them together were absolute torture. It meant, somewhere along the way, she'd developed *feelings* for the bastard.

But now he was here, and *not* with Madison. When she'd opened her door and seen his dumb, gorgeous face on the other side, the wave of relief she'd felt had been terrifying.

She didn't want to want him. She certainly didn't want to need him. Part of her brain told her she should tell him to go. *Don't fall for me. I'll only disappoint you.*

But when she opened her mouth to say it, the words just wouldn't come out. The other words, the ones telling him that she was in deeper than intended, too, also wouldn't come out yet.

All she knew was that she was indescribably happy that he was here. And she knew she didn't want him to leave again.

Pushing off the bar, she crossed the room to where he sat on the edge of the bed, leaning forward on his elbows, eyes on the floor.

She stopped in front of him. "Hey."

He looked up at her and she felt a pang all the way through her chest, staring down at his pitch-dark eyes, the golden angles of his face, his jaw dusted with several days' worth of dark stubble. She reached out and laid her hand along his jaw, her thumb rubbing across the roughness. His lips parted slightly. His mouth was indescribably beautiful. She'd thought so from the very first time she saw him.

"Violet—"

She reached for his hand and tugged him to his feet. He rose slowly, dark eyes fixed on hers.

"I'm glad you came back," she whispered.

"You are?"

She nodded tightly.

Then Chase brought his hands up to her face. She forced herself to raise her eyes to his. His nearness was setting off sparks across her skin, little tingles lighting her up from the inside out. His lips hadn't touched hers yet, but she felt like she could almost see the energy arcing between them, like an electrical charge.

His thumbs swept across her cheekbones and he smiled, just the slightest tightening of the corner of his beautiful lips. Finally, he leaned in and kissed her. He'd kissed her so many times at this point. Deep, hungry kisses, and quick, teasing ones as he brought her body right to the edge, and filthy kisses between her legs that left her shaking. This kiss was different, soft and simple. It felt like his words had that night back in Austin, when he'd told her that he liked her, that she mattered.

When the kiss ended, he looped one arm around her waist so he could pull her body in close to his while his other hand cradled her cheek.

She rested her hands on his biceps, eyes fixed on the top button of his shirt, on the triangle of golden skin revealed by his open shirt collar. "I'm not sure what you want." Even though she wanted this, she really should try to warn him that it wouldn't be easy, not for either of them.

"I'm not asking you for anything, Violet. Just stop trying to chase me away, okay?" He dipped his head and brushed another kiss across her lips. Her fingers tightened on his biceps. "Hold still and let me be with you."

"I'm not good at this," she whispered as he kissed his way down the side of her neck.

"I'm not that great at it, either," he said. His hand skated up her rib cage, caressing her through the soft fabric of her robe. His thumb found her nipple through the silk and flicked across it.

She dragged in a deep breath. "I'll probably fuck it up."

He bent down, scooped an arm behind her knees, swept her up into his arms, and pressed another brief kiss to her mouth. "You have so little faith in me." He started carrying her around the side of the bed. "Maybe I'll fuck it up first. Let's try it and find out, okay?"

36

As Violet slicked on her favorite shade of red lipstick—Stiletto Red—the bathroom door opened behind her. Chase wandered in, wearing just his boxer briefs, with his black hair a sleep-rumpled mess, looking barely awake and hot as hell.

Her phone was on the counter, playing music at a low volume, and he stopped, pointing a finger at it. "Don't tell me . . . Poly Styrene."

"That's the lead singer. The band is X-Ray Spex. But that's very good." He'd insisted she make him a playlist of her favorite music, and she was embarrassed to admit how long she'd spent on it. Every song on it reminded her of him, like she was some dumb, lovesick teenager. She hadn't thought it would be to his taste, but surprisingly, he liked to listen to it before he had to drive. He said her music put him in "the right aggressive headspace," which seemed like a compliment.

"Where're you off to so early?" He rubbed a hand across his face and stretched in a way that made every muscle in his upper body flex. He was unreal.

She checked him out in the mirror as she unscrewed her liquid liner. "Conference call with Europe. You didn't have to get up."

"And miss a glimpse of you all dressed up and ready for work?" He sidled up behind her and set his hands on her hips. "Have I told you how much I like it when you wear suits? You look like a sexy corporate villain. In a good way."

She carefully touched up her winged eyeliner. "You like it when I wear anything. Or nothing."

He hooked his hand around her hair and slid it to one side, then leaned in and kissed the back of her neck. "I like it best when you're wearing nothing."

"Don't start that now. I'm late. My car's already waiting downstairs."

His hands slid up to her waist and tightened. "Guess I'll just have to finish it tonight."

She turned in his grasp and he pressed her back, bracing his arms on the counter behind her.

"I have to go," she murmured.

"I'm heading to the track for qualifying at noon."

"I'll stop by the garage."

He grinned, that wicked pirate's smile that made her toes curl. "See you then."

She hesitated a beat, then reached up and pressed a quick kiss to his mouth. "Bye." It felt . . . domestic. Intimate and familiar, which was wildly *unfamiliar* to her. But she tried her best not to overthink it. She liked this. She was happy. For now, that was enough.

The sun was intense as Violet made her way through the paddock toward the Pinnacle garage. They were between qualifying sessions so dance music was thumping through the loudspeakers, echoing through the track.

In the garage, everyone was bustling around with brisk efficiency. Rabia was discussing something with Imogen, who was busily taking notes. When Rabia looked up and saw her, she waved her over.

"Got an update for you, Violet." Beside her, Imogen looked positively thrilled.

Rabia cast a quick glance around the garage, but no one was close enough to hear. She leaned in closer and lowered her voice. "Leon and I massaged our contacts at Sokia and worked out a deal to get our power unit from them. Imogen slid that contract under Junior's nose and got him to sign off on it without even glancing at it."

Violet looked from Rabia to Imogen. "That is seriously underhanded. It sounds like something I'd do. Imogen, I'm so proud of you."

Imogen blushed and shrugged. "If it's got one of those 'sign here' stickies on it, he'll sign anything. He *could* have read it, if he bothered."

Rabia snickered. "Yeah, Veben was mad at first, but . . . Sokia provides units for Lennox, Allegri, and Hansbach. This will give us a much better chance."

Sure would. They were ranked first, second, and third on the grid.

"Your new design is brilliant, too, Rabia," Imogen said.

Rabia tilted her chin down and looked at Violet over her glasses. "We couldn't have afforded that Sokia power unit without that influx of cash from Carillon."

"That part was all Chase. Carillon wants him for their watch ads and they were willing to invest in Pinnacle to lure him in."

"And who made Chase? You're the new power behind the throne, Violet."

Was she . . . blushing?

"Oh, hush. I think it might be all of us. Team spirit. Ra!" she said awkwardly.

Oh my god, who *was* she?

Rabia and Imogen turned back to their conversation and Violet headed out of the garage. Up ahead in the paddock, she saw a familiar face coming from the opposite direction.

"Simon!" she called out when he was close enough. "I haven't seen you in ages."

"Violet. You look stunning, as always." He leaned in to kiss her cheek, and lingered a beat too long before pulling back.

She hadn't seen Simon since that night on the yacht in Monte Carlo. It amazed her to remember it now, but she'd been halfway intending to sleep with him that night, had things worked out differently. But then Chase had crossed her path and . . . well, everything had changed.

"How are you?" she asked.

Simon gave an elegant shrug. "Keeping busy with the team. You know how it is. How about you?"

"Same. I'm run off my feet, actually."

"Right. I'm sure you've got your hands full now that your driver's dumped his movie star girlfriend."

She fought back the urge to laugh. "It was a very amicable parting of the ways," she said, quoting the press release Horace had drafted. "No dumping involved."

"Whatever you say. Hey, I hope you're not too busy for a little fun." Simon smiled at her, slow and seductive, and reached out to brush his fingertips across the back of her hand. "I seemed to have lost track of you in Monaco, which is a shame. Maybe I can make it up to you now."

"I, ah . . ." She laughed awkwardly and hooked her hair behind her ear. Oh, god, she hadn't been in this position in a while. She'd almost forgotten how it worked. "Actually, I'm seeing someone now." The same someone they'd just been discussing, but she'd leave that bit out for now.

Simon stared at her for a beat, then he let out a bark of laughter.

She scowled. "What's so funny?"

Simon's laughter trailed off. "Oh, shit, are you serious?"

"Yeah, I'm serious. I'm seeing someone."

Simon shook his head and let out a low whistle. "I never thought I'd see the day when someone managed to put a rope on Violet Harper. Never took you as the monogamous type."

Her face flushed with unexpected anger. "You don't know me, Simon—"

He put his hands up in mock surrender. "I meant it as a compliment, Violet. It's all good. I'll see you around."

He gave her a smile and walked off. But his *I'll see you around* had undertones. Like he expected her to blow this up. Like he knew what she would do.

How dare that fucker? But her fury mixed with a wriggling doubt, and a horrible recognition.

Up until now, that *was* exactly who she was and how she operated. And Simon had been around the track. He'd seen it all.

Yes, relationships had felt like a trap, but part of her also feared she'd be bad at it. She and Ian had always been a little dysfunctional, so maybe normal relationships were just beyond her. Maybe an endless string of hookups was the most she was capable of. The most she could give. And she had a feeling Chase could give a lot more.

Her phone buzzed in her pocket. Carter Hammond. Of course. Just what she needed right now.

She swiped to answer, ignoring the flush in her cheeks. "Mr. Hammond, hello."

"Hello, Ms. Harper. Is my son with you?"

"No, he's entertaining some corporate sponsors over at hospitality."

"That sounds like Reece," Carter grumbled. "That's fine. I wanted to speak to you alone. I understand my son had some . . . unexpected guests at his little party in Las Vegas last week."

Violet closed her eyes and cursed silently. Fuck, fuck, *fuck.* She'd thought she'd managed to bury that incident, but Savannah and Brook must have blabbed to someone.

"How did you hear about that?" she asked when she'd recovered.

"Now that you know Reece, it probably won't surprise you to know that I have eyes on him all the time. Just to be safe."

"That's . . . good to know." It was *horrifying* to know. Carter had a spy on Reece? What had Carter's spy seen? What had he reported back?

"My source informed me that you dealt with Reece's . . . ill-advised female guests very efficiently. There wasn't so much as a whisper about it anywhere. Reece isn't always easy to manage, I know. You did well."

"Thank you."

"And I understand you've been hard at work raising the team's profile. This new driver my son chose . . . Chase Navarro. He's getting quite a lot of positive press."

Did he just call her to compliment her? What was going on?

"Strategically, I felt it was important to push Chase forward. He plays well to the media. What's good for Chase is good for Pinnacle. Every time he's mentioned, Pinnacle is mentioned, too."

"I agree. You've done a lot of good work in a short period of time. Ms. Harper, you've clearly got a good head on your shoulders. That's why I've called to let you know that I'm nearing a deal to sell the team."

All the air rushed out of her lungs in a whoosh, leaving her lightheaded. Suddenly the sun felt like it was just inches away, baking the world and everything in it. "You're *selling* us? To who?"

"Howard Capital."

She frowned in confusion. "I don't know them . . ."

"They're a private equity group. If they decide to go ahead with the sale, they'll be looking to cut operating costs while they maximize return on their investment, before eventually selling the team on to other owners."

Violet closed her eyes and pressed her hand against her chest. Her heart was pounding like a bass drum. Fuck. A private equity firm. Yes, they'd sell the team on, but they'd sell it for parts, after they'd starved it of resources and sucked every ounce of value from it.

Affinity Motorsport had been bought by a private equity firm a few years back. They fired half the staff and cut salaries for the rest, so the best and brightest from the team all took jobs elsewhere. They invested almost nothing in development, and their performance was accordingly dismal. Limping along, Affinity had been sold on to someone else before finally folding entirely.

Being sold to private equity was a death sentence.

Her throat felt like it was in a vise, but she managed to spit out, "I see."

"Ms. Harper, I've been very impressed with your performance. I doubt Pinnacle would look nearly as appealing to Howard without your hard work. They're not particularly interested in entering sports management, but the team's increased profile excited them."

She pressed her palm to her forehead as she suppressed a bubble of hysterical laughter. Wasn't this just fucking ironic?

"Should the sale go through and Howard Capital restructures as I expect they will, I'd like you to come to work for me. It would be a shame for your considerable skills to go to waste."

"That's . . . thank you for the offer, Mr. Hammond," she said, because this was still her boss and she wasn't stupid enough to say what she was really thinking.

"We'll talk more once things are settled. In the meantime, I'm sure I can count on you to keep this information strictly confidential. Pinnacle's worth right now rests in its public image. We wouldn't want that tarnished."

"I understand."

"Thank you, Ms. Harper. We'll speak again soon."

Then he was gone. Violet stared at her phone, dread settling in her limbs like concrete.

She turned back toward the garage, but stopped abruptly. Up ahead, she could see Leon pointing something out to two of the mechanics, and behind him, Rabia laughing at something Imogen had just told her.

Everything she'd done here . . . everything *everyone* was doing to turn this team around, to give them a shot at becoming serious contenders . . . it was all about to be wiped away. And there was nothing she could do to stop it.

37

Chase was in the tiny office assigned to him at the track, changing out of his race gear after qualifying, when his phone vibrated with a call from his agent.

"Hi, Phil. What's up?"

Most communications came via email and usually from one of Phil's assistants. He wasn't sure Phil had ever called him directly.

"Chase! How was qualifying?"

Phil never checked in to see how his races had gone.

"P twelve," he said cautiously.

"Q two! Excellent, excellent. Listen, I just got off the phone with Antonio Cenelli. We've got official interest."

Chase sat down hard on the folding chair behind him, blinking at the opposite wall. Fuck. This was actually happening. Allegri wanted him to drive for them next season.

He'd stopped by Allegri's garage on Thursday, as asked. Eric had introduced him to Karl Aurbach, the head of design, and a handful of other Allegri team members. It had been a brief, superficial conversation, but now the legendary Antonio Cenelli, the owner of Allegri, had just *called his agent.*

"Now, there's a long way to go between this and a formal contract," Phil continued. "But it's a good sign that Antonio reached out to me personally to initiate the conversation. I'm drawing up a list of items I think should be a part of any negotiation. If you could let me know what you'd like to have included—"

"What about Pinnacle?"

"Pinnacle?" Phil echoed. "You've already got an offer from them—"

"I do?"

"Of course. There was a clause in your contract automatically triggered when you moved up from reserve. And they'd be fools not to re-sign you with the increased funding you're bringing to the table. But they can't offer you what Allegri can."

"I know that." He'd been so blown away by the idea that Allegri wanted him that he hadn't even stopped to think about Pinnacle. But now, thinking about Rabia and Leon, the amazing new car Rabia was designing, the pit crew and staff who'd rallied around him this season . . . Violet.

He glanced at the mirror in the corner, at himself in Pinnacle's "silver and pewter" race suit and imagined trading it for Allegri's red. Part of him wanted to scream in triumph at having made it, after all the struggles. But it wasn't *all* of him, and that was surprising. This was much more complicated than he'd imagined.

"So start thinking about what you want out of this deal, Chase. This is the moment to think big." Phil was still chattering, despite Chase having gone silent. "Feel free to ring me up if there's anything you want to discuss."

"Sure thing. Thanks, Phil."

He ended the call and sat staring at his phone for several minutes. There were so many people he should probably call.

Dad. Sam and Tyler. His grandmother and the aunts. But there was only one person he really wanted to tell first: Violet.

He needed to talk it through with her. She was so much smarter about this stuff than he was. She'd be able to pick through all this conflicting shit in his head and help him see it clearly.

He stood up, stripping out of his race suit and Nomex long underwear and changing back into his street clothes. Grabbing his bag, he headed out through the garage. The pit crew was there, still working on the cars ahead of tomorrow's race. Someone had put music on—something by the Stooges. Seemed Violet's musical taste had worked its way through the whole team. The crew was talking and laughing as they worked. The scene was a far cry from when he'd first arrived at Pinnacle, everyone silent, sullen, and distrusting.

Rabia and Leon were on the far side of the garage, heads together as they discussed something on Rabia's laptop. Some other driver would be taking advantage of Rabia's new design. He'd be in Allegri's car, an undeniable marvel, but right now he didn't feel that same thrill imagining it.

HE WAS LYING on Violet's bed, hands behind his head, staring at the ceiling of her hotel room, trying and failing to picture what the next year of his life would look like, when the door clicked open and she came in.

His eyes skated over her appreciatively. She was wearing another one of her killer suits, this one in dark purple, with skinny pants that showed off her ass in ways that should be illegal.

She registered him on the bed, surprise showing in her eyes. "I thought you'd still be at the track," she said, setting her bag down on the desk.

He watched her back as she fiddled with her things, plugging in her phone and pulling some stuff out of her bag. Something seemed off about her, different from this morning in the bathroom. When she'd come in just now, there hadn't been even a hint of a smile when she saw him, and there was a tension in the set of her shoulders and the ramrod straightness of her back.

"You okay?"

"Yeah, fine," she said quickly.

He sat up, swinging his legs over the edge of the bed. "I have something to tell you." He leaned forward, propping his elbows on his knees. "It's early still, but my agent got a call from Antonio Cenelli."

She finally turned around to face him, eyes wide. "Does that mean . . ."

"They want me for next season."

"That's . . ." She looked down at the floor and hooked her hair behind her ear. "That's excellent. Congratulations."

This wasn't the reaction he'd expected from her. Something was definitely off.

"Yeah, but I'm not sure."

She leaned back against the desk and crossed her arms over her chest. "What aren't you sure about? It's *Allegri.*"

"I know. I should be ecstatic. And I am. It's amazing. But—there's Pinnacle to think about."

Violet shook her head firmly. "No. Forget fucking Pinnacle. If you have an offer from Allegri you need to take it."

The force of her pushback surprised him. She'd spent so much time and energy turning him into a star, all for the sake of Pinnacle. Now she was okay with just watching him walk away from all that?

"Violet, what about all your hard work?"

"What's that got to do with anything?"

He stood up, running a hand through his hair. "Everything you've done for me, turning me into this big star, all the sponsorship money it's brought in. You're seriously okay with it walking back out the door to another team?"

"Your sponsorship deals are yours, not the team's. That's the deal. This is your *career.*"

"But . . . it's more than *my* deals. Carillon, ILM, HeatTech . . . they all want to sponsor Pinnacle next season because of me. If I leave, that might not happen."

Violet was clenching her teeth so hard he could see a little muscle in her jaw flexing. He could feel the tension radiating off her and he didn't understand it. "What happens to Pinnacle isn't your concern. You need to look out for yourself."

He scoffed. "Come on, Violet. What happens at Pinnacle matters to me, regardless of where I end up."

"Why?"

"Because . . ." He crossed over to her and touched her shoulder, picking up a silky lock of her black hair and rubbing it between two fingers. "Because it affects you. I care about you. You built this. Not for me, for Pinnacle. I'm not going to be the one to tear it apart."

Violet squeezed her eyes shut and drew in a deep breath. Chase was too close, and he was too . . . *good,* putting her first and looking at her like she was his *everything.* Her, the girl who hadn't had a relationship last longer than six hours in years. Her, the girl who hadn't even been able to save this fucking team.

She was going to fuck this up eventually. There was no way she wouldn't. So why should he give up a single thing for her sake? And certainly not for the team's sake. Pinnacle probably wouldn't even exist in a few years, and he would have spent the peak of his career tethered to this sinking ship.

"Please don't make me a part of this," she whispered. She couldn't handle that kind of pressure, couldn't handle being responsible when his career was in tatters in two years' time.

He scoffed, bringing his hands up to cradle either side of her neck. His thumbs rubbed along the length of her jaw. "Come on, Violet, you're already a part of this. I care about you." He paused, pressing his eyes closed briefly and swallowing hard. She could feel the words coming even before he opened his mouth. "I love you," he murmured.

No, oh please, no. Not like this, not now. She wasn't ready for this. She couldn't say it back. She didn't even know how to. That part of her had died years ago, and would probably stay that way forever. She'd known that. It was why she didn't commit, why she never let anything get serious. It's why she shouldn't have tried this with him. Because eventually it was going to end up here, and she knew going in that she wouldn't be able to see it through.

Panic flooded her limbs, and adrenaline had her heart trying to beat its way out of her ribs. Her throat closed up around the breath she tried to draw.

Shoving at his chest, she pushed herself away from him. "Just stop."

He jerked back in shock, and she had to turn away from that stunned look on his face, that pain in his eyes.

She rounded on him, trying to make him see. He needed to understand what a mistake he would be making . . . with

Pinnacle. With her. "Listen to me. You need to take that fucking contract with Allegri. Get out of here and don't look back."

He blinked, those glittering dark eyes full of pain as he stared at her. A muscle in his jaw worked as he ground his teeth together.

"And you and me?" he finally asked, voice hoarse.

She *couldn't* be a part of this. If he stayed here for her, he'd lose everything. She'd already made that mistake.

"I can't do this . . . I thought I could, but I can't."

"But I thought things had changed."

Yes, everything had changed. Her chest felt so tight that she could barely breathe. The panic felt so intense that she couldn't even look him in the eye.

"I said no strings for a reason. Strings get tangled. You're thinking about turning down Allegri for Pinnacle. That's insane."

"I'm thinking about turning them down for *us*!" he shouted.

"And I am cutting the fucking strings! Stop trying to make me what I'm not." This is who she was. Hard, cold, unattached. Only capable of a one-night stand. No matter how much she may have wanted to believe otherwise.

He scoffed and shook his head. "Guess it was too good to be true after all, you committing to something. Some*one*."

That hurt. Badly. But she didn't let him see it, because he was exactly right.

"Believe me," she said. "You're going to look back and be glad."

He took another step back and his expression shifted, and she realized that in all this time she'd spent with him, she'd never seen him truly angry at someone. It just wasn't in his nature. Except that's how he was looking at her now, so hard and cold.

She'd never felt this small and ugly before.

"Fine," he spat, before he turned and headed for the door. "You don't want to matter to me, Violet? Then fine, you don't matter anymore. You're free, just like you wanted."

Then he jerked the door open and he was gone.

She stood in the same spot, unmoving, staring at the door he'd just disappeared through, for a long time. When her arms and legs could move again, she slowly sank to the floor, drawing her knees up to her chest and wrapping her arms around her legs.

It seemed that at some point in the past weeks with Chase, her bloody *heart* had started beating again. And now she remembered why she'd worked so hard to avoid that. Because it hurt like hell.

38

The last fucking thing Chase felt like doing was going to some sponsor party, shaking hands and making a lot of bullshit small talk. But Rally Fuel was considering shoveling a shit ton of sponsorship money into his lap and no matter how he felt right now, business was business. The party was at an upscale restaurant, and no expense had been spared. The food was sublime, and the drinks were flowing, but he wasn't interested in any of it.

He hadn't seen or heard from Violet since that fight the day before. If she'd been at the track for the race this afternoon, she'd steered clear of the garage. It fucking figured. The first time he'd attempted to date someone since Sophie and he had to pick Violet Harper. That was like choosing a wild animal as a pet. When you did something like that, you had no business complaining you got bitten.

But he hadn't chosen her. She'd just *happened* to him. She'd blown into his life and before he knew it, she'd filled up every corner of it, impossible to resist. All he could see, all he wanted, was her.

So here he stood in the middle of this crowded, loud party, every burst of laughter scraping across his nerves like broken glass, every polite smile and handshake seeming to last a thousand years. She was gone and she'd left a hollowed-out shell in his life where she used to be. His head felt thick and his eyes burned, like he'd been awake for weeks. He'd forgotten just how miserable heartbreak could make you feel.

"Chase! Hi!"

He blinked, coming out of his fog, and turned at the mention of his name. Mira Wentworth was weaving through the crowd in his direction.

"Hi, Mira. What's got you here?"

She hooked a thumb over her shoulder. "Dad. Rally's one of our sponsors." She peered over his shoulder. "Is Violet with you? City after city together and I barely see her."

"No, she's not. Why the hell would she be with me?" The words just fell out of his mouth, sharp, sarcastic, and unintended.

Mira blinked in surprise.

"Sorry," he said, rubbing a hand over his face. "I didn't mean—"

"Is something wrong?" she interjected. "What happened?"

He blew out a long, frustrated breath. "I wish I knew!"

Mira cast a quick look around them, then snagged his elbow and towed him through the crowd to an empty booth in the corner of the restaurant. When they were seated, she leaned forward on her elbows. "So, what's going on?"

"I thought things were going okay. It got weird in Vegas when Ian showed up—"

"Ian?"

"That guy she used to date?" Had Violet really never told Mira about Ian? Did it mean anything that she'd told *him* about

Ian? Who the hell knew? And it didn't even fucking matter anymore.

"Is that his name? The rock star?"

Chase scoffed. "*Rock star.* He wishes. But yeah, that's him. And I thought she'd invited him, but apparently he just did that on his own. So she told Ian to go fuck himself and I got myself out of that weird situation with Madison, and we decided to give it a go. Me and her. A real relationship."

Mira's big green eyes got bigger. "You did? *Violet* did?"

"Yeah. And it lasted all of five fucking days." Now that he'd started talking about it, he couldn't seem to stop. "I don't know what happened. She turned so cold. Last night I went to tell her about . . ." He broke off, remembering that as cool as Mira seemed, she worked for a rival team. "Never mind. Team stuff I shouldn't talk about."

"Maraschino cherry."

He looked up at Mira and scowled. "Excuse me?"

"It's what Violet and I say when we need to unload about something at work. Once we say it, we're in a cone of silence. Nothing we say about our teams leaves the cone. So, I'm offering you the cone of silence. Nothing you tell me leaves this table."

Despite how shitty he felt, he cracked a smile. "Okay, maraschino cherry. I've got . . . interest from another team. A good team."

Mira nodded. "With your raised profile and the way you've been driving, I'm not at all surprised to hear that."

"Thanks. So I went to discuss this with Violet, to debate the options—"

"What options?"

"Staying where I am? I mean, she's worked so hard to turn me into this huge thing, and it was all to pull in sponsorship money, for the good of the team. I can't just pull that out from under her."

Mira smiled and tilted her head to the side. "That is so sweet, Chase. Unnecessary, but really sweet."

His anger had already started to ebb, but Mira's words lit it up again, throbbing and hot, like an open wound. "Well, Violet sure as fuck didn't think so. She basically told me I shouldn't factor her into any decision I make."

"I'm sure she just wants you to take the deal that's best for you."

"She said strings were messy and that eventually I'd be grateful she cut them for me." Just saying it felt almost as bad as hearing it had been. He hadn't realized words could sting like that, like a whip cracking across his skin. "And after I told her . . ." *I love you.* ". . . after I told her how much she meant to me."

Mira winced. "Okay, I admit that wasn't great—"

"I don't know what I was thinking. She's never made any secret of who she is and how she operates. I don't know why I thought she might be different with me."

"See, that's the thing," Mira said, leaning closer. "This *isn't* how she is. I've seen Violet with men and she's ruthless."

He chuckled grimly. "Yeah, I know. I can still feel the shiv between my ribs."

"No, Chase." She reached across the table to grip his wrist. "I think you *are* different. Just the fact that you're still here is different. How long has it been? Since you guys started?"

"Since I started at Pinnacle, sort of."

"Violet is the queen of one-and-done. Nobody sticks around for months. *Nobody.*"

"But—"

"Look, she's spent a long time keeping everybody at arm's length. It's probably hard for her to let someone in. Scary, too."

"Violet isn't afraid of anything."

Mira shot him a look. "I know you don't believe that."

"Maybe not. But what does it matter? I put myself on the line and she fucking sent me packing. What am I supposed to do here?"

"Just don't give up on her," Mira said, her eyes all full of earnest pleading. "Not yet."

With a sigh, he slid out of the booth and stood up. "Mira, look, I like you. And I'm glad Violet's got you in her life. But I'm not the one who gave up. I tried. And she's pushed me away over and over. I'm not waiting around to let her kick me in the teeth again."

That Violet-shaped hole in his life felt like it was growing by the minute. He prayed it wasn't permanent. Because it felt like the kind of loss he'd feel forever.

"Chase—"

He held up his hands to cut her off. "Sorry, Mira. I'm out."

Then he turned around and left. Left Mira, and left the whole fucking party. Because he really couldn't handle another minute of talking about some mythical version of Violet, a version that cared about him, and wanted him as much as he'd wanted her. Because it was pretty obvious that version of Violet was all in his head.

39

As a rule, Violet did her best to cut through life like a knife. Cut through the bullshit and do what you have to do to get what you need. It worked for pleasure as well as business, and in both worlds, she didn't bother with guilt. It just wasted time, and left you worse off. As she saw it, at work her ruthlessness was just ambition, and no man would ever be faulted for it. And as for her personal life—men and sex—well, it was exactly the same. She never felt guilt about it because she was up-front about it.

But she'd stayed in the hospitality center for the whole of race day, to avoid crossing paths with Chase. It wasn't guilt, she told herself. It was just . . . cleaner this way. She stayed busy, too. Chatting up sponsors and arranging press events for the upcoming race in Miami. As long as she kept moving, she was fine.

If she had one moment to sit with this, she felt like she was crawling out of her skin.

Which was why, when Rabia found her in hospitality, she was staring into space, picking at a pastry she suddenly had no appetite for.

"Hey, mind if I join you?"

Violet waved her into a chair. *Please, distract me.*

"We had one of the reserve drivers trying out the new design in the simulator back at the factory last week." She passed her iPad across the table. "Check out these times."

Violet scanned the chart and her eyebrows shot up. "Can you replicate this in the car?"

Rabia shrugged. "You never know. Gremlins can always sneak in and fuck you up. But right now there's no reason to believe we can't." She shook her head, smiling. "When we get our hands on that Sokia power unit, and with Chase behind the wheel, next season could get very interesting."

Violet's stomach knotted up with misery.

When Carter's sale went through, the flow of money would stop. They could very likely be forced to race this year's car next season, with no upgrades at all. They'd tread water for a season or two, until they finally went under for good.

But at least Chase would be okay. He was free now to go to Allegri.

Chase.

It felt like someone was sitting on her chest. She took a breath and refocused on Rabia.

Rabia, whose tablet glowed with plans that would never come to fruition. Carter had made her promise not to spread the word of the potential sale, but fuck that. What did it matter now?

I should have just told Chase.

She pushed the thought aside. Well, she couldn't undo that, but she could help Rabia. Rabia deserved to know that none of this was going to happen.

She passed the iPad back across the table. "Rabia, I have something to tell you."

When Violet had finished sharing the bad news, Rabia sat back in her chair, deflated. "Fuck."

"I know. Fuck. Double fuck."

Rabia's eyes skated over the glowing screen of her iPad. Usually she was so no-nonsense and unsentimental, but for a second, Violet saw a flash of genuine sorrow in the other woman's eyes. The look on Rabia's face was like a knife to her chest.

"Guess that's that, then." Rabia sighed, pressing a button to shut down her iPad. "I should have known."

"You couldn't have seen this coming, Rab."

"Not this, but I've been beating my head against the wall in this industry long enough to know better. Do you have any idea the kind of shit I've put up with to get here? There are more women in the garages these days, but when I was starting out, that wasn't the case. And Brown women? Forget it. I was top in my class at uni, and yet I took a job at *Pinnacle*, because it was the only team that would hire me."

"I'm sorry." Violet tore her pastry into pieces. "And I can't imagine Oscar made it any easier."

Rabia scoffed. "He was a fucking nightmare. And I didn't dare say a word because as bad as this team was, at least I was *here*. But if Hammond's decided he's done with us . . . honestly, I should just give it up. Move over to aerospace and be done with all this racing nonsense. Nine to five in an office, home with Rajan every night, watch the races on the telly like normal people."

Her words were at odds with her eyes, so full of frustration and sadness. Walking away from racing would kill her, for all those same reasons Chase had given her back at that bar in Eldham months ago. People who worked in racing did it for one reason—because this sport was buried in their souls. Their hearts beat in time with the roar of the engines.

Fuck this. Fuck all of it. They'd all worked so hard, and for nothing. So some investor class assholes could strip them for parts. It wasn't fair, and she hated—absolutely *hated*—feeling helpless to prevent it.

She was good at one thing. And that was her job.

If she wanted or needed something done, she just kept pushing until it happened, like making Chase a star, like yeeting Oscar Davies into the sun, like pummeling this ragtag team into something marginally competitive. So why not now?

"Rabia, maybe I'm delusional, but what if we could convince Carter not to sell?"

"You want Carter Hammond to keep running a Formula One team?"

"Why not? We're figuring out how to make it work, aren't we?"

"Carter's not interested in racing, Violet. I can't imagine finding an angle that suddenly makes him interested."

Violet's mind raced as she flew through every angle she could think of. "He likes good press, though. He's been paying attention. What if we pitched him? On what we could be? Every Pinnacle success is a Hammond success."

"Do you think he'd really go for that?"

"I have no idea, but we won't know until we try. Are you in?"

Rabia threw her hands in the air. "Why not? What the fuck do we have to lose?"

The jolt of inspiration, of purpose, had powered her through the rest of the afternoon, but once she was back in her hotel room, all alone, the walls began to press in on her. She put in her earbuds and blasted some Black Flag, but it didn't bring the release it usually did. A vodka on the rocks didn't help. Neither did two. She felt restless and unsettled.

So she decided to do what she always did when she wanted to get out of her own head—she went out.

ILM Cloud Storage was considering sponsoring Pinnacle next season, and Zak, the company rep who'd come to the race weekend, had invited her to a party they were hosting at Mexico City's Museum of Modern Art. She hadn't planned on going, but as she pulled up, she was sure this was just what she needed. It was hard to get lost in your own head when you were lost in a crowd.

Inside the museum, the lights had been dimmed, and throbbing techno music was being piped into every room. The crowd was pretty sedate, but at least there was a crowd. And champagne. She plucked a flute from the tray of a passing server as she made her way through the room.

"Hey, look who it is!" Zak's eyes lit up when he spotted her. She didn't miss the quick perusal he'd made of her body. She'd thought she'd caught a vibe from him earlier, and now she was sure of it.

He wasn't bad-looking. Decently tall, with thick dark brown hair and a square jaw. He was a bit sporty and laddish for her taste, but he'd be a distraction, at least.

"Couldn't stay away," she said.

He reached out to wrap a hand around her upper arm as he leaned in to kiss her cheek. The warm rasp of his palm and the pressure of his fingertips sent an unpleasant jolt through her body, and suddenly she had to fight down the impulse to yank her arm back.

"You're looking stunning tonight, Violet."

Her throat closed up around any witty reply she might have made, so she just forced out a smile and threw back the rest of her champagne.

Surely this would get easier? She was just out of practice after no one but Chase for all these months.

Chase.

Suddenly it was hard to draw in a full breath, like her chest was caving in on itself.

Zak had moved closer, all into her personal space. "What do you say we get out of here?" he murmured in her ear.

Hot, moist breath on her neck, his fingers caressing her arm . . . a shudder ripped down her spine and she squeezed her eyes shut against the sensation, against the almost overwhelming urge to run away from Zak, run away from this party, run away from—

"Violet?"

Her eyes snapped back open. "Will!"

He was standing a few feet away, one hand casually stuffed in his pocket, the other gripping a champagne flute. The stupid flood of relief she felt at the sight of him was unreal.

He glanced between her and Zak. "You okay?"

Zak held his hands up and grinned. "Sorry. Didn't realize I was poaching on the world champion's turf."

Another shudder of revulsion rippled through her. Honestly, what the *fuck* was she thinking?

"I'm not *turf*. He's my friend's fiancé."

"Oh, well then—"

When he reached out for her again, she sidestepped him, grabbing for Will's arm instead. "Glad I found you, Will. Something to . . . um, discuss."

"Sure thing," he said, turning them both away and propelling them through the crowd.

"Hey, Violet—"

Zak's protest was swallowed up by the crowd.

"Thanks for that," she muttered.

Will shrugged. "You looked like you needed a rescue."

Had she? She could always handle herself with men. Why had that suddenly felt so different? So wrong?

"Um, is Mira here?" Maybe she just needed to spill her guts to Mira and get her take.

"She's at an event with her dad tonight. Do you need me to call her for you?"

She shook her head and forced out a smile. "It's not that serious."

Will stopped walking and turned to face her, eyeing her in a way that made her feel twitchy. All that *concern.*

"You sure?" he asked.

"I think I need another drink," she muttered.

"I think you need more than a drink, but we'll start there."

As a waiter passed, Will snagged a glass of champagne from his tray and pressed it into her hands. "Now, wanna tell me what's bothering you? Where's Chase?"

At the mention of his name, she had that same breathless chest-caving-in feeling, and most alarmingly, her eyes burned . . . almost like she might fucking *cry.* What was *wrong* with her?

"Okay," Will said on an exhale, like he could see the chaos all over her face. "Over here." He took her by the elbow and led her through a crowd to a small side gallery. The mass of people were back there in the main hall. In this dimly lit little room, there was just the two of them and a very large piece of modern art that she didn't understand at all.

Will crossed his arms over his chest. "Violet, I can tell you're freaked out. What's this about?"

God, this was embarrassing. Here she was, all cut up and full of angst over some *boy.* Hadn't she spent the past three years

working hard to make sure she was never in this position again?
"Um, I think it might be about . . . Chase."

"What happened?"

"Just me being me." She meant it to be flippant, a joke, but it didn't come out that way.

Will said nothing. He just stood there, arms crossed, waiting her out. If she was looking for a sounding board, she wouldn't have picked Will, but now that she thought about it, he probably had the most relevant experience.

She kept her eyes on her hands as she twisted the stem of her glass. "So, you were a manwhore once."

He sputtered out a laugh. "Umm . . . I guess it's all in your perspective—"

She shot him a glance. "You were."

"Okay. Yeah, I guess I was."

She tossed back half a glass of champagne in one gulp, but alcohol wasn't helping. It tasted cloyingly sweet and wasn't doing a goddamned thing to shut down the noise in her head, the panicky thoughts clamoring to get out. God, why was this so hard? Why did she feel like one big, exposed nerve right now?

"How did that work?" she finally forced out. "When you met Mira?"

"What do you mean?"

"Like, there you were, sleeping with one girl after another, tossing them out like used tissues when you were done, and suddenly you meet the one who changed everything?"

"Jesus, you make me sound like a total dirtbag."

"If you were, then I am, too," she muttered.

He paused, looking closely at her. "So first of all, neither one of us is a dirtbag. We were both single, and we enjoyed being single, right?"

"I'm not apologizing for who I am, and I don't feel bad about a single thing I've done. Except maybe this one thing."

"You guys have been together for a while now, right?"

Were they? She'd fought like hell to avoid putting any sort of name to it. But now that it was over, looking back on it, yes, they had been. They'd been *together* almost from the beginning.

"Yes, we were. I . . . um. I ended it. Yesterday."

"Why?"

"He was getting too attached. He was making decisions based on me, not on what was best for him."

"Well, when you're with someone, and it's serious, usually you do factor the other person into your plans. Because it's a partnership. You're supposed to get attached."

"But what if you make those choices based on another person and it all falls apart?" She'd done that—poured years of her life and all her hard work into someone else and in the end, she'd been left with nothing to show for it.

"What if it *doesn't* fall apart?"

"It *always* falls apart."

"Not always," Will said, with a shrug. "To answer your earlier question, I didn't necessarily know Mira was the end of my *man-whore* days, as you put it. I just . . . wanted her. And then I *only* wanted her. And then I realized my life wouldn't be the same if she wasn't in it."

Violet considered that for a minute. When was the last time she'd wanted someone other than Chase? Not since before Chase. Since he'd come along, she hadn't so much as glanced at another man. Just now with Zak . . . that should have been easy. Instead, all she could think of was getting away from him. The only thing she felt was that it all felt wrong.

Leaving a guy behind had never been a problem before. Why now? Why Chase? And for the love of god, how did she make it *stop*? When she tried to imagine the next season, the next month, even the next few days, without Chase around, her mind went blank and that awful twisty hollow feeling started up in her chest again.

"Oh, fuck." She dropped her head and squeezed her eyes shut. "I think I love him."

Will chuckled.

"This isn't funny, you bastard," she growled.

"Sorry, but it kind of is. Violet, listen, this isn't a bad thing."

She lifted her head to glare at him. "The hell it's not. I promised myself I'd never do this again."

"What? Care about someone?"

"Yes! Because if you care about someone, you're giving them the power to destroy you. Trust me, I've been there. I don't want to do it again."

He nodded slowly. "I guess that's true, but the power can go the other way, too."

"What do you mean?"

"That power can make you . . . better, stronger, *happier*. With Mira . . ." Will paused and shook his head, a soft, sappy smile on his dopey face. "She makes me better. I make her better. We're better together than either of us on our own. There's stuff in my life that I never would have been able to handle without her."

"Your shit parents?" She'd met Will's parents once and they were the worst. Puffed up, snobby wankers.

"Them and a whole lot more. With her, I just know I can deal with anything that comes along. And I like to think I do the same for her."

Violet thought back to last season, and all the bullshit Mira had to weather. "You do."

He made a good point. The two of them definitely complemented each other. She thought about Chase, that impulsiveness that made him so good on the track but had left him with a scattershot career, until she'd come along and pulled it all together. That was kind of her thing, right?

But what about her? She'd been so steadfastly single for all this time because she wasn't about to let another man take from her. But what if someone *gave* instead? Suddenly she remembered what she'd told Ian that night in Vegas, when she'd finally sent him packing. She felt valued now. Chase valued her. He appreciated her insight and her skills. Wasn't that all she'd ever wanted from Ian? And Chase had been giving it to her from the start.

He'd given her so much more, though. Everything else she'd said to Ian . . . about being a part of the team, part of something bigger. She'd had that once with Ian and lost it all. Now, without even realizing it, she'd gotten it back with Chase and Pinnacle.

"Listen, Violet," Will was saying. "Yeah, there's always a chance that it all goes to hell and you get hurt. But there's also a chance it doesn't. And if you really do love him, maybe it's worth taking that chance. Because when it works out, it's fucking great. And you pushed him away, and you don't seem so great right now. So why not?"

"Because I fucked up. Badly. I sent him away and I was kind of mean about it, because . . . well, I'm me."

Will waved a hand dismissively. "Chase knows you. He can handle you at your meanest. If he feels the same way about you, you can fix it."

"What if he doesn't feel the same way?" It came out almost at a whisper, because it felt like giving voice to the thing she feared the most. Maybe he'd meant what he said. *You don't matter anymore.*

"Was he upset when you sent him packing?"

"Yeah, he was upset."

"Then he cares. You just gotta tell him how you feel."

She scoffed, because that was literally the hardest thing she could imagine doing. But if she wanted him back, she was going to have to figure out how to do it. And she did. She wanted him back.

She'd had something with him . . . and it had been amazing. And she'd thrown it away with both hands because she was too scared to acknowledge how much she really cared about him.

"It's not going to be easy," she murmured.

"No," Will acknowledged. "But it'll be worth it. I promise."

40

Miami, Florida

Chase let himself back into his luxury hotel suite and dropped his shoulder bag with a sigh, surveying the room. Across from him, through a wall of glass, the skyline of Miami glittered.

He crossed to the glossy black bar where liquor bottles glinted subtly under the recessed lighting, and poured himself a finger of scotch. Then he dropped onto the plush white leather sofa and propped his feet on the glass-topped coffee table. There was a massive flat-screen on the wall, but he didn't turn it on. Instead, he just tipped his head back, staring at the ceiling.

If someone had told him a year ago that he'd be here in this suite, flush with new sponsor money, driving for one Formula One team with an offer from another team—one of the best teams—on the table, he'd have laughed in their face.

He'd done it. He'd achieved everything he'd ever wanted. Before Miami, he'd stopped in New York for a round of meetings with Jeff. He was about to line up enough in sponsorship deals to make his head spin. He hadn't just hung on to his spot in F1; he was about to ascend to the apex of the sport.

So why was he sitting here filled with misery?

Because she was still gone.

He hadn't heard a word from Violet since he'd walked out of her hotel room in Mexico City. Today had been open practice, so he thought he might finally see her at the track, but she never showed.

He scrubbed his hands over his face and growled in frustration before shoving himself back up to his feet. It was time to quit mooning over her. He was in Miami to race, and that's what he needed to focus on. Tomorrow was qualifying. He'd order some room service and get a decent night's sleep, and he would absolutely *not* keep obsessing over Violet.

He was in the bedroom, in the middle of digging sleep pants and a T-shirt out of his suitcase, when he heard a knock at the door of the suite. Immediately his pulse picked up. These days, for security reasons, only a small handful of people knew where his hotel suite was, and an even smaller handful would show up unannounced.

It might be her. It was probably her. God, he wanted it to be her.

When he swung the door open, Violet was standing on the other side and something clenched tight inside his chest suddenly released. She was *here.*

This was a different Violet, the one he remembered from last season. She was wearing shredded black jeans and a faded Ramones T-shirt. She hadn't straightened her hair, and it tumbled in tousled black waves around her shoulders.

"Hi," she said, eyes wide and fixed on him.

"Hey."

She swallowed hard enough that he could see her throat move. "Can I come in?" He was usually the one to ask that.

Wordlessly, he moved aside. When he'd fastened the security latch, he turned to see her over by the wall of glass, looking out at the view.

"Nice room."

"Formula One doesn't suck."

She didn't reply, just rubbed her palms down her thighs.

"What's up, Violet?" he finally said, to break the silence. Violet wasn't one for lingering goodbyes, so just the fact that she was here sent a tendril of hope sprouting up in his heart, but he couldn't bear to get ahead of himself. She'd been pretty final when she'd sent him packing. If she'd changed her mind, she was going to have to say so, and explain why.

"I'm not good at this," she murmured, running one fingertip down the glass.

"At what?"

"Apologies. I owe you one."

Part of him wanted to accept it immediately. Fine. All is forgiven. Just come back. But as impulsive as he was on the track, some sense of self-preservation had him hesitating now. He needed more than "I'm sorry," which she hadn't said yet. So instead of pulling her into his arms and keeping her there, he stayed silent, leaning against the back of the sofa, watching her shoulders rise and fall as she considered.

"I, um . . . things are complicated. It's about more than just you. And me." She paused and cleared her throat. "You and me."

"What else is it about?" he finally asked. If she said Ian's name, he was going to start breaking shit.

She bowed her head, inhaled deeply, then turned to face him. "Carter's about to sell the team."

That was . . . not at all what he was expecting her to say.

He absorbed that piece of information. "Not all that surprising. He never wanted Pinnacle, right? And maybe it's a good thing. If Carter goes, so does Reece, and—"

"He wants to sell us to some private equity outfit."

"Shit." He knew what that meant. Everyone had seen what happened to Affinity.

"So you see," Violet continued. "I couldn't let you fuck around with an offer from Allegri. If they wanted to sign you, you needed to take it. I couldn't let you make that kind of mistake, not when I knew what was coming."

"Why didn't you just tell me?"

"Carter made me promise to keep it confidential. But fuck that." She lifted her hands and let them drop. "None of us might have jobs in a year's time. Fuck the rules."

He considered her words, scowling at the floor. "But that doesn't explain why you pushed me away. Only why you wanted me to take that job, and—"

She cut him off. "The rest was just me being . . . me." She squeezed her eyes shut briefly and tipped her head back. "Somebody said something to me—"

"Who?" Who was the asshole who'd caused this nightmare? Chase wanted to track them down and—

"It was nobody who mattered. And what they said shouldn't have mattered. But it just . . ." She shook her head in frustration. "It got inside my head. It made me . . . doubt."

"Doubt me?" Surely she must see how wild he was for her.

"No, not you. He made me doubt myself. Who I am. And . . . what I'm capable of."

"What are you trying to say, Violet?"

"I'm sorry," she said softly. "I'm sorry I'm the way I am. I'm sorry I'm so angry and mean and . . . scared." Finally, she looked directly at him, her dark blue eyes meeting his. "Mostly I'm just scared."

"Of what?"

"Me. Losing myself in you. I've done that before and I've spent all this time since then trying to make up for that mistake."

She paused, and the instinct to rush in and reassure her was strong, but he resisted, staying quiet, letting her say what she had to say. As hopeful as her arrival made him feel, he was still smarting, feeling the ache of this past week.

"But I've been doing some thinking," she finally said. "And I've figured some things out."

"Like what?"

She lifted her eyes to his again, a quick, anxious glance that told him all he needed to know about how hard this was for her. "You've never tried to erase me. You've never taken what I've done for you for granted."

"Of course not. Who would do that?"

At that, she cracked a small smile. She looked tired, stressed, like the week apart had been as hard on her as it had been on him. "Guess."

"That fucking wanker," Chase groaned.

"You stole my word." Her small smile grew, and he felt himself smiling in return, like the distance between them had shrunk and the coldness had thawed. "There's something else I want to say," she said.

"What's that?"

"You've made me feel like I'm a part of something. The team, but also . . . me and you. It's important, and it matters to me. A lot. I mean, you should have seen me talking to Rabia the other day. I was all 'hope' and 'team spirit.' Bloody disgusting." But she was still smiling.

And he was too, mostly because he felt like he couldn't stop. That coldness had turned to warmth, a huge swell of it in his chest, threatening to spill out all over the place. "And me?"

She met his eyes again, and this time she didn't look away. "You matter. More than you can imagine."

He pushed off the back of the couch and crossed to where she still stood by the windows, like she'd grown roots. She was so tense all over, her expression anxious and her body rigid, like she was still half expecting disaster.

"You matter to me, too," he said gently, trying to reassure her. He took a step closer and reached for her hand. She let him take it, but her fingers were curled in tight against her palm. He turned her hand over and began smoothing out each finger.

"I'm sorry I hurt you," she said quietly. "I'll probably do it again at some point. I'm not good at this. But I promise, I'll try."

"You're better than you think, Violet. It's a chance I'm willing to take."

Her hand was splayed open now, and he rubbed his thumb across her palm. She was chewing on her bottom lip, watching his fingers tangling with hers. Then her eyes lifted to his again. "What if you hurt me?" she whispered, almost too soft to hear.

Ah, there it was. The root of all of it. Her armor was off now and he could see what was underneath, a girl so scared of being hurt that she never gave anyone a chance to do it to her. He reached out a hand to cup her cheek, rubbing his thumb across her full bottom lip. "I promise, I don't want to ever hurt you. I know I'm asking a lot, asking you to trust me."

"I trust you," she said, holding on to his wrist. "I really do. But it's not easy. Trust."

"I think it might get easier the more you do it."

Resolve flickered across her face, an expression he was much more familiar with coming from Violet. Then she reached up and took his face in her hands. "I care about you, Chase. I want to try this again."

He let out a gusty sigh. "Oh, thank god. Being sad and angsty really doesn't work for me."

She laughed, just a soft huff, but her whole face transformed when she did it. She gazed up at him with something he was coming to recognize as fondness. "No, it doesn't. You should never be sad. It's not who you are."

Then she leaned up and pressed her lips against his. He wrapped his arms around her and pulled her in tight against his body.

"I missed you," he murmured against her mouth when they briefly broke apart.

"It's only been four days." She started kissing her way down his neck, and the feeling of her lips skimming across his skin made him drop his head back and groan.

"Four nights, too. We have some catching up to do."

Violet pulled away from him and took a step back. She looked up into his face for a beat, then held her hand out to him. He put his in hers, palm to palm, and she tangled their fingers together. It felt like a different kind of connection, one that promised more than physical pleasure. This felt like companionship, caring, and a partnership, one that might last for a very long time.

Violet turned and led him toward the bedroom. Once inside he pressed up against her back, circling his arms around her and bending down to kiss the side of her neck. She let him for a minute before she turned back around. Her hands slid up under his T-shirt, the warmth of her palms sending sparks through his system as she ran them up his rib cage, pushing his shirt up as she went. He lifted his arms and let her whip it over his head.

"You're so beautiful," she murmured, running her hands back down over his shoulders and arms.

He started working her faded black T-shirt up as well. "So are you." When it was gone, his eyes ran over every inch of her exposed upper body, her long, pale arms, and the swells of her gorgeous breasts above the black lace of her bra. Reaching behind her, he unhooked her bra and slid the straps down her arms, his eyes feasting on her bare breasts. "All of you."

"I know you like them."

His hands came up to cup them and her eyelids fluttered down. "I love them."

She let him play with them for a few minutes before she brushed his hands aside and reached for the button on his jeans.

"I like parts of you, too," she said.

"Oh, really?" He couldn't help but smile, because all of this, the playfulness and familiarity now mixed into their sex, felt so right. "Which part specifically?"

Her hand slid into the open fly of his jeans and wrapped around him through his boxer briefs. "This part, for a start."

"It likes you a lot, too," he groaned, reaching for her. Wrapping his arms around her, he lifted her off her feet and crossed the room toward the edge of the bed before tossing her back onto it. She landed with a bounce and he came down over her, bracing himself with his arms as he leaned in to kiss her. Her hand found him again, stroking him at the same pace as his tongue stroked hers. His hips began to flex with each stroke until he was about to lose his mind from it.

He broke their kiss and pulled her hand free, pressing a kiss to her palm. "I wanna be inside you when I come."

She stared up at him with that tender affection he was rapidly getting addicted to. "I want you there, too."

Rearing back off her, he grabbed the cuffs of her jeans and wriggled them down, watching her long, silky legs emerge inch by creamy inch. He wanted to kiss his way up each one to the hot, wet center of her. He wanted to feel her come on his tongue, on his fingers, on his cock. He wanted all of it, and all with her.

When she was lying naked on the bed, he stood up and shucked his own jeans and boxers, then, retrieving a condom, he rolled it on his aching, swollen cock. Violet propped herself up on her elbows, watching with unabashed interest as he did. He gave himself an extra stroke just for her. She bit her lip and squirmed, rubbing her thighs together. God, he might explode if he didn't get inside her right now.

Leaning back over her, he put his hands on her knees and spread her thighs. Then he leaned down and pressed one quick, soft kiss right on her clit. She moaned, writhing against his restraining hands. "So pretty," he murmured.

"Chase . . ." Her voice was raspy and strained, almost pleading.

"Almost, baby."

He climbed up her body, fitting his hips between her thighs and sliding one arm under her shoulders to brace her body. He pressed himself into her hot wetness, just an inch and then pulled back out. Her legs wrapped tight around him, her heels digging into the backs of his thighs, urging him forward. This time he gave her what she wanted, what *he* wanted, and thrust in deep. She moaned, her nails digging into his shoulders.

He'd intended to drag this out, but he wanted her too much, his body was too desperate for hers. Instead, he dropped his forehead to her shoulder and started to move. Her body seemed to instinctively respond in that way it had since their very first night together, an alchemy he'd never known with anyone else. She matched his pace, tightening around him as he brought them both closer to the edge.

His body started spiraling tighter in on itself just before the eventual explosive release. He lifted his head just enough to see her face, to look into her eyes.

Usually she did her best to look away at this moment, or to shut her eyes, anything to keep him out, to keep him from seeing her at her most vulnerable. This time she didn't.

She looked back into his eyes, even as he felt her start to come undone. He brought a hand up to cup her cheek, to stroke his thumb across her cheekbone, and he brushed his lips briefly across hers as she gasped and cried out. Feeling her body shaking underneath him was all it took to send him tumbling over the edge, and pleasure rushed through him like a tidal wave.

He dropped his head into the hollow between her neck and shoulder, breathing in the soft, slightly spicy smell of her skin as he slowly came back to earth.

"I love you, Violet," he said against her shoulder. Then he lifted his head to look at her. Her eyes were heavy-lidded, and her expression was soft. "You don't have to say it back if you're not ready. But I am, and I want you to know that. Know that I love you."

She ran a hand down the side of his face and smiled. The gentle gesture said everything he could tell she wasn't quite ready to say out loud. Then she leaned up and kissed him, and if he hadn't been sure before, he was once she kissed him. She could take all the time she needed to say it out loud. He could feel it here, in her kiss.

41

As a rule, Chase wasn't prone to superstition, but from the moment he woke up Sunday morning, he could feel something tingling through his bloodstream. Not quite anticipation, not really nerves. It had to be the weather that was putting him on edge. It was that weird changeable Florida weather, hot and humid, but with thunderstorms threatening at any moment.

The track had already been soaked down once this morning and spot thunderstorms were anticipated through the afternoon as well. The Formula Three race was currently underway and three cars had already crashed out because of the wet conditions.

He cast a glance up at the sky overhead, then turned his attention back to Emil, who was going over race strategy with him.

". . . there might be a chance to jump ahead of Schlosser and Bang on the start. They've both been struggling to launch. So keep on top of that—"

"Emil, the track is soaking wet. I can make all the plans I want, but you and I both know it's all going to go to shit the first time somebody's tires lock up."

Emil smiled and shrugged. "Then our only plan is 'don't crash.'"

"That's always the plan."

Rabia had been checking over a bunch of stats with Leon on the bank of monitors in the garage, but now she came over to join him and Emil. She looked up at the sky just outside the garage.

"I don't like this. It feels weird."

"It's Florida," Chase replied. "It's always weird."

Luckily, he'd spent a lot of time driving in the wet conditions.

Back in his karting days, when rain chased most of the kids off the track, he usually stayed out, because it was the only time he'd had the track to himself and could open it up and see what he was capable of. In the rain, he'd found out what kind of driver he really was. He wasn't afraid of the rain.

"Not that you're going to be able to pay attention to anything other than not dying today, but I tweaked the steering again. Conditions might make it hard to evaluate, but see if you notice a difference."

"Will do, boss. You seen Violet?" He smiled when he said her name. Fuck, he had it so bad for her.

"She's up in the VIP lounge with Carter Hammond."

He glanced up at her in surprise. "Carter Hammond's here?"

Carter Hammond wasn't the least bit interested in racing. Or his son. If he was here, it was important.

"Ah . . . yeah."

Rabia's poker face was terrible. He could tell in an instant that she was up to something. And that something probably had a whole lot to do with Violet.

"Rabia, what are you two up to?"

"Ask her yourself." Rabia nodded her chin toward the crowd out in the paddock. Violet was weaving her way quickly through the crowds. Chase took a minute to appreciate the view, the long legs in her fitted poison-green suit, the swing of her glossy black hair as she walked . . . He felt almost weak in the knees from it.

"How's it going in VIP?" Rabia looked at her over the rim of her glasses.

Violet nodded briskly. "Good so far. I managed to get some celebrities here for this one. His wife, Corrine, is having an absolute blast. She took a selfie with a Kardashian, so well done there. Carter was surprised to see so many business execs here. I explained how many movers and shakers follow Formula One, and he seemed intrigued by the idea of doing deals in the VIP stands instead of on the golf course."

"What about Junior?"

"Imogen corralled him with the sponsor rep from ILM and a bottle of bourbon. Hopefully that keeps him out of the way until after the race."

"Are we up?" Rabia asked quietly.

Violet nodded.

Chase looked from Violet to Rabia and back again. "I know that look in your eyes, Violet. What are you plotting?"

She leaned in close and murmured in his ear. "Rabia and I are going to try to convince him to keep the team."

"How are you going to do that?"

She ran a finger up his chest then tapped his chin with it. "By showing him how amazing Pinnacle is, and how amazing you are, and how much he'd be missing if he let us go."

"I'm slightly afraid. But if anybody can do it, it's you." He reached up and touched his fingertip to her bottom lip, where he'd kiss her if they were alone.

She smiled, a new sort of smile he hadn't seen from her before. It was soft and intimate, like it was meant just for him. "Wish me luck."

He could feel himself smiling back, impossible to contain. "You don't need luck, Violet. You make your own magic."

She reached out and snagged his hand. He glanced down at their entwined fingers and smiled. "Really? Right here in the garage? What is everybody going to think?"

She stepped closer. "I guess they're going to think you're my boyfriend."

His smile exploded into a grin, still only half as big as this emotion swelling up in his chest. "Damn right, I am."

She sobered slightly. "Be careful out there."

"I'll be fine. You know I'm hard to keep down."

The corner of her mouth tugged up. "I do know that. Have a good race."

He looked into her eyes. "You, too."

Because Violet was definitely running her own race today, one that everyone's futures were riding on.

VIOLET SURVEYED THE Pinnacle VIP hospitality room, checking in on all the major players.

She'd had to do the tap dance of her life to get Carter Hammond down here. In the end, she'd hit up his administrative assistant, who she'd discovered was also personal friends with Corrine Hammond, his wife.

Corrine Hammond, a statuesque woman in her sixties in a stunning ivory suit, with impeccably styled blond hair, was currently chatting with Dean Morley, a mid-list movie actor and racing fan Violet had invited to the box. Corrine, she'd been told, loved a good party and a chance to rub elbows with celebrities.

Carter himself was talking to both the CEO and CFO of Rally Fuel, one of their sponsors.

Rabia slipped into the VIP box and stood beside her. "Is it time?"

Rabia looked as nervous as she felt.

"It's now or never."

"Do you really think we have a shot at this?" Rabia asked.

Violet shrugged. "Probably not? But look at it this way, if we fail, we're no worse off than we already are." And Violet felt weirdly . . . hopeful, after everything with Chase.

Rabia drew in a deep breath. "Right. I've updated my CV. Just in case."

Violet barked a laugh. "Good plan. Wait here. I'll see if I can get him."

She summoned every ounce of her confidence—earned and aspirational—and strode toward Carter's group. She was going to need all of it to pull this off.

Carter Hammond was tall, over six feet, with broad shoulders and a barrel chest. His hair had gone completely white, but it didn't age him. She knew he was nearly seventy, but he carried himself like a man two decades younger. There were hints of Reece in his face, but where Reece was soft and flushed, Carter was lean and as chiseled as granite.

He turned to face her as she approached.

"Mr. Hammond, I have a few things I'd like to discuss with you. Could we steal you for a few minutes?"

He gave one brisk nod of his chin. "Gentlemen, business calls. Lead the way, Ms. Harper."

She ignored the butterflies in her stomach as she led Carter down a hallway to a small conference room at the back of the hospitality suite. Usually, it was where department heads met when they needed to work through lunch or dinner, or if a sponsor had a pitch to make. Today it was carefully set up for a very different sort of presentation.

"Can I get you a drink?" she asked Carter. Behind him, Rabia nervously stuffed her hands into her pockets, then pulled them back out and smoothed down the front of her gray Pinnacle button-down shirt.

"Whiskey, please."

Violet licked her lips, trying to dispel her nerves as she poured him a hefty glass of thirty-year Laphroaig. Might as well grease the wheels with the good stuff.

She handed him his glass and motioned to Rabia. "You've met Rabia Dar, Pinnacle's chief technical officer."

"Briefly. Replaced Davies after that ugliness came to light, right?"

"Rabia's been with Pinnacle for ten years. She's instrumental to our success so far this season."

"Not much of that, is there? Pinnacle's what . . . last?"

"The team is currently ranked ninth, actually, but Dieter Gruber is ranked seventeenth and Chase Navarro is currently twelfth, which is remarkable, considering how new he is to the team."

Carter chuckled. "Okay, Ms. Harper, let's have it."

"Excuse me, sir?"

"I know the windup to a pitch when I hear it. What are you here to propose?"

Violet glanced to Rabia, who nodded tightly.

"Why don't we sit down, Mr. Hammond?" Rabia said, motioning to the glossy mahogany conference table behind them. "We have some information we'd like to go over with you."

Forty minutes later, the conference table was littered with printouts, and the wide-screen TVs mounted around the room, which usually just aired the race live stream, were populated with spreadsheets and design specs cast from Rabia's iPad.

Despite not knowing a single thing about auto racing, Carter Hammond had kept up with the dense flood of information admirably. Violet had to concede, he'd earned his place in the business world with his brains. Nothing got by him.

"I will admit, Ms. Dar, that the designs you've shown me for next year's car do look intriguing, to the extent I understand them. That's some pretty sophisticated engineering."

"You've picked up a lot more than most newbies do."

"And you don't really need to understand the mechanics of it to appreciate the data coming out of the simulator sessions." Violet slid the spreadsheet of sim times back in front of him. "Compared to this year's times, you can see the remarkable improvement."

"But as I understand it, this car"—he tapped the paper—"is still theoretical?"

"We've started manufacture," Rabia explained. "But it won't hit the track in physical form until next March, in Bahrain. But we're very optimistic."

Carter slid an artist's rendering of next year's car, complete with livery, closer and sighed. "Always was a sucker for muscle cars when I was young."

Violet and Rabia exchanged a brief hopeful look. Formula One was a business, but it was powered by a sheer, irrational passion for cars.

"But the budget you've shown me . . . forgive me, but this sport seems like a money pit. What you want me to do . . . keep ownership of the team . . . what's in it for Hammond Holdings? Where does the profitability come from?"

Violet jumped in with her promotional spread. "The team is basically a dedicated promotional space for Hammond Holdings. Between live races, broadcasting, and online and social media coverage, any brand sponsoring Pinnacle Motorsports or one of its drivers has unprecedented ad reach. Formula One is one of the most popular sports in the world. I've looked at the companies in Hammond Holdings. Their presence is strong in America, but you haven't made much headway with overseas consumers. This is how you can do that."

Carter nodded, conceding the point. "I can see the international reach, and it's appealing. But for the kind of visibility you're pitching, Ms. Harper, a team needs results. Nobody talks about the guys in last place. Can you promise that kind of attention?"

"Nothing's a guarantee," Rabia said. "But with this new design and our current team, on and off the track, I feel more confident than I have in my ten years at Pinnacle. We're doing something special here."

"I appreciate the confidence you both bring to the table. But what I'd like to see is a measurable result. Something that gets the media talking about Pinnacle's potential, beyond just Chase Navarro."

"And if we do that?" Violet asked, lacing her fingers together so tightly they hurt.

Carter smiled. "Well, let's see how the race goes, shall we? We'll talk after." He pushed back from the table and stood.

Violet stood up, too. "We appreciate you taking the time to listen to us."

He headed toward the door, but paused and turned back. "Good luck today. I do mean that. I'm a businessman, and I respond to results. But regardless of what I ultimately decide, you've both impressed me."

Once Carter was gone, Violet turned to face Rabia. "That wasn't a no?" she said, as brightly as she could manage. Some of Chase's ridiculous optimism must have infected her.

"It wasn't a yes, either," Rabia groused. "He wants a result. *Today*. How do we pull that off?"

"We tell Dieter and Chase to drive for their lives. And beyond that . . ."

"Yeah?"

"We pray for a miracle."

The start of the race neared, and the VIP suite had gotten more crowded. The atmosphere was notably more festive.

Violet cast a worried glance outside, where the vast stretch of Florida sky was growing darker. It was raining again, and the wind had picked up. Not hard enough to delay, but hard enough to turn it into an ice rink down there. And it may be getting worse.

No one was out on the balcony. Wide-screen TVs mounted all around the room displayed a constantly changing stream from the cameras positioned all around the track, but nobody was paying them much attention yet. Waiters moved seamlessly through the well-dressed crowd, refilling champagne flutes and offering gourmet appetizers, while everyone laughed and chatted.

Carter and another man were sitting on a sofa inside. As Violet passed, he noticed her and wheeled around.

"Ms. Harper, what are you doing back there? Come sit."

It wasn't like she could tell him no, so she perched on the edge of the sofa next to him.

"This is Harrison, Violet."

Violet didn't know who the hell Harrison was, but his bespoke suit and Patek Philippe watch screamed money.

"I've been telling him," Harrison told her, "once Formula One gets in your blood, there's no getting it out."

God bless you, Harrison, keep it up.

"I need you to explain this to me," Carter said jovially. At least he was enjoying himself. She feared the VIP experience in the lounge might be the most exciting part of the day.

"The rain changes things," she warned him. "The drivers will be exercising a lot of caution."

"Here we go!" Harrison called out on the other side of Carter. "Hang on to your ass, Hammond!"

On the monitor, the lights were clicking on one by one as rain splattered against the camera lens and the light grew dimmer. Just then, a particularly strong gust of wind buffeted the VIP lounge, rattling the glass walls, and nervous laughter rippled through the crowd.

The last light came on, and the roar of the engines down on the track below them revved ever higher. This was the moment in every race when Violet's pulse began to race with the engines, and anticipation began to simmer through her veins.

This was the moment when she remembered, over and over again, how much she loved this sport.

The crowd in the VIP lounge quieted as the tension ramped up. And then the lights flashed out and the cars shot forward down the start/finish straight toward the first turn. It wasn't quite a hairpin, but it was tighter than ninety degrees. The race leaders had gotten off fast . . . Will Hawley, René Denis, and Michael Pinman headed into the turn in the clear. Behind them, the midfield clumped up, half obscured by the spray of water thrown up by their tires as they hit the brakes.

Something happened—there was a collision and a skid, blurred by distance and rain. In the next instant, five cars had been shoved off the track. The room erupted in shouts.

Violet held her breath as she frantically scanned the rain-misted chaos on screen for the silver of Pinnacle's livery. Orange. That was Kodama. And there was a flash of Allegri's red, Hansbach's copper, Lennox blue . . .

No Pinnacle cars. *It wasn't him.* He was safe.

She was still trying to identify Chase in the mess when it happened again, halfway through the turn. One of the drivers forced off the track by the initial collision came back on track and swerved into the path of another car.

A silver car. *No.*

The world slowed down as that streak of silver spun out across the track and hit the wall.

Violet stopped breathing. Her heart stopped beating as the camera zoomed in on the two cars up against the track wall. The driver of the Pinnacle car was already climbing out, and in an instant she knew.

Not Chase. She knew him so well at this point. The angle of his shoulders, the length of his torso . . . even the way he turned his head. Even at this distance, in his drive suit, helmet, and HANS device, and through the rain.

But fuck . . . Dieter was out of his car, which meant he was out of the race.

When she blinked and looked around, the room was as chaotic as the track, everyone talking and gesturing at the monitors. And Carter was gripping her hand. Or she was gripping his. Had she reached for him in the middle of all that chaos?

She snatched her hand back. "Oh, god. I'm so sorry—I apologize, Mr. Hammond. I wasn't thinking for a minute there."

"Not a problem." He chuckled, not unkindly. "Was that one of ours?"

She nodded tightly. "That was Dieter. He's out."

"Where's the other one? Mr. Navarro?"

She swallowed thickly. "I think Chase made it through." *Thank you, thank you, thank you.* Now that her heart had started beating again, it was pounding its way out of her chest, and the adrenaline coursing through her veins left her feeling shaky. If anything happened to him, she wouldn't be able to handle it. She couldn't handle even *thinking* about it.

By now, the red flag had been called and the announcers were running through the compound collision in slow motion, identifying who was who and what, exactly, had happened.

On the approach to the turn, Elian Peña rammed into the back of Gunnar Larsson from Optima, sending them both sliding straight across the track just as half a dozen cars were entering the turn.

They took out three other drivers like bowling pins—Laurent Demarche from Hansbach, Qian Hai, also from Optima, and Matteo Gatone, whom she knew well from back at Lennox.

Just as they were picking apart that collision, Rolando Castenada from Hunter had collided with Dieter and sent him into the wall.

Violet checked the Pinnacle WhatsApp chat for any kind of update, but unsurprisingly, everyone was busy. In minutes, though, the damage was clear. Dieter was forced to retire the car from the race, along with Matteo, Laurent Demarche, Elian Peña, and Gunnar Larsson.

Half the front-runners and half the midfield, out of the race in the first minute. They still had fifty-seven laps to race.

"It's exciting, that's for sure," Carter said.

Races like this made for exciting viewing, but they were dangerous as fuck for every driver out there. She'd gone into today praying for some miracle that allowed one of the Pinnacle drivers to score big. Now all she was praying for was Chase to walk away in one piece.

CHASE'S NECK ACHED in unfamiliar places. His shoulder muscles felt locked into position. Even his hands ached after gripping the wheel for so long.

It had been a long and brutal race, starting with that fucking ridiculous double pileup thirty seconds after the start, and the fifteen-minute red flag while they'd cleared the *five cars* disabled in the wrecks.

Then, in Lap Thirty, as if there hadn't already been enough carnage out here, Michael Pinman and Giulio Conti got a little too close taking Turn Seventeen. In these conditions, all it had taken was Giulio's nose clipping Michael's tire and they were both off the track, into the wall, and out of the race.

The field had bunched back up behind the safety car, then Bence Takács, who was literally last on the grid at present, had misjudged a turn and sent himself into the wall.

Eight cars out of the race. *Eight.* There were only twelve of them left with ten laps to go. It was practically like fucking qualifying. The rain had ended and the sun had come out, but the previous forty-six laps had taken far longer than the usual ninety minutes.

"Nine laps to go," Emil barked in his ear, as he crossed over the start/finish line. As he dipped into the Marina section of the grandstands, he glanced in his mirrors and caught a glimpse of a towering black cloud formation behind him, just north of the circuit. If that caught them, they'd have another run in the wet before all was said and done.

The first fat plop of rain hit his visor as he exited Turn Sixteen. In seconds, when he was halfway down the straight, the skies opened up. Rain fell so hard and fast it was ricocheting off the track and back up. The sky was still blue over most of the circuit. It was a classic Florida pocket thunderstorm.

Up ahead, he saw Liam and Kai Nolan hit Turn Seventeen and slide off the track. Though they managed to recover, his instincts kicked in.

"I'm boxing."

There was no way his current slick tires would be usable in the next lap if this rain continued.

"Confirm, boxing," Emil replied. "Which tires?"

"Inters," he replied, again on instinct.

Emil paused. "Inters. You sure?"

No. Maybe.

"Yes." He'd seen loads of these storms when he'd run a racing series in Florida as a teenager. Brutal, but brief, which meant he might be driving on a dry track again before the race was over. If that happened, he'd be glad to be on inters.

As Chase entered the pit, the team garages were all in utter chaos. Teams were struggling to get tires out of blankets and crew into the pit lane in preparation for panicked drivers arriving for an unexpected stop. Every driver had called in to box, but nearly everyone had been past the pit lane when the rain started.

Only he, Liam, Axel Nyström, and Kai Nolan had made it in on the current lap.

It took under three seconds, despite the late warning. As they dropped him off the jacks and he accelerated back out, he spotted both Axel and Kai still up on jacks.

Fuck yes.

Emil crackled over the radio, "You just jumped up two spots—ninth place, Chase."

But could he hold it?

VIOLET STOOD AT Carter's side, chewing on her thumbnail, destroying her manicure, while Chase flew through his last pit stop a few feet away.

Earlier, when the rain had stopped, she'd brought Carter and Corrine down to watch the rest of the race from the garage. Then the rain had started again and so had the chaos.

Inters. Chase had asked to go onto intermediate tires instead of full wets, while the rain was still coming down in rivers. God, she hoped he knew what he was doing.

"What's happening there?" Carter asked her, pointing to one of the monitors trained on the other teams' garages. Axel Nyström and Kai Nolan had both gotten tangled up during their pit stops. Their crews had been scrambling to get new tires ready, and they weren't in position yet when the drivers had come in for the swap. Those few seconds lost them both spots in the race.

"Holy shit," she muttered under her breath. Then she looked at Carter. "Chase is now in ninth place. We're in the top ten." Which, when there were only twelve cars left in the race, wasn't *that* impressive, but Carter didn't need to know that.

Violet was too nervous to smile, but Carter did it for her, grinning as he watched the chaos unfold on the monitors. "Watch closely," she told him. "This race is about to get very interesting."

Keeping one eye on Chase out on the track, she explained the different kinds of tires to Carter, as concisely as possible, and how that would affect what he was about to see happening. The other cars had already passed the pit lane exit. They wouldn't be able to change their slick tires for another lap.

"So Chase is on the right tires now?"

She shook her head. "Not exactly. I think he's betting on the rain stopping before the end of the race. If the track dries out enough, *then* he'll be on the right tires, and no one else will be."

Carter looked outside at the rain still coming down. "That's quite a gamble."

She sighed and shook her head. "That's Chase." All reckless optimism and faith. Whatever happened out there, she wouldn't want him any other way. He was perfect just as he was.

As Chase approached Turn Four, everyone else in the garage seemed to realize the situation at the same moment, coming to cluster around the monitors with Violet and Carter.

"Shit, Chase just overtook Olivier," one of the pit crew said.

"Chase is going to take them all out," another one said in wonder.

Every time Chase passed another car, the garage erupted in shouts, the energy ratcheting up higher and higher. First Olivier, then Rolando, Haneul, and Qian, all of them still struggling along on dry tires; Chase passed them all. She couldn't believe what she was seeing, couldn't believe this could possibly be happening.

Unthinking, she reached out to clutch Carter's forearm.

"Oh my god . . ."

CHASE WAS NAVIGATING Turn Nine and Ten when Emil broke onto the race radio.

"Uh, I don't want to alarm you, Chase, but you are currently in fifth place."

His whole body jerked, an involuntary response to a truly staggering piece of information.

"Copy," he said. Understatement of the fucking year. But this race wasn't done, and his gamble could still go spectacularly sideways on him. He'd only managed to pass those guys because they were stuck out here on the wrong tires. Once they hit the pits, that would change.

Up ahead, another group of cars—the fucking race leaders, he realized—were limping through Turn Seventeen, just trying to make it to the pits.

Emil crackled in his ear again as he blew past the pit lane. "Race leaders are in the pit. You are now in second place."

Holy fuck. He was currently on the podium. Wherever Violet and Carter Hammond were right now, he hoped they were freaking the fuck out.

This one's for you, Carter. And for you, Violet.

This might not last. The race leaders might be able to catch back up after their pit and steal this moment of glory from him. But maybe not.

Then, just like he'd hoped it would, the rain began to ease off. Typical mercurial Florida weather. Horrific downpour and ten minutes later, the sun was coming out like it never happened. His tires were finding their grip now that they'd warmed up and the rain eased.

"Eight laps to go," Emil said. "Let's keep it clean and bring it home. You're in second, Chase. No need to blow it out."

Except Liam fucking O'Neill was the only one ahead of him in first, so yes, he *did* need to blow it out.

Up ahead he could see Liam working like hell to keep his tires cool. Liam had made it into the pits when Chase had, and he'd made it back out before him. Liam had opted for full wet tires, but now that the track was beginning to dry, they'd be like driving on tank treads.

Liam took a big detour through the turn, hitting puddles in an attempt to keep his tires alive. Chase, on his inters, flew straight into the sweet spot of the apex and powered back out. He'd already taken half a second out of Liam and he wasn't done yet.

The thing about coming up through racing alongside a guy is, you knew how he raced almost as well as you knew yourself. Chase was on the tires he liked, racing in conditions he liked, and he knew every muscle twitch Liam would make.

The rain disappeared entirely, making the track conditions wildly unpredictable, still soaking wet in spots, the rain steaming off the asphalt in others.

"Three laps to go," Emil said. "On the last lap, you were a second faster than Liam. At this pace you should catch him with a lap to go."

His earlier exhaustion was a distant memory. Now there was nothing but adrenaline pumping through his veins. He couldn't afford a single mistake in these final laps.

Ahead of him, Liam's car grew larger and larger as he closed down the gap. He was so motherfucking close he could taste it. The whipping white flag indicated they were in the last lap. He was almost out of time to make a miracle happen.

Liam was holding him off, but just barely. His tires were dragging him back as the track dried out.

They were closing fast on that motherfucking Turn Seventeen. This was it, his last chance to overtake. Chase positioned himself so Liam could see him in his mirrors. *Yeah, I'm right behind you, asshole.*

Liam dove to the inside to cut him off, just like in the old days. The inside of the track was terrible for Liam's tires, but Chase knew he wouldn't be able to resist making his trademark asshole move. Chase swung wide to the outside.

He could feel it, that subtle sensation that let him know his car was glued to the track. He had this. The car had this.

He rolled onto the throttle exiting Seventeen, and the power of the acceleration pinned him back in his seat. For a heartbeat he could see the yellow blur of Liam's car to the left in his peripheral vision, but he stayed focused, willing the car to stick to the road, burying the accelerator to drag every last ounce of speed out of it . . .

Halfway to Turn Eighteen, he lost sight of Liam, but that didn't mean he wasn't there, ready to surge back and overtake. He stayed on the accelerator, ripping through the curve, this time hard on the inside.

All at once, the fog lifted and he could hear it—the overwhelming roar of the crowd. The stands were on their feet, the ground vibrating with their stomping and cheering as he rounded the last turn into the start/finish straight.

It hit him in a rush, elation like he'd never known before. He wasn't hallucinating. This was real. There might be a huge asterisk beside his name and this victory, but right now, he didn't fucking care. Somehow, impossibly, he'd just made every dream he'd ever had come true.

Liam was gone, back behind him somewhere. It was just him and the car, an endless expanse of open track, and a waving checkered flag to lead him home to victory.

■

THE PINNACLE GARAGE erupted in elated screams all around Violet. The pit crew raced out to the pit wall to cheer Chase on as the checkered flag came down. The next thing she knew, Carter had swept her up in a bear hug, laughing and whooping with delight. After that it was a blur. She hugged Leon and Imogen. Then she hauled Rabia into her arms, both of them screaming and laughing as they gripped each other. When Violet let go of Rabia and turned, Carter was there, watching them, still smiling broadly.

"Well, Mr. Hammond?" she asked, still breathing hard, feeling the triumphant smile glued to her face. "How'd we do?"

He laughed and shook his head, then extended his hand to hers to shake. "You've got two years, Ms. Harper. Let's see how it goes."

Inside, a wave of relief and euphoria rushed through her, but she returned his shake with the same level of confidence. "Thank you. I can't promise you another day like this, but I promise it'll be exciting."

"I don't doubt it. My god, what a thrill . . ."

He started to turn away. She should leave it. They'd gotten two more years, which was everything they'd dare hope for. She ought to be satisfied with that win. But fuck it. If you didn't ask for it, you'd never get it.

"Mr. Hammond, there's one more thing . . ."

Carter hiked his eyebrow. "I just gave you your team. What else do you want?"

"A *real* team principal. No offense," she added quickly.

He chuckled again and dipped his head. "Understood. None taken."

Bye, Reece, Violet thought.

Then Carter turned and extended a hand to Rabia. "Ms. Dar, congratulations. The team is yours. Now if you'll excuse me, I should go find Corrine. I believe we've got some celebrating to do."

"Don't go too far," Violet said. "You're the team owner. The media is going to want to talk to you."

Carter thought about that for a beat, then smiled. "So they will. Come find me when you need me, Ms. Harper."

When he'd gone, Violet looked at Rabia. Rabia was still shaking her head, wide-eyed.

"Did he just make me team principal? It sounded like he did, but maybe I have an undiagnosed head injury and I'm just hallucinating."

"He did. Congrats, Rabia. You've earned this."

Rabia smiled at her. "So we have two years to prove ourselves, huh?"

Violet scoffed. "Not a problem. Hammond will get his money's worth and then some. Pinnacle just became *legendary*. This is *Miracle on Ice* shit. They're going to make a fucking movie about our team and this season. I'll make sure it happens."

She was almost delirious with elation. Did she know anyone with connections in Hollywood? She must. How did you go about pitching a movie there? Who knew, but she'd figure that out, the way she did everything else.

Her phone was already blowing up. Every journalist who had her contact info was reaching out, begging for an interview. Every media outlet in the world would be talking about Chase Navarro and Pinnacle tonight.

Suddenly Emil shouted over the din of the garage. "Uh, does anybody have the FIA regulations handy? I never read the podium procedure because I didn't think we'd ever need it. I have to tell Chase what to do next."

"I have it!" Imogen shouted, racing across the garage and waving her iPad over her head.

"You have to keep Imogen as your assistant," Violet said to Rabia.

"Obviously. She's the smartest person here."

When Chase finally climbed out of the car and pulled off his helmet, the entirety of the Pinnacle pit crew and every staffer on site clamored at the pit wall.

Violet watched from the back of the crowd as he ran down the track toward them, all unconscious grace and barely contained energy. She wanted to remember every inch of him in this moment, high on his triumph, his eyes bright with adrenaline, his smile glowing. Even though he still had pressure marks from his helmet on his cheekbones and his hair was a sweaty wreck, she'd never seen anything more beautiful.

He reached the pit crew and launched himself at them, laughing when they lifted him up and dragged him over the barricades. The pit crew chanted his name as they passed him over their heads, and finally deposited him on the other side, right in front of her.

"Hi," he said, his smile wide and his dark eyes glowing.

"Hi."

"Thank you, Violet. This . . . I can't thank you enough for what you've done for me."

She shook her head. "I just made you a star. This? Today? You did this all by yourself. You're a champion."

"And you gave me the chance to be one. I love you. So much I can hardly stand it."

"You are . . ." She shook her head, unable to find the words. Then she forgot all about words and simply flung herself at him, wrapping her arms around his waist and hugging him as tightly to her body as she could. Her fingers curled into the rough canvas of his race suit, and she buried her face into the crook of his neck, pressing a kiss to his sweat-slicked skin.

"I love you, too," she whispered.

She felt him chuckle and he dipped his head so he could whisper in her ear. "So I just had to win a Grand Prix to get you to fall in love with me, huh? Why didn't I do this sooner?"

She pulled back enough to look up at him and reached up to take his face in her hands. This face, this man, who'd become so unbearably precious to her. She was so, so grateful that he hadn't given up on her, that he'd given her time to catch up to him.

"I was already in love with you, Chase. I have been for ages. I just didn't realize it."

The smile on his face grew impossibly wider, and the expression in his eyes softened.

"You'd better go. There's a podium and a first-place trophy with your name on it."

He ducked his head and pressed his lips to hers. "I've already got the best prize."

43

Five months later
Sakhir, Bahrain

As twilight descended across the desert and the stadium lights came on, flooding the track in bright white light, Chase attached his HANS device to his helmet.

"Let's go." Leon clapped him on the shoulder.

He started rattling off a laundry list of things the engineers wanted feedback on tonight, the first race of the season. Chase half listened while he scanned the cluster of Pinnacle staffers at the back of the garage. His mom and dad were there, chatting with Imogen, and beside them he spotted Violet, a vision in a fitted dark red suit. She was talking to Carter Hammond, pointing out different things in the garage so he'd understand everything he was seeing.

Carter nodded along, eyes sharp, expression focused. Since he'd committed to ownership, he'd proved to be a quick study, learning the ins and outs of high-end motorsport engineering and aerodynamics in a remarkably short span of time. He and Rabia had been having lengthy phone calls nearly every day during the offseason.

But now they were back for the new season, with a new team principal and a brand-new, fucking *awesome* car. Testing last week had been good, but Rabia was never satisfied with good. The factory had worked day and night since then on a list of improvements, and qualifying yesterday had been fucking fantastic. His starting position tonight, fourth, had thrown down a gauntlet. Pinnacle was back, and this year, they were in it to win it.

He took a second to run his fingers down the elegant sweeping side of the car, the surface glittering like graphite in the stadium lights. There were more sponsor logos than open paint.

"You ready?" Leon asked.

"As I'll ever be."

He looked back at Violet. This time she was watching him and when their eyes met, a slow, sexy smile curled her blood-red lips. She couldn't really see his expression under his helmet, but he winked at her just the same. She touched a finger to her bottom lip, the little gesture she made when she was thinking about him, but one or the both of them was busy with work.

He felt the touch of that finger on his own bottom lip and he smiled. He had a good feeling about tonight, this car, and the rest of the season, but no matter how it worked out, he had *her*, and in the end, that was all that really mattered.

Turning his attention back to the job, he climbed into the cockpit and slid down until he was settled in his custom seat. A couple of guys from the crew reached in to tighten his straps. There were a few more bits of business to get through, adjustments to be made, and words of wisdom from Leon.

"Okay, out for your reconnaissance laps," Rabia said over headset. "Let's see how she does."

"She's gonna kick ass, Rabia, because you built me a brilliant car."

Rabia laughed. "She's only as good as her driver."

"Then you better clear some space for that Constructor's Championship trophy, because I'm winning it for you."

Then it was thumbs-up from Leon and he fired the engine.

The smooth roar vibrated through his bloodstream like the beat of his heart. This was the magic the simulator could never capture. Rabia and the engineers would be judging the car based on stats and algorithms, but he always went with his gut. Maybe it wasn't science, but his gut was telling him this car was a winner.

On his recce laps, the car felt flawless, lithe and sleek through the corners, poised and easy in the braking zones . . . alive with the sense of barely restrained power. The engineers and aerodynamic specialists liked to tout the fact that Formula One cars generated such downforce at full speed that they could theoretically drive upside down, defying gravity. He'd never felt the truth of that until he'd driven this car. In this car, he felt like he could fly.

He rolled to a stop at his spot on the grid, in front of the lights that would signal the start of the race. They had a break now, and the pit crew surrounded his car like a swarm of insects to make a few last-minute adjustments. Violet sauntered up to him, all long-legged grace and sexy sway.

"The media chatter is that you might be on the podium tonight."

He hiked one eyebrow. "Did you maybe *start* that chatter, Violet?"

She laughed. "Well, it *is* my job to talk you up, but in this case, I didn't need to. You'll get there."

He looked out across the track, right now just an empty strip of asphalt, soon to be full of engineering masterpieces battling it out at top speed for a spot at the summit. He'd made it there in Miami, and that felt great, but there was that *asterisk*. Tonight he wanted to win it fair and square, up against the best drivers in the world. And tonight, he really felt like he could. "You know what? I think I will."

Violet touched her bottom lip again. "I'll be waiting for you on the other side."

He grinned and touched his own lip. "Guess I better hurry back then."

"Good thing you drive fast."

EPILOGUE

Four months later
Cloveshire Manor, England

"Before this congregation, William and Miranda have given their consent and made their marriage vows to each other. They have declared their marriage by the joining of hands and by the giving and receiving of rings. I therefore proclaim that they are husband and wife."

By the time the officiant said the words, twilight had deepened into night and fairy lights had twinkled on over the heads of the two hundred guests assembled on the grass for the wedding. Behind Mira and Will, the ivy-covered walls of Cloveshire Manor provided a gorgeous backdrop for their wedding.

Violet stood at the front of the congregation behind Mira, who she thought looked like a proper princess in her lace sheath dress, her blond hair in a riot of curls down her back. Will, looking sharp as anything in a black tux, held her hands and gazed down at her like she was a miracle.

Will leaned in to kiss her and everyone erupted in applause. Violet scanned the crowd, past Mira's father, Paul Wentworth, and his new wife, Natalia, and past Will's sour-faced, insufferable parents, the Hawleys, who couldn't even be bothered to smile at their son's wedding.

She finally spotted Chase sitting in the row behind Will's sister, Jemima, and her girlfriend. He looked absolutely edible in a fitted black suit and crisp white dress shirt, open at the neck. She wanted to grab fistfuls of that gorgeous tousled black hair, climb onto his lap, and do unspeakable things to him. She'd start a mental list of them for when they were back in their hotel suite later.

After the ceremony concluded and the guests were streaming across the lawn toward a huge white tent for the reception in, Chase found her.

He reached out and ran a finger over her hip. "Nice dress."

"Mira said I could wear what I wanted." She smoothed a hand down the emerald-green silk sheath.

"Lucky me." His eyes were lit up with hunger as he sidled closer to her and grabbed her hips with both hands.

Laughing, she pushed on his chest with two fingers. "I've got a speech to give at the reception, so whatever filthy thing you're imagining, it's going to have to wait."

"Is that my favorite PR person in the whole world??"

Violet heard the words, called out in a broad Texas accent, and turned to see Mira's mother, the former supermodel Cherie Delain, descending on her with arms spread wide.

"Hi, Cherie."

Cherie swept her up in a bone-crushing hug. "It's so good to see you, honey."

"You, too, Cherie." Last year back at Lennox, Mira had done her tell-all interview about Brody McKnight, then closed the book on that miserable chapter of her life and moved on. Violet and Cherie, however, had been far from done with him. They'd texted back and forth whenever another shitty thing he'd done came to light, and Violet did what she could to make sure every major media outlet reported about it. It had bonded them for life.

"Who's this handsome friend of yours?" Cherie asked, all mischievous smiles and twinkling green eyes, just like Mira's.

"Cherie, this is my boyfriend, Chase Navarro. Chase, this is Mira's mum, Cherie."

That word . . . "boyfriend" . . . had been hard to say at first, but it was coming easier to her now. All of this was coming easier. She'd let Chase slip through one crack in her armor, and it seemed like a flood of people had flowed in with him. Mira and Will, Rabia and Rajan, who had turned out to be *hilarious* and awesome, Imogen, Leon, Chase's parents and siblings . . . Nicole was texting her almost daily, just to chat, and next month she was finally going to meet Samantha, Chase's sister. She'd even been added to the Navarro family WhatsApp, although she could barely keep up with the chaos.

"So nice to meet you, Chase. You take good care of my girl, Violet. She's special."

Chase looped his arm around her waist and tugged her closer. "She sure is."

"Ah, you two. You're adorable together." Cherie sighed. "I'm gonna go catch up with my baby girl. Enjoy yourselves tonight."

"See you inside, Cherie."

"She's sweet," Chase said as she left.

"Until you fuck with her, then watch out. But, yes, she's really sweet. She's a good mom to Mira."

"And you."

Violet pivoted around to look at him. "What are you talking about?"

"She thinks of you as one of hers."

"Cherie? You think so?"

"It's obvious, Violet. She adores you. So does my mom. Because you're adorable, I guess."

She nudged her elbow into his side as they walked across the lawn. "The last thing I am is adorable."

"Maybe not, but you're lovable. They love you. And so do I."

She nudged him again, but this nudge was softer and ended in a sideways hug.

"Looks like Mira and Will are heading in," Chase said, pointing toward the tent. After the ceremony, the two of them had been whisked away by the photographer for a few more formal portraits but now they were back for the reception.

"They look really happy together," Violet said, watching as Mira looked up at Will, her face glowing.

"Forever looks good on them."

Violet sighed, feeling a very rare pang of sentimentality. "It does."

Beside her, Chase ducked to murmur near her ear. "I think it would look good on us, too."

She stopped walking and turned to face him, heart pounding. "Are you—"

Chase grinned, holding his hands up. "I'm not asking anything. Yet." Then he reached out for her hand and brought it up to brush a kiss across her knuckles. "I'm just planting the seed."

"Planting the seed," she repeated.

He slid his arm around her shoulders and turned them both toward the reception again. "Because I know that with you, seeds take some time to blossom."

As they walked, his arm holding her against his side, she absorbed that idea—forever. And she found—shockingly—that it wasn't as terrifying as she'd thought it would be. Not now, and not tomorrow. But maybe in the future . . .

"Maybe," she said out loud, very quietly.

Chase let out a soft huff of laughter and tightened his grip on her. "Take all the time you need, Violet. For you, I've got forever."

ACKNOWLEDGMENTS

I had so much fun creating these characters and writing this book, and for that, I have to thank Hayley Wagreich, Nicole Otto, and Sierra Stovall at Slowburn. From the start, they sensed Violet jumping off the pages of *Fast & Reckless*, demanding her own story, and with their invaluable assistance, I think we gave her a great one. Nicole's spot-on editorial guidance made these characters and this book so much stronger.

I'd be nowhere without Rebecca Strauss, my brilliant agent. With her in my corner, advocating for me, I know I have nothing to worry about. I'm so glad to know her, both professionally and personally.

Many thanks to Melissa Panio-Petersen for keeping my ducks in a row and guiding me through all the stuff I still don't know!

Thank you to FS Meurinne for the years of online friendship and support, and for making sure I didn't make a hash out of Chase's Spanish.

Thanks, as always, to my husband, Matthew Ragsdale. Without his passion and expertise supporting me, I wouldn't dare attempt to write about Formula One. And thanks to the Missed Apex Podcast crew and community, always willing to weigh in when I need information or feedback.

I value Matt for his racing expertise, but as my husband, I value him beyond measure. Holding down a demanding full-time job while also pursuing a writing career is no easy feat, but he has always, from the very first, done everything he can to make it easier for me. My daughter, Lilith, has grown up understanding that sometimes Mom has to spend the weekend writing, but she's never once complained. The two of them make the best pair of cheerleaders in the world.

And speaking of the demanding full-time job, this year, I finally shared my writing career fully with the people in my "real life," and every single person I've told about it has been nothing but excited and supportive. I'm very touched.

And, finally, thanks to the hardworking, talented, and dedicated staff of Zando Projects. Julia McGarry, Zoey Cole, Natalie Ullman, TJ Ohler, Emily Morris, and everyone at Slowburn and Zando have given me such amazing support, and I'm so very grateful.

ABOUT THE AUTHOR

AMANDA WEAVER has written everything from steamy contemporaries to swoony historicals, and can now add sports romance to that list with the Racing Hearts series, after her husband's job as a Formula One journalist sparked a whole new obsession. In her "other life," Amanda is a costume designer working on Broadway and in opera. Born and raised in Florida, she now considers New York City home, and she lives with her family and cats in Brooklyn. Find her at amandaweavernovels.com and @amanda_weaver_author.